PENGUIN BOOKS

THE YEAR AT THRUSH GREEN

Miss Read, or in real life Mrs Dora Saint, is a teacher by profession who started writing after the Second World War, beginning with light essays written for *Punch* and other journals. She has written on educational and country matters, and worked as a script-writer for the BBC. Miss Read is married to a retired schoolmaster and they have one daughter. They live in a tiny Berkshire hamlet. She is a local magistrate and her hobbies are theatre-going, listening to music and reading.

Miss Read is the author of numerous books, which have gained immense popularity for their humorous and honest depictions of English rural life, including, most recently, *The Year at Thrush Green* and *A Peaceful Retirement*. Many of her books are published by Penguin, together with seven omnibus editions. She has also written several books for children, including the Red Bus series for the very young (published in one volume by Puffin as *The Little Red Bus and Other Stories*), a cookery book, *Miss Read's Country Cooking*, and two auto-biograpical works, *A Fortunate Grandchild* and *Time Remembered*, published together in one volume as *Early Days*, with a new foreword by the author.

THE YEAR AT
THRUSH GREEN

MISS READ

ILLUSTRATIONS BY JOHN S. GOODALL

PENGUIN BOOKS

PENGUIN BOOKS

Published by the Penguin Group
Penguin Books Ltd, 27 Wrights Lane, London W8 5TZ, England
Penguin Putnam Inc., 375 Hudson Street, New York, New York 10014, USA
Penguin Books Australia Ltd, Ringwood, Victoria, Australia
Penguin Books Canada Ltd, 10 Alcorn Avenue, Toronto, Ontario, Canada M4V 3B2
Penguin Books (NZ) Ltd, 182–190 Wairau Road, Auckland 10, New Zealand

Penguin Books Ltd, Registered Offices: Harmondsworth, Middlesex, England

First published by Michael Joseph 1995
Published in Penguin Books 1996
5 7 9 10 8 6 4

Copyright © Miss Read, 1996
All rights reserved

To Beryl and Ray

With love

January

Snow had fallen, snow on snow,
Snow on snow.

Christina Rossetti

The snow came on Twelfth Night.
Dusk was thickening over Thrush Green, and the lights in the nearby High Street at Lulling were already flickering into action.

The first flakes fluttered down so sparsely that Winnie Bailey, the doctor's widow, thought that the last pale leaf was floating by from the wisteria by the front door, as she drew the curtains against the bitter cold which had gripped Thrush Green for days.

Near by, at the most beautiful house in this Cotswold hamlet, Winnie's neighbour, Joan Young, hurrying in from the garden, caught sight of a pale fragment descending slowly. A feather, she wondered, or a particle of ash from a recent bonfire? Somehow she, in common with other Thrush Green residents, gave no thought to snow at that time.

Only Albert Piggott, the gloomy sexton at St Andrew's church on the green, realized what was falling, as he shuffled back to his cottage close by.

'It's begun,' he told his cat, as he unwound the muffler from his skinny neck. 'There'll be a foot of the dratted stuff before long.'

*

Albert Piggott had been expecting snow for weeks. So, for that matter, had the rest of the community, but they had waited so long for its arrival that when at last it came, on that bleak January evening, it was barely noticed.

The gripping cold had taken hold early in December, and the general talk had been about a white Christmas. The children everywhere were full of hope. Old sledges had been dug out from lofts, garden sheds and garages, dusted and oiled and put by to await a white world which failed to materialize during the whole of the Christmas holidays.

The school at Thrush Green had opened for the spring term the day before those first tentative flakes had floated down.

Alan Lester, the headmaster, heard the children's bitter comments with mixed feelings of sympathy and amusement.

'It's not *fair*!' cried one six-year-old. 'I was going to make a snowman.'

'So was I. My dad give me an old pipe for it. And a cap.'

'I'd got my sledge oiled up lovely, to go down the slope to Lulling Woods,' grumbled a third.

'Well,' said Alan reasonably, 'you can play with all those things after school. Or on Saturday, for that matter.'

'It's not the *same*!' wailed another child. 'You need *all day* to play in the snow!'

Clearly, there was going to be no comforting of the younger generation in the face of such injustice.

Alan Lester ushered them from the playground back to the warmth of the classroom.

His charges did not appear grateful.

It had snowed intermittently throughout Twelfth Night, but only an inch covered the iron-cold earth by morning.

But the sky was covered with dark grey clouds, and there was an ominous stillness everywhere as though the world awaited something menacing.

Joan Young, well muffled against the cold from woolly hat to wellington boots, crossed the corner of the green to take some magazines to Winnie Bailey, who welcomed her.

'No,' said Joan, 'I won't come in, but I'm going down to Lulling and I thought I'd bring back anything you needed. Don't go out, Winnie, it's so slippery.'

'Well, you are kind! I remember Donald always said that if the wind came from Oxford or Woodstock it was time to get in the potatoes and an extra bag of flour.'

'The wind's certainly going to be there soon,' agreed Joan. 'Shall I get those potatoes and the flour?'

Winnie laughed. 'It might be as well. Then we can withstand the siege if need be.'

She watched her neighbour returning to her house, leaving black footprints in the new snow. Shivering, she returned to the warm kitchen, where Jenny, her maid and friend, was chopping onions.

'Onions keep the cold out,' said Jenny.

'We shall need a good supply then,' Winnie forecast.

Equally prudent residents of Thrush Green and Lulling were also stocking their larders.

Across the green, opposite Winnie Bailey's house, Harold Shoosmith and his wife Isobel were making a shopping list while coffee cups steamed near by.

The Shoosmiths were relative newcomers to Thrush Green. Harold had arrived first, some years earlier, a single middle-aged man of handsome appearance, recently retired from a post abroad.

He was a lifelong admirer of a former Thrush Green resident, one Nathaniel Patten, a missionary in Africa who had formed a school there and been greatly loved by all who met him. Nathaniel had long been dead when Harold came across his good works, but his influence still flourished in the African settlement, and when Harold discovered that a house in Nathaniel's birthplace was on the market, when he was house-hunting, he quickly put in his bid, and soon found himself living happily at Thrush Green.

Next door to his house was the village school, and the headmistress at that time was a competent woman, Dorothy Watson, who lived in the schoolhouse with her friend and fellow-teacher Agnes Fogerty.

All three were good friends and neighbours, and it was through Agnes that Harold eventually met his wife Isobel. She had been at college with Agnes, and the two had kept in touch throughout the years.

When she came to stay at Thrush Green with her old friend, Isobel was recently widowed. The friendship which sprang up between Harold and Isobel flourished, grew warmer, and led to an exceedingly happy marriage, to the delight of their friends at Thrush Green.

It was Harold who had instigated the setting-up of a fine statue of Nathaniel Patten on the green. He had been shocked to find that so little was known about the Victorian missionary who had done so much good overseas, and he set about educating his neighbours.

Harold's enthusiasm had been infectious, and now the memory of one of Thrush Green's most famous sons was a source of pride in the community, and his statue and memory greatly revered.

This morning a sprinkling of snow spattered Nathaniel's head and shoulders, and a noisy family of starlings squabbled on the white ground around him. Near by, the children's voices, as noisy as the starlings', had suddenly ceased.

'Alan's getting the children in,' commented Harold,

looking at the kitchen clock. 'I'll get down to Lulling before things get too busy.'

He went to wrap up well before crunching his way to the garage through the bitter cold.

An hour later, his shopping done, Harold pushed open the door of the Fuchsia Bush, Lulling's most notable restaurant in the High Street.

Harold was not a frequent visitor to this establishment, but he was so cold that he felt that a cup of coffee would thaw him before he visited the bank and the local building society, the last duties to perform before driving home.

The Fuchsia Bush·was warm and welcoming. Coffee was provided promptly, and soon the ample form of Nelly Piggott appeared from the kitchen bearing a tray of scones hot from the oven.

She greeted Harold with affection. 'Nice to see you, Mr Shoosmith. Parky today, isn't it?'

'That's putting it mildly,' said Harold. 'May I have one of those delicious scones? I can't resist your cooking.'

Nelly beamed at the compliment, and Harold wondered, yet again, how such an attractive woman as this buxom one before him could ever have taken miserable Albert Piggott for a husband.

It had always been a mystery to Thrush Green, this marriage of two such opposites. Even Charles Henstock, the much-loved rector of Thrush Green, had doubted if the marriage would last.

In fact, it was the Fuchsia Bush which had rescued that marriage from the rocks some years earlier. Nelly had always been a first-class cook, and had very little chance to use her skill when catering for Albert. He suffered from peptic ulcers, and Nelly's use of cream, butter, plenty of sugar, honey and golden syrup did nothing to help his digestion. It was a happy day for her when the owner of the Fuchsia Bush appeared on Nelly's doorstep to ask if she could help at the restaurant while the cook was ill.

This had led eventually to a thriving partnership between Nelly and Mrs Peters and to the Fuchsia Bush gaining a name in the neighbourhood for delicious food.

To Nelly it was her whole life. She set off for work every day in the highest of spirits. The kitchen at the Fuchsia Bush was her kingdom, the compliments from customers balm to her spirit. Nelly was probably the happiest worker in Lulling, and even Albert's gloomy company could not quell her new-found ebullience.

'And how's Mrs Shoosmith?' asked Nelly, putting a plate before him. 'Had her flu jabs, I hope. They say this new flu's a real killer.'

'Months ago,' Harold assured her, spreading butter.

'Good,' said Nelly. 'Well, I must get back to the oven. I've got some brandysnaps in at the moment, and you know how quickly they catch.'

Harold did not, but watched her bustle away to her duties.

As he put the car away in the garage, he saw his friend and neighbour Edward Young emerging from his house.

'I was just coming to see you,' called Edward.

'Come indoors,' said Harold, but Edward, who always seemed to be in a hurry, refused the invitation.

'It's about the fête,' said Edward, banging his gloved hands together to keep warm.

'But that's not till July,' protested Harold.

'I know, I know! But the fact is that we are trying to plan a holiday while young Paul's home from school, and I don't want to be tied down this year with fête arrangements. Could you possibly have the administration side at your house?'

'No bother at all,' replied Harold. 'You go ahead and leave the fête to me this time.'

Edward clapped his friend rather painfully on his shoulder. 'That's a great relief. Terribly grateful, old boy. Must dash now. I've got some urgent posting to do, and I want to get back by the fire pretty soon.'

'Don't we all,' agreed Harold, turning home.

By midday a vicious little wind had sprung up. It threw a spattering of dead leaves against the window of the Youngs' house where Joan was watering a bowl of early hyacinths.

She looked across the garden, and saw the branches of a lime tree tossing in the wind, and its last few leaves being swept away.

She heard the slamming of the back door, and her husband's voice, and went to greet him in the kitchen.

He was standing with his back to the Aga, rubbing his cold hands together. Molly Curdle, once Molly Piggott, daughter of Albert, was rolling out pastry at the kitchen table. She and her husband Ben Curdle lived in a cottage which the Youngs had converted from their stables for Joan's parents, now both dead.

Molly had started working for Edward and Joan when their son Paul was a little boy. She had taken him for walks, played with him, bathed him and put him to bed. The bond between them had strengthened over the years, and although Paul was now away at boarding school, it was Molly he rushed to greet first on coming home.

'Wind's getting up,' commented Edward. 'And due north-east too.'

The sky grew darker. Black clouds gathered ominously, swept along by a bitter and relentless wind. Dead leaves, twigs and a couple of paper bags eddied across Thrush Green, now airborne, now dashed spasmodically along the ground.

There was a howling in the trees in the garden, and an even more intense roaring in the avenue of horse chestnut trees outside the Youngs' house.

By three o'clock the snow was whirling across the scene, blotting out the view of St Andrew's church and the wind-tossed trees surrounding it. It was a wild and fearsome landscape, suddenly devoid of human figures. Joan Young, watching from her windows, thought of arctic wastes, of the cruelty of nature and of man's sudden diminution in the face of weather extremes.

But, as she watched the fury of the blizzard sweeping across Thrush Green, she saw signs of humanity.

From the school on her right a few small figures emerged, as two cars drew up at the gate. The children were bundled up in coats with upturned collars and hats pulled down over their ears, and some had long scarves round their necks, tied crosswise round their swaddled bodies to form a bustle at the back. They clambered into the cars, and drove away through the whirling maelstrom, out of Joan's sight.

Soon, she knew, others would be collected, and for the few who lived along the lane to Nod and Nidden, no doubt, kind and conscientious Alan Lester would act as taxi-man in his own car. The numbers at Thrush Green school did not warrant a school bus.

Shivering in the draught from the window, Joan crossed the room to add logs to the fire. She reviewed the food situation as she went about her duties. Had she forgotten anything vital should the snow keep them penned indoors?

Bread, flour, potatoes, root vegetables and all those things which her old friend Donald Bailey had advised his neighbours to get in, once the wind had taken up its unwelcome quarter in the north-east, she thought she had remembered. But it was other vital things which invariably escaped the memory. Salt, sugar, the special Frank Cooper's marmalade which Edward so much relished – all these, in the past, had been casualties of the demands of emergencies, and no doubt would be again sometime.

The wind howled in the chimney, and every now and again there would be a sharp hiss from the logs on the fire as a snowflake descended to a fiery death. A particularly violent gust sent a puff of smoke into the room, and Joan went across to pull the curtains against the bitter world outside.

It was almost dark, and one or two lights were showing in the houses round the empty green. The children had gone, though the lights showed in the schoolroom. Normally, Betty Bell from Lulling Woods arrived to clean up at about this time, but Joan doubted if she would be able to make the journey in such conditions.

She drew the heavy velvet curtains together, grieving for any living thing that had to endure that world behind the windows, and thankful that she had warmth and shelter and, she hoped, adequate provisions under her own roof.

The violent wind continued to batter all in its path until the early hours of the morning.

Then it died down, but still the snow fell, thickly and silently, for the rest of the night. It was still coming down when the first grey light appeared.

Harold Shoosmith woke to see the strange light upon his bedroom ceiling, and knew at once what caused it. He slipped from his bed and went to look upon the white world of Thrush Green through the snow-spattered window. Behind him his wife Isobel still lay in sleep.

The view was awe-inspiring in its strange beauty. Snow had drifted in the fierce winds into fantastic shapes of varying depths. The statue of Nathaniel Patten close by wore a deep skirt of snow, covering the base and extending halfway up the plinth. Nathaniel's shoulders wore a cape of snow and his head a round white cap.

The railings of St Andrew's church were engulfed and the oak tubs, which stood each side of the doorway into the Two Pheasants hard by, were also hidden beneath a snowy blanket. Swirls and hillocks, gullies and valleys, banks and little cliffs stretched in every direction. It was an arctic landscape which Harold viewed with mixed wonder and fear. What damage, he mused, would the Cotswold world discover when the short hours of daylight finally arrived?

He looked down upon his own front garden, now a smooth white sheet of snow covering path, flower beds and lawn. Only the tops of the gateposts broke that surface, and brought home to the watcher the necessity of getting downstairs and finding a spade for a good deal of hard work.

At that moment, Isobel sat up and stretched her arms.

'Well, what's it like?'

'Siberia! But superb,' said her husband.

Later that morning there was plenty of activity on Thrush Green, as Harold and his neighbours set out to clear their paths to the road.

It was a Saturday, so the school was empty, but Alan Lester was hard at work, digging with the rest to clear the access to the schoolhouse which was next door to Harold's home.

Occasionally they stopped to rest on their spades, their breath blowing out in small clouds in the frosty air.

'I've asked the Cooke boys to give me a hand with the playground,' said Alan surveying the vast waste behind them. 'I only hope we don't get more tonight.'

'How did you get in touch? Are the phones still working?'

'Luckily, yes. But Albert Piggott says they're sagging dangerously across to Lulling Woods.'

'Well, you know Albert!' commented Harold, looking farther along the road to where the bent figure of the sexton of St Andrew's was plying a stiff broom.

'Always looking on the bright side,' agreed Alan, with a smile.

They returned to their labours.

Turning over this brief exchange as he made his arduous

way towards the gateposts, Harold thought of his old friend Dotty Harmer who lived at Lulling Woods. Would she be engulfed? The house was in a lonely spot, and years before, he remembered, in just such weather, he had collected a rescue party to fetch the old lady on a sledge.

That, of course, was when she lived there alone. Things were better now, for her niece Connie and her husband lived with her, and would look after her.

Nevertheless, Harold promised himself that he would telephone Dotty as soon as he went back to the house.

'Coffee!' called his wife from the window.

And thankfully Harold set aside the spade.

At the Youngs' house there was equal activity. Ben Curdle and Edward Young had cleared a pathway between their houses, and Molly was already in the kitchen of the big house. With her, clutching a doll, was her youngest child Anne. George, her first-born, now eight years old, was busy with his father and Edward Young dealing with the snow.

'I had a Christmas card this morning,' said Molly, tying her apron round her.

'Rather late in the day,' commented Joan.

'It had a funny stamp on it,' contributed Anne, now settled comfortably at the kitchen table undressing the doll.

'It had been around a bit,' said Molly. 'In fact, it was sent down from the Drovers' Arms, and it's years since I worked there, as you know.'

'How strange!'

'Very. And from someone I don't really know. He says he's a vague relation, an American.'

'Can you place him? Did any of your relations go to America?'

'Not as far as I know. Old Grandma Curdle had only the

one boy George, and he was killed in the war, leaving only one son, my Ben. It's a mystery.'

'Any address?'

'No. So I can't do much about it. Ah well! I'm not a great hand at writing anyway, so I shall just forget about it.'

'Except that George wants the stamp,' Anne reminded her mother, tugging a petticoat from the doll.

At midday Molly had finished her time at the Youngs' house, and returned with Anne to her own, on paths newly cleared.

Although she had told Joan that she was not going to think about the late Christmas card, she found herself speculating about the identity of the sender.

Molly had met her husband Ben when the annual fair arrived at Thrush Green on May Day. Old Mrs Curdle, head of her tribe, a real gypsy queen, of awe-inspiring dignity, ruled her business with an iron hand.

The travelling fair stayed only a few days at the most in each place, but Ben had fallen in love with Molly at first sight. He had to wait another year before he could seek her out again.

Albert Piggott had not approved. He did not want to part with a daughter who was also housekeeper, cook and occasionally, when he had drunk too much, nurse.

Mrs Curdle was more sympathetic. Ben, her only grandchild, son of George who had been killed in battle, had been brought up by the old lady, and was the apple of her eye. If Molly could make him happy, and was willing to throw in her lot with her travelling band, then she would be welcomed.

Thrush Green was Mrs Curdle's favourite stopping place on her travels. She had been befriended by the local doctor Donald Bailey, and never forgot the kindness he and his wife had shown her. Each year, at the beginning of May, she called at the Baileys' house bearing a large bouquet of artificial flowers which she had made from finely pared wood dyed in brilliant colours.

The Baileys greatly loved the old lady, but her bouquets, being indestructible, were a source of some embarrassment as the years passed and storage places grew fewer for Mrs Curdle's bounty.

When Mrs Curdle died she left instructions for her body to be put to rest in St Andrew's churchyard, where Molly and Ben faithfully tended the grave.

Ben had been left the fair by his grandmother, but parted with it a few years after her death. Their first child was expected, Molly's father was ailing, and it seemed best to settle at Thrush Green.

Before long, the Youngs invited them to take over the converted stable. Ben carried on his work as a motor mechanic in Lulling, and Molly was glad to help in the house she knew so well.

When the second child arrived, they called her Anne after her redoubtable great-grandmother, and everyone hoped that the child would grow up as fine a character as her forebear.

For two days the skies were clear, and the countryside was transformed into a white glistening wonderland.

It was freezing all day long so that the winter sunshine melted nothing, and the trees spread tracery like white lace against the clear blue of the sky.

The icicles fringing the roof of the Two Pheasants shone like glass fingers, and an icy shape reared from the upthrust lid of Mr Jones' water-butt where the water had frozen solid and pushed outward to find release.

All sound was muffled. Cars, inching their way through

the piles of snow at each side of the road, made little noise. Those on foot walked as quietly as if they trod upon fleecy white blankets.

Shapes too were softened by the snow. Roof ridges were veiled by a snowy sheet. Gateposts, steps and porches wore cushions of white. In the forks of the chestnut trees were soft beds of snow.

The light was dazzling. As far as the eye could see the whiteness stretched away, across the fields towards Lulling Woods, a dark blue smudge on the skyline against the paler blue.

The snow ploughs came out, chugging along the main road from Lulling, and clearing a way for the sparse traffic. The side roads, such as the one which joined Thrush Green from Nidden and Nod further west, remained piled with snow. Only the tractor from Percy Hodge's farm had drawn dark lines across the snowy wastes from his gate as far as the Two Pheasants where custom took him daily.

There was general relief at the opening of the road to Lulling, for the Christmas bounty was running out, and householders were looking forward to replenishing stocks of fresh food and vegetables.

At the Fuchsia Bush the customers became more plentiful, not only those who were doing everyday shopping, but also the bargain-hunters who had braved the elements to attend the High Street sales, which were having an extended season because of the weather.

Mrs Peters, the proprietor of the Fuchsia Bush, came to the assistance of her young waitresses one morning at coffee-time. Delicious smells of baking scones drifted from the kitchen where Nelly Piggott was hard at work. The three aged Lovelock sisters had arrived and were unexpectedly treating themselves to morning coffee.

They had been born, and lived all their long lives, in the beautiful Georgian house next door to Mrs Peters' premises. As neighbours they had presented difficulties. They complained about cooking smells, the sight of tea towels blowing in the yard at the rear of the restaurant and, chiefly, about the charges for anything purchased there.

The Misses Lovelock were renowned for their parsimony, and when Miss Bertha took to shoplifting, which included the occasional scone or shortbread finger from the Fuchsia Bush itself, no one was really surprised.

Mrs Peters, who was a magnanimous woman and had borne with her trying neighbours with exemplary patience and forbearance, had felt compelled to point out the matter to Miss Violet, who was really the only one approaching normality.

Violet had done her best to curb her sister's deplorable lapses, but Mrs Peters still kept a sharp eye on easily removed objects when Bertha was around.

She greeted the old ladies warmly, and summoned Gloria to take the order, as she proffered the menu.

Gloria, reluctant to be called away from the shop window which gave an absorbing view of Lulling High Street, ambled over to the table.

'I don't think we really need the menu,' said Violet. 'Just coffee for the three of us, don't you agree?'

She looked at her two sisters, who were busy uncoiling loops of scarves from their skinny necks and gloves from their claw-like hands. Mrs Peters could not help wishing that they would attend to their noses, all three of which sported a glistening drop of moisture.

'Perhaps a biscuit,' murmured Bertha, 'or just *half* a scone.'

'We'll have one each,' pronounced Ada with unusual firmness. 'We have been to the sale at the new draper's, and it really is quite exhausting in this cold weather.'

Gloria licked her pencil and wrote laboriously before making slow progress to the kitchen.

'Well,' said Mrs Peters brightly, 'and did you have any success with your shopping?'

'I was somewhat surprised,' said Bertha, 'to find that *hat elastic* was not included in the "Everything half-price" notice.'

'Hat elastic?' echoed Mrs Peters. She looked bewildered.

Violet sent a sharp glance around the shop before lowering her voice to answer. 'Latterly, I believe, it was called "knicker elastic", but that is *not* the sort of thing we like to ask for in public.'

'Quite,' agreed Mrs Peters, still wondering if it was possible to buy knickers which had elastic threaded at the waist. Surely such garments had vanished thirty or forty years ago?

'Ada looked at a very nice dress which was much reduced in price,' said Violet, speaking in her normal voice now that knickers had been dismissed from the conversation. 'Unfortunately it had a white collar.'

'We've given up things with touches of white at the neck,' explained Ada. 'In the old days our maid used to remove little collars, and cuffs too, of course, and wash them out and starch and iron them, and sew them back after use. We find that rather tiring, don't we?'

The other two nodded in agreement, and Mrs Peters noted, yet again, the number of brooches which the three were wearing pinned to their headgear. At least two of Bertha's were embellished with diamonds, she guessed, which flashed fire as she moved.

Ada had a splendid gold arrow among the half dozen which decorated her fur hat. Violet, more restrained in her decorations, simply sported a silver-mounted monkey's paw pinned across her velvet tam-o'-shanter.

'A pity in some ways,' continued Ada. 'I always liked a touch of white, but one has to forgo these little pleasures when one has no staff.'

At that moment, Gloria appeared with the tray, and Mrs Peters made her escape to take up a strategic position behind the counter, which offered a great many temptations to kleptomaniacs.

She felt a pang of pity for the three venerable figures intent on their refreshment. How their world had changed! No *hat* elastic, not even *knicker* elastic, and no maid to remove, wash, starch, iron and replace those little touches of white last thing at night!

She looked indulgently upon her neighbours. Poor dears, she thought.

Mrs Peters was a thoroughly nice woman.

While the Misses Lovelock were enjoying their coffee, Albert Piggott was making slow progress from his cottage along the snowy lane which led to Lulling Woods. He was bent upon calling to see Dotty Harmer.

These two odd characters shared strong bonds. They both liked animals. They did not care a fig about other people's opinions of them. Sturdy independent individuals, they found a strange comfort in each other's company.

He made his way to the end of the house where Dotty had her quarters. The larger part of the home was now occupied by Dotty's niece Connie and her husband Kit, but Dotty relished her independence and muddled along in what she refused to call 'her granny flat'. She was lucky in that Connie and Kit respected the old lady's feelings whilst still keeping a loving eye on their sprightly relative.

Dotty welcomed Albert and invited him into her cluttered kitchen.

'I'll take off me boots,' said Albert, hopping about in the porch, before sitting down at the kitchen table. It was strewn with a variety of objects ranging from an onion cut in half, a saucer of peanuts, various tins and a collection of papers at one end upon which Dotty appeared to be working.

She pushed them to one side, almost capsizing a glass jar containing a cloudy liquid in which floated some yellow objects which Albert could not identify.

'Fungi,' Dotty said, following his gaze. 'A very nutritious type of bracket fungus which grows on those wild plum trees at the southern end of Lulling Woods. Delicious with cold meat. I'll give you a jar.'

'Thank you,' said Albert, realizing that this offering would join many others in the hedge as he went home. 'Dotty's Collywobbles' was a common local complaint, familiar to Dr Lovell and his partners, and the inhabitants of Thrush Green and Lulling had soon learned that it was wiser not to broach any of Dotty's sinister brews. No one had actually died, but many had hoped to, when suffering from sampling Dotty's offerings.

'Kettle's on,' said Dotty briskly. 'I shan't offer you coffee. It's bad for that ulcer of yours, but I'll give you some of my hot blackcurrant.'

Albert's heart sank, but obviously there was no obliging hedge to hand, and he resolved to take evasive action as best he could.

The kettle gave an ear-splitting scream and Dotty switched it off whilst she bent to rummage in a low cupboard. Several sinister-looking bottles emerged, and from one of them Dotty poured an inky fluid into two mugs.

'There,' said Dotty triumphantly, putting two steaming mugs on the table. 'Just try that! That'll tone up your innards, Albert.'

He took an exploratory sip, repressed a shudder, and watched his hostess attack her own mug.

'You been busy?' enquired Albert, eyeing the profusion of papers.

'Trying to sort out my funeral arrangements,' said Dotty.

'You don't want to start thinkin' about such things,' said Albert. 'It's morbid, that is.'

'Rubbish!' replied Dotty. 'I think one should leave matters as tidy as possible. I'm not so much concerned with the actual *funeral* arrangements. Connie has very good taste in music and choice of hymns, although I have made sure that we don't have 'Ur-bide with me', which I detest.'

'I like it meself,' said Albert.

'It reminds me of the *Titanic* disaster,' reminisced Dotty. 'Those poor people singing that hymn – unless it was 'Nearer my God to thee', equally lugubrious – as they slid into that awful Atlantic. I find it terribly upsetting.'

Albert was dismayed to see that his old friend's eyes were brimming with tears.

Before he could decide how best to cope with this strange behaviour, Dotty had recovered herself and was rattling on again about her demise.

'It's the disposal of the *body* which is the difficulty, as murderers always find. I should *really* like to be buried in the vegetable garden. All that good humus and those minerals being released slowly into the soil would do so much for the plant growth. However, there seems to be a great reluctance to let me have my way about this, and I suppose it must be cremation after all.'

'They do it very nice,' said Albert comfortingly.

'Well, I hope so,' said Dotty doubtfully. She picked up her mug and drank deeply.

'I suppose the ashes would contribute a certain amount of nourishment,' she continued more cheerfully. 'I shall tell Connie to put most of it by the rhubarb.'

Albert felt it was time to change the subject. 'I really come along to see if I could do any little job outside for you. How's the goats? And how's the hens?'

'Most kind of you, Albert! Kit has cleared the snow from the pens, I know, but I should appreciate it if you would check that they all have plenty of dry bedding. And I've got some cabbage leaves here which they'll all enjoy.'

She made her way into the larder, and Albert was about to nip to the sink with his unwanted drink when Dotty returned with a large basket.

'I'll do it right away,' promised Albert, taking the basket and making for the door.

Dotty watched him stumping towards the chicken run, and then turned back to the table.

'There!' she exclaimed, seeing Albert's mug. 'He forgot his delicious blackcurrant!'

For the rest of January the fields around Thrush Green lay white and unblemished, stretching their glistening purity as far as the eye could see.

But at Thrush Green and Lulling the scene was different.

Here the snow was pock-marked with drips from the trees, and stained by the traffic which had thrown slush upon it.

Each day it shrank a little in the hour or two of comparative warmth at midday. The piles of besmirched snow at the roadsides dwindled slowly. The crisp crunchiness had vanished, and boots now squelched rather than squeaked as their wearers went their way.

It was still bitterly cold at night when frost came with the darkness. The first excitement about the snow had long vanished, giving way to a feeling of endurance and a longing for spring.

On the last evening of the month Harold Shoosmith went upstairs to draw the curtains in the bedroom. A new moon, a silver crescent, was rising above the houses across Thrush Green. He opened a window and looked out.

Everything was still. The lights from the Two Pheasants shone upon a black-and-white world. Nathaniel Patten's statue threw a black stain across the snow around him.

Harold's face grew cold. His breath blew a little cloud into the silence about him.

Suddenly, from the bare branches of a lilac tree the stillness was broken by the sweet sad song of a robin.

Gently, Harold shut the window.

February

And in green underwood and cover
Blossom by blossom the spring begins.

A.C. Swinburne

On the second day of the new month the wind changed course and turned from north-east to south-west, much to the relief of everyone.

Now the snow shrank faster, revealing the brown ploughed fields around Thrush Green, and the gardens which had been hidden for so long.

With the thaw came floods. The River Pleshy which bisected Lulling overflowed its banks and spread sheets of water across the meadows beside it. At the lowest point in the town, near the ancient bridge which spanned the Pleshy, the water was two feet deep at one time, and the cellars of the adjacent houses were full of muddy water in which floated such things as deck chairs, garden tables, demoted chests of drawers and other household flotsam, together with beer barrels and smaller kegs.

At Thrush Green the last of the snow slid from the roofs with soft plops, and little rivers gurgled along the gutters and down the hill to join the floods in Lulling High Street. Wellington boots were the only sensible foot-wear as people slid and squelched their way around.

But it was warm again. The sun shone, lighting the

dripping trees into chandeliers of shining droplets. The snowdrops were out, and the stubby green noses of later bulbs pushed above the glistening earth. Nature was on the move again, and everyone rejoiced.

Molly Curdle, making her way across the green from her house to her father's, breathed in the fresh air with rapture. It seemed a very long time since she had been outside and able to enjoy a world beyond that of her own kitchen and that of Joan Young's. The return of colour to the view was particularly welcome. The harsh light from the unrelenting snow everywhere had had a depressing effect, and to see green grass, brown earth, and one or two brave early flowers such as snowdrops and the yellow fronds of witch-hazel raised the spirits of all who had been housebound for so long.

Albert Piggott was not in, but Molly had a key and let herself into her old home. It was warm and quiet. Tired after struggling through the mud of the green, Molly sat down to rest for a moment before seeking her father in the church which she could see through the cottage window.

She looked appreciatively at the room which she knew so well. Everything was in apple-pie order, and shone from Nelly's ministrations.

She had not approved of Nelly when they first met. Her own mother had died when Molly was in her teens, and she had automatically taken over as housekeeper to her curmudgeonly father.

They had not been happy years for Molly, and the fact that she could escape into the welcoming Youngs' household every afternoon was her salvation. Later, after meeting Ben Curdle at one May Day fair on the green, life really took on some meaning, and the happy marriage which followed had transformed her outlook.

Her dislike of her stepmother Nelly began to change to

appreciation. It was true that she still regarded Nelly as over-boisterous and vulgar. She suspected that Nelly was the one who brought Albert to the altar, and not the other way round. In this she was right, and her own natural modesty and feeling for what was correct could never come to terms with this knowledge.

Nevertheless, as time passed, Molly began to realize that Nelly's sterling qualities had been a blessing to all. For one thing, she had released Molly from bondage. She had, within limits, done much to improve Albert's lot. His home was clean and warm, his meals superb, even if too rich and abundant for Albert's ailing digestion, and her income was the only money which really contributed to the household funds.

There was no doubt about it, reflected Molly, noting the shining pans on the hob, the thriving cyclamen on the window sill – her own Christmas present to Nelly – and the spotless walls and floor, Nelly was a first-class manager and deserved the wages and appreciation which her work at the Fuchsia Bush gave her.

She rose to cross the road to the church to find Albert, but at that moment the door opened, and her father appeared.

His welcome was typical. 'Ain't you got the kettle on? I'm fair shrammed with the cold.'

Molly shifted the kettle to the centre of the stove. It began to hum immediately, and she went to the wall cupboard.

'Tea or coffee, Dad?'

'Coffee.'

He sat down with a sigh, and began to blow his nose into a red-and-white spotted handkerchief.

Molly made the coffee and put his mug on the table.

'And what brings you over?' asked Albert. 'Want something, I suppose?'

Molly ignored the churlishness, as she had done so often, and put a Christmas card in front of him.

'I've been meaning to ask you for weeks about this man,' said Molly, 'and kept forgetting.'

Albert studied the card, turning it back and forth.

'What's so special about it?'

'I just wondered if you knew anything about this fellow. He's an American. Anyway, it had an American stamp.'

'Don't mean nothin' to me,' announced Albert, pushing the card across the table. 'What does Ben say? I take it that this was addressed to you two Curdles.'

'That's right.'

'Well, I've done me best to keep away from gypos,' said Albert nastily. 'One of the blighters stole my daughter. In marriage, in case you've forgot!'

Silently, Molly put the card back in her bag, and drank her coffee. It was clear that her father was in one of his more spiteful and truculent moods.

Once again, she decided that the small mystery of the Christmas card should be ignored.

As soon as she had finished her coffee, she made her departure, wishing Albert goodbye at the door.

By this time he was immersed in the local newspaper, and made no reply. Molly relieved her feelings by slamming the door shut as noisily as she could, and set off again across the slippery green.

For once, sympathy for her stepmother was her dominant feeling, but Albert's remark about 'gypos' still rankled.

He had never forgiven her for marrying into the Curdle family. It was plain he never would.

Well, thought Molly robustly, he'd just have to lump it! If it ever came to a choice between her father and her husband, it would be Albert who would go to the wall.

As the flood water subsided and the ground began to dry out, the people of Thrush Green and Lulling started to venture forth from their homes and to meet their friends again.

The news, naturally, was of the weather and all its attendant horrors. Tales of leaking roofs, ruined carpets, power cuts, and the prevalent wave of coughs and colds resulting from such conditions, were exchanged with the greatest animation and exaggeration.

Shopkeepers rejoiced in the return of customers, farmers went out into their fields again, and the Reverend Charles Henstock, vicar of Lulling and rector of Thrush Green, set out with joy to visit those who had been kept from his care by snow and water.

He decided to walk the mile from his home at St John's vicarage through Lulling High Street to Thrush Green. He did not hurry. Everyone stopped to speak to him. He was hailed by the shopkeepers, the dustmen, the window cleaner and his friends at the garage near the river's bridge.

Charles Henstock had no enemies. There was an inno-

cence, a modesty, and a genuine love of his fellow men which protected him from malice of any sort.

He had lived at Thrush Green for many years in a hideous Victorian house which had caused his neighbours, and particularly Edward Young, the architect, considerable pain and loathing.

Charles was not upset by the ugliness nor the discomfort of his home. He had met his second wife, Dimity, at Thrush Green, and they had lived in their uncomfortable

quarters in the greatest harmony, until the house burnt
down, to the relief of Edward Young, and Charles was
given the living of Lulling, Thrush Green and two other
adjoining parishes.

Some of his closest friends lived at Thrush Green.
Harold Shoosmith was a tower of strength when financial
affairs had to be tackled. Dr Lovell and Winnie Bailey
were two more, and Ella Bembridge was yet another.

His wife Dimity had lived with Ella for several years,
and they were near neighbours and friends during Charles's
widowerhood. All three remained close friends.

On this particular morning, he called at Ella's first. She
opened her door, inviting him in, but Charles was a little
dismayed to see that she was dressed ready to go out.

'No, no!' he protested. 'You are just off somewhere, I
can see.'

'Come in for half a minute,' said Ella, in her gruff voice.
'I've got a letter for Dim. From Australia. Came just after
Christmas, and I keep forgetting to send it on.'

She made her way to the kitchen, and Charles followed
her. Whilst she rummaged through a dresser drawer which
appeared to hold dusters, string, jam-pot covers and a
collapsible lacy affair which Charles could not place, he
looked happily about him.

In this very room he had proposed marriage to his dear
Dimity. For him it would always be a hallowed place.

'There we are!' cried Ella triumphantly. She began to
shovel the clutter back into the drawer.

Charles put the letter in his pocket.

'And what is that?' he asked, as Ella was about to thrust
the white lacy bundle into the drawer.

Ella snapped it open. 'It's a cover to keep off the flies,'
she explained. 'Very useful when we have tea in the
garden, or leave meat out for second helpings.'

'Most intriguing,' murmered Charles, his eyes wide with
wonder behind his spectacles.

Ella laughed indulgently at Charle's naivety. Who else
would be so impressed by such a simple contrivance?

They went together through the front door. Ella turned
left to Lulling, leaving Charles gazing happily about him,
wondering whom to visit next.

Before him stood the attractive collection of old people's
homes, built on the site of his own burnt-out house. Here
were several of his friends and parishioners, under the care
of Jane and Bill Cartwright who were joint wardens.

Should he call now, or leave that visit to the afternoon?
He consulted his watch, and was dismayed to find that it
was almost noon.

That decided it. He would call on the Shoosmiths first.

He set off across the green, passed his church where
Albert appeared to be in a state of meditation as he leant
on a broom by the porch, and made his way in high spirits.

It was good to be home again.

From her bedroom window Joan Young had seen Charles
Henstock making his brisk way to the Shoosmiths.

She and Molly were sorting out garments for the next
jumble sale. It had seemed, at the outset, to be a simple
straightforward task, but it was proving to be uncommonly
difficult.

Joan had been the more ruthless of the pair, holding up
jumpers and cardigans and ready to put them on a mount-
ing pile on the bed. But Molly, brought up to be more
prudent, acted as a brake upon such hasty progress.

'That's too good to give away. You always looked nice
in that pink. I'd keep it for a bit.'

Reluctantly, Joan removed it from what she thought of
as 'the slush pile' and put it on a chair.

A heap of Paul's outgrown clothes had to be tackled, and here Joan was firmer in her approach. The better items of school uniform were destined for the school's second-hand shop, but such things as shabby pants, vests and holiday wear were being sorted quickly.

'My George could use those,' said Molly as some things were being held up.

'Then do take them,' said Joan. 'In fact, anything you can make use of, Molly, just put on one side. Most of these are going to end up as dusters.'

It was at this stage that she caught sight of the rector crossing the green, and left her labours to gaze upon the scene she loved.

Thrush Green had changed little since she came to live there as a married woman. She and her sister Ruth had known the place from childhood and she hoped that she would never have to leave it.

The old rectory had gone of course, but few had mourned that architectural monstrosity. Now Rectory Cottages, the homes designed by her husband, stood in its place, and Joan looked upon the buildings with affection. Edward had done a good job, and Jane and Bill Cartwright were equally successful in their care of the old people who lived there.

She had known Jane as a child and followed her career as a nurse with admiration. She was indeed 'a chip off the old block', for her mother Mrs Jennings had been the local nurse and midwife for many years. Old Dr Bailey had relied on her skills hundreds of times, and his successor John Lovell also knew her worth. It had been a great satisfaction to Dr Lovell, as a trustee of Rectory Cottages, when Jane Cartwright and her Yorkshire-born husband had been appointed as wardens.

'Mr Henstock's around,' said Joan.

'Going to see the old folk?'

'Not at the moment. I think he's calling on Harold Shoosmith.'

'Well, he'll be welcome wherever he goes,' said Molly, joining Joan at the window.

'Could my Ben have this cotton T-shirt for cleaning the car windows? Nothing like a bit of real cotton, Ben always says.'

'It's his,' said Joan, turning back to her task, refreshed as always by a glimpse of Thrush Green.

Charles Henstock found Isobel Shoosmith setting the table for lunch, and began his apologies.

'Join us,' said Isobel. 'It's not quite time yet, but do stay.'

'Well –' began Charles diffidently.

'Or is Dimity expecting you back?'

'Well –' said Charles again.

'What's wrong?'

'I don't like to intrude.'

'Charles! Really!'

'But the truth is,' said honest Charles Henstock, 'Dimity's gone shopping in Oxford, and she's having lunch there with an old schoolfriend.'

'Then you can stop,' said Isobel firmly. 'That's settled.'

'She left me something cold,' went on the rector, looking worried.

'Have it this evening,' said Isobel briskly. 'Now, if you want Harold, he's in the garden.'

He found his friend tending a bonfire which seemed reluctant to burn. His sleeves were rolled up, his grey hair on end, and his face decorated with a few black streaks, but he seemed very content.

'Nice to see you. I'm not making much headway with

this – everything's so wet after the snow. But what brings you here?'

'The pleasure of seeing Thrush Green again,' said Charles, 'and one or two little parish matters.'

'Come in and have a drink,' said Harold, abandoning his work and leading the way to the house.

'It's about this summer's fête,' said Charles, when they were settled with their glasses.

'You're the second person to mention the fête,' commented Harold. 'Heavens, man, it's not till July! Edward Young wants me to do his usual job, by the way, as he's hoping to go away during Paul's summer holidays.'

'Well, we shall have to bring it up at the committee meeting,' said Charles, 'but I just wondered if you had any strong feelings about where the proceeds should go this year.'

'I hadn't thought about it. It's usually the church roof or the organ that's in need. What's in your mind?'

'Rectory Cottages.'

'But surely they are in good nick? We're both trustees. There's no doubt there, is there?'

'Well, no. But Jane Cartwright has been wondering if the communal room is really big enough. You see, it's not just the residents of the seven cottages that use it, but their visitors sometimes. And, of course, if they have a party of any sort, it does get rather crowded.'

'But Edward Young went into all that very carefully when he designed it. And also when the conservatory was added.'

The rector began to look unhappy. 'I know. and I should not like to hurt his feelings by suggesting that it is too small, but as a matter of fact, Mrs Thurgood rang me about the matter the other day.'

'Oh!' said Harold, with feeling. 'I begin to see.'

Mrs Thurgood was also one of the trustees. She was an elderly woman who spoke her mind, irrespective of the feelings of others, and was a power to be reckoned with. Mrs Thurgood usually got her way.

The rector had crossed swords with her before over the matter of kneelers at St John's church at Lulling, where she and her daughter were regular worshippers. It had been a doughty battle which the rector had won, for despite his gentle manner, which some took for weakness, when it came to sticking to his guns Charles Henstock was as ferocious as the next.

Nevertheless, his heart sank when Mrs Thurgood approached. It usually meant that there was trouble ahead.

'I thought I'd have a word with Jane,' he told Harold, 'when I call there this afternoon. It is best to find out at root level if there is any need for an enlargement. It would cost a great deal, and mean quite an upheaval while the building was going on.'

'Too true. And then there is Edward.'

Charles sighed. 'Yes indeed. There is Edward.'

They sat surveying their glasses for a moment.

'He'd probably understand,' said Harold at last.

'He's very sensitive,' responded Charles. 'I suppose it is because he is *creative*.'

'Well, aren't we all? I'm creative when I'm gardening, Isobel is creative when she's cooking, but we don't throw tantrums about it.'

Charles laughed. 'You're quite right of course. Nevertheless, I don't like upsetting Edward. He's a good man, but just a little – what shall I say?'

'Touchy?' suggested Harold. 'He was a real pain in the neck when John Lovell said his steps at the Cottages weren't safe. He just can't bear criticism.'

'I know.'

The rector looked sad, and Harold adopted a rallying tone.

'Cheer up! It may never happen. Cross that bridge when you come to it, and all that.'

The rector nodded, and put down his empty glass.

'In any case,' went on Harold, 'I'd sooner face Edward than Mrs Thurgood.'

Isobel put her head round the door. 'Ready for lunch?'

'Always,' smiled Charles.

The mild weather continued, and heart-lifting signs of spring were everywhere.

Yellow tassels of the hazel catkins fluttered from the hedge. Yellow aconites, with ruffs of green, appeared with the snowdrops. Yellow early dwarf irises and early crocuses were about to burst into bloom, and over all spread the kindly yellow sunlight.

Soon yellow primroses would star the woods, and the daffodils would blow their trumpets in the gardens of Thrush Green. Yellow, gold and green, spring's particular colours, would bring hope again after the bleak black and white of winter.

On one of these hopeful mornings, Winnie Bailey and Jenny were discussing the possibility of a lunch party for a few of their old friends.

'We can't seat more than ten,' said Winnie, 'and as far as I can see it will really be a hen party.'

'And what's wrong with that?' asked Jenny.

'Nothing, I suppose. I mean I must ask the three Love-locks, and Ella and Joan Young. They've been so good, fetching and carrying for me through the bad weather. I think Dimity would come too, but that means two men as well. What do you think?'

'I'd let the men fend for themselves that day,' said

Jenny. 'Besides they wouldn't want to be swamped by all of us women.'

'Fair enough. Well, that's eight counting us. What about Dotty and Connie?'

'Ideal,' responded Jenny. 'Now, it's just the food to think about.'

'I'll ring them today and arrange a date,' said Winnie, 'and then we can work out some menus. Something *soft*, I think.'

'*Soft?*'

'Jenny, dear,' explained Winnie patiently. 'Half of us have lost a great many teeth, and the other half have unreliable dentures.'

'I never thought of that,' confessed Jenny.

'You don't when you've got plenty of your own,' said Winnie sadly.

'We might have tapioca,' suggested Jenny.

Winnie snorted. 'I'm not sinking to *tapioca*, teeth or no teeth,' she declared.

It was that same night which hid some very mysterious goings-on in the peaceful confines of Thrush Green.

Later, no one could recall anything unusual during the hours of darkness. Joan Young had stirred at about three in the morning, being obliged to visit the bathroom, much to her annoyance. Harold Shoosmith had padded downstairs at much the same time to switch off the porch light which had been forgotten. Nelly Piggott, asleep in the back bedroom of her home, was dead to the world from twelve until six in the morning, and Albert, in the only other upstairs room, facing the green, was equally oblivious to what was happening across the road.

For something certainly had happened, and it was Albert who made the discovery.

It was nearly half past six when he awoke to the sound of Nelly moving about below. He heard the kettle being filled, the stove being riddled, and the cat mewing for its breakfast.

He also became conscious of the squeaking and banging of the church gate. Someone had left it open, he thought morosely. One of them Cooke lot as like as not.

It was beginning to get light as he crossed the road to shut the gate. Behind him the appetizing smell of rashers frying wafted from the kitchen, and he looked forward to his breakfast.

The gate was damp. There might have been a shower in the night, but the air was mild and it was going to be another pleasant spring day.

Albert sniffed the morning freshness with relish, and was about to return to his cottage when he noticed a strange object in the church porch.

At first sight he thought it might be a large basket or trug left by the flower ladies. So often, heady with the floral displays they had just created, the church floral arrangers left their impedimenta behind, and Albert was quite used to retrieving secateurs, unwanted twigs, lengths of wire and, as in this case, baskets of varying size and shape.

Grumbling to himself, Albert reopened the gate and made his way to the church porch. The sight which met his eyes stopped him dead in his tracks.

The object certainly was a basket. It was a large one with a kind of hood covering half the base, and it was lined with a tartan blanket. Fast asleep in this shelter lay a curled-up dog, no more than a puppy.

It wore a collar from which a long piece of rope led to the iron ring of the church door handle. Albert bent to look more closely, fumbling with the dog's collar to see if there were any signs of identification. There was none.

Albert stood up and reviewed the situation. It was a nice little dog, a white Highland terrier, obviously well cared-for, and in an expensive basket. What worried Albert was its complete inertia. It had scarcely stirred when he had moved its collar round. It had not so much as blinked an eye. Could it be ill?

Deciding that there was nothing to be done immediately, Albert began to shuffle back to his breakfast. The dog was in a safe sheltered place, deeply asleep, and Albert needed time to come to terms with this extraordinary situation. Perhaps Nelly could help?

Nelly put Albert's breakfast on the hob to keep warm and returned with him to the church porch.

'The little love!' she exclaimed on seeing the sleeping puppy.

'But what's to be done?' asked Albert. 'The police?'

Nelly was on her knees stroking the white head. 'Poor little soul! It don't seem to be very lively.' She looked up at Albert. 'Why don't you see Dotty? She's the best one for a job like this. She'll know what to do.'

'I'll go down straightaway,' said Albert.

Nelly struggled to her feet.

'Not till you've had your breakfast you won't,' she said firmly. 'For one thing, Dotty won't be up, and more important, there's a good plate of food waiting for you.'

Even in a crisis Nelly's first thoughts were of her cooking.

The lunch party which Winnie planned took longer to arrange than was first envisaged.

One would have imagined that collecting eight women guests, all apparently free from regular outside employment or the demands of young children or invalids at home, would be a simple affair.

Winnie spent the best part of two days trying to find a time which was convenient to all.

Bertha Lovelock had a doctor's appointment. The dentist was doing something which demanded Violet's attendance and co-operation. Ella Bembridge had an embroidery class. Joan Young, as a magistrate, had to go to her duties on the bench.

Only Dotty and Connie, it seemed, were delightfully free to come whenever it could be arranged.

At last the date was fixed for 1 March, which, as they all reminded each other over the telephone, was not far off, and wasn't it incredible how time flew? Here we were almost at the end of February! Almost into March! Quite astounding.

Much relieved to have the date settled, Jenny and Winnie got down to the serious business of catering for a lunch party for ten elderly ladies with, possibly, dental troubles.

'I suppose a nice round of beef is out?' said Jenny wistfully. 'Can't beat a nice roast, with Yorkshire pudding and horseradish sauce.'

'I know, but I think something in a casserole, or some minced dish would fit the bill. What about a really luscious fish pie? With shrimps in it?'

'I know for a fact Miss Harmer's averse to fish. Percy Hodge took her down a lovely trout last summer, and she never gave him so much as a thank-you.'

'Oh dear! Shepherd's pie? A dish of minced beef?'

'Not very *festive*, is it? *Mince*, I mean. Sounds like school dinners.'

Winnie was obliged to agree, and silence fell.

'Tell you what,' said Jenny at last. 'What about those tube things you like? Pasta things stuffed with mince? We shouldn't need potatoes with those, but have lots of interesting vegetables.'

'Cannelloni?' cried Winnie. 'Why, I think that's a very good idea, Jenny.'

'And the cauliflowers are lovely just now,' continued Jenny, 'and we've lots of our own spinach in the freezer and runner beans.'

'And a starter? Something simple, I think.'

'Grapefruit?'

'Too acid for Ella. Let's have half an avocado pear apiece. Always looks rather luxurious, and should suit everyone.'

'Particularly the Lovelocks,' agreed Jenny. 'They'd never pay out for an avocado pear, even if they split it three ways!'

Much cheered they began to draft the menu.

Nelly Piggott had to depart for her work at the Fuchsia Bush, but Albert made his way to Dotty's cottage as St Andrew's clock chimed half past eight.

He guessed that Dotty would be about, and he was right. He found her clearing away her breakfast things, and twirling a spoon which she had just removed from a jar of honey.

'Want to lick it?' asked Dotty hospitably.

Albert shuddered, and Dotty put the spoon into her own mouth with evident relish.

'So good for one,' said Dotty when she had removed the spoon and flung it into the sink. 'Now, Albert, what brings you here so early?'

Albert told her. Dotty listened attentively until he finished his account.

'And it is still asleep?'

'Well, it was when I had a look just afore I come down, but I think it had moved round in its basket. Looked more lively-like.'

'Very odd,' mused Dotty. 'I shall get Kit to bring me up as soon as he's ready, and we will bring the poor thing here. Leave it with me, Albert. I will get in touch with the police, and the vet too, if need be.'

'But what about old Flossie?' he asked, nodding to Dotty's ancient golden cocker spaniel, a former derelict who had lived happily with Dotty for many years.

'Flossie won't make any trouble,' said her mistress. 'She's got quite enough to worry her with her arthritis, poor love, and in any case, her sight is not what it was.'

'You don't want fightin' and all that,' pointed out Albert.

'There will be no hostility in this house,' Dotty told him firmly. It might have been her redoutable old schoolmaster father speaking, thought Albert, as he went on his way.

Within an hour Kit, Connie and Dotty had met Albert in the church porch, and stood surveying the puppy. It was now attempting to get out of its basket, but was very wobbly on its legs. It was also whining in a very pathetic manner.

'I think,' said Dotty, 'the poor thing has been sedated.'

'Been what?' asked Albert bewildered.

'Drugged. He's now coming round.'

'He?' echoed Albert, peering short-sightedly.

'Indeed it is. A fine young dog,' insisted Dotty, 'and I think the best thing to do is to take him to my kitchen and give the poor chap some hot milk.'

All four set about transferring the animal and his basket to the waiting estate car, and within minutes Albert was watching it make its way home.

'Be all right with Dotty,' he murmured to himself as he shut the church gate firmly.

*

Dotty was at her most energetic in her kitchen. The newcomer had been given a light meal, a long drink of water, and been introduced to Flossie.

She had behaved admirably after the initial sniffing had been done. She wagged her plumed tail and then repaired to her basket and fell asleep. Flossie was accustomed to stray animals in the kitchen, from orphaned lambs, goat kids and ailing kittens, to injured birds and small reptiles. She took the newcomer's presence philosophically.

Dotty settled down to her telephoning and rang her old friend, the local vet. She explained the position and requested an early visit.

'I'm going to Percy Hodge about midday. He's got a cow off colour. I'll pop in and see you between twelve and one.'

'Oh good,' exclaimed Dotty, 'you could have some lunch with me.'

'Very kind of you,' replied the vet hastily, 'but I really can't spare the time.'

He had once suffered from 'Dotty's Collywobbles' after drinking one of Dotty's brews, and had learnt to be prudent.

Her next telephone call was to Lulling police station, a charming building near the great parish church of St John's.

The local police had a reputation as good gardeners as well, of course, as of being exemplary officers, and the police station was adorned with climbing roses and wisteria, and tubs of fine fuchsias each side of the front door, as well as hanging baskets dripping with lobelias, geraniums and petunias in the summer.

In February there was not quite the same pressure on the force's horticultural pursuits, so Dotty was attended to by the sergeant on duty within seconds.

He listened to Dotty's account, and put a few questions.

'In good health, you say, madam?'

'Splendid, apart from some drowsiness still after sedation.'

'And you would like us to take it into custody? I mean, into care?'

Dotty became agitated. 'No, no, no! I am quite capable of caring for him here, as you know. *All* my animals thrive. It is simply that I want you to have the facts so that the owners can be found.'

'We'll do our best, madam,' replied the sergeant, holding the telephone some distance from his ear.

'I can't think why the poor little thing has been abandoned,' went on Dotty, in full blast now. 'He has obviously been looked after very well, coat in excellent condition, nose just the right degree of dampness, and the most expensive basket and rug. It is a complete mystery, officer. A complete mystery!'

The sergeant acknowledged a mug of coffee being put before him by one of his younger colleagues, rolling his eyes heavenward at the same time to show how much he was enduring.

'Leave it with me, Miss Harmer,' he said at last. 'I'd better send someone along to make a few notes later today. For our records, you know.'

'Of course, of course. I shall be at your disposal for the rest of the day. If you are here about four I can offer you a cup of fresh herbal tea. I know you must not take alcohol on duty.'

'Thank you, madam, but no doubt one of us will call before four.'

He put down the telephone with a sigh. 'John,' he said to the younger policeman. 'There's a job for you up at Lulling Woods early afternoon. A Miss Dotty Harmer.

And whatever you do don't eat or drink anything while you're there.'

'Why not?'

His superior officer told him.

March

. . . daffodils
That come before the swallow dares, and take
The winds of March with beauty.

William Shakespeare

March came to Thrush Green like a lamb rather than a lion.

The mild weather of February continued during the first few days of the new month. The sun shone, the birds began a flurry of mating and nest-building, and the flowers of spring began to appear in woods, meadows and cottage gardens.

At Winnie Bailey's house the new month was greeted with more than usual activity, for this was the day on which her old friends were coming to lunch.

After much cogitation and rearranging, the menu had been settled. Avocado pears would be followed by cannelloni served with spinach and runner beans from the freezer and cauliflower from the Women's Institute stall.

The dessert course had proved more difficult. Jenny was loud in her praises of 'a good crumble-top', and cited the home-grown gooseberries and plums bottled last summer.

'Rather *searching* perhaps?' mused Winnie, still anxious about the digestive efficiency of her aged guests. 'I think a well-sweetened apple meringue would be better, and perhaps a fruit jelly as well. And we must remember to order plenty of cream from Percy Hodge.'

'Cream might be too rich,' commented Jenny, slightly piqued at being denied the pleasure of making a large crumble-top, and the undoubted compliments she would have received on bringing it to the table.

'We might have yoghurt,' said Winnie doubtfully. 'What do you think?'

'Things are quite fancy enough with avocado pears and cannelloni,' said Jenny firmly. 'Yoghurt as well would put some of the old ladies into a proper tizz-wazz. They'll like a nice English dish like your apple meringue and cream.'

And no doubt, she thought rebelliously, they would have preferred a nice gooseberry crumble-top if they'd been given it.

By twelve o'clock on the great day the table was spread with a fine pink cloth and matching napkins. The silver was dazzling after Jenny's ministrations, pink candles added to the ensemble, and a low pot of dwarf pink tulips stood in the centre. The sun shone upon all this splendour, the cannelloni was ready for the oven, and Winnie and Jenny hovered by the windows awaiting their guests.

Ella and Dimity were the first to arrive, each bearing a pot of recently made marmalade, and were greeted affectionately, and while they were being helped with their coats, Joan Young's car drew up and the three Misses Lovelock were assisted from it.

'I'll fetch them,' Joan had said when she had heard about the invitation. 'The thought of having to hire a taxi would spoil the whole day for them.'

This was probably true, Winnie realized, but only someone as forthright as Joan would have said so. And no one as generous, thought Winnie, would have so readily have offered to fetch the ancient sisters.

Soon they were all ensconced in the sitting-room sipping sherry, or mineral water, or orange juice, while Jenny shuttled between the kitchen and the visitors, keeping an eye on the cooking.

Dotty and Connie were the last to arrive, and the conversation turned naturally to the extraordinary affair of the abandoned dog.

'Doing very nicely,' Dotty assured them. 'Very friendly, eats well, gets on with Flossie, though of course she finds him rather boisterous.'

'But whose was he?' queried Bertha Lovelock.

'Still a mystery,' Dotty told her. She dipped a finger in her orange juice and sucked it.

'Do you think I might have a knob of sugar, or preferably a little honey in this?' she enquired. 'It seems a little sharp.'

Without a word Jenny went from the room and reappeared bearing a pot of honey on a saucer flanked by a teaspoon.

Oblivious of all eyes upon her, Dotty scooped out a spoonful and stirred it briskly into her glass. The spoon she sucked with relish before replacing it on the saucer.

Amidst a stunned silence Dotty took a sip.

'Delicious!' she announced, and took up her tale again.

'So far we've had no reply to all the questions we've asked. As you probably saw, the local paper had a paragraph about the dear thing, asking for help in tracing the owners.'

'And a charming photograph,' said Winnie. There was a polite murmur of assent, though in truth the photograph had been rather fuzzy, and as the photographer had posed them with the dog held close to Dotty's face, it was quite difficult to distinguish the rough white hair of one from the other. Luckily, Dotty's spectacles came out clearly, which helped a little.

'Could it have been stolen, and then dumped because the thieves were scared off?' asked Dimity.

Ella pointed out that thieves would hardly take the trouble to bring a basket and rug for their captive, and to make sure it was humanely secure in the church porch, and comment was brisk and wildly conjectural until Jenny announced that lunch was ready, and with much fluttering and cries of appreciation the ladies took their places.

The mystery of Dotty's dog was left, as other local topics were discussed over the avocado pears.

'Was it true,' asked Violet Lovelock of Joan Young, 'that there might be an addition to Rectory Cottages?'

She had heard, she said, that the original common room, or drawing-room, or whatever it was called, was turning out to be too small, even with the added extension.

Joan, fiercely protective of her husband's reputation as an architect, parried the question.

'It's the first I've heard of it,' she replied. 'That room has always seemed adequate to me, and I know Edward went into the dimensions most carefully when the building was designed.'

'Oh, I'm quite sure of that!' agreed Violet, helping herself to a spoonful of spinach. She was conscious that she had made a gaffe, which was particularly unfortunate as Joan had been kind enough to collect her and her sisters, and would be needed very soon to return them to Lulling.

'If they do want more room,' said Dotty brightly, 'those glasshouses you stick on the end of one room might be just the thing.'

'But that's been done,' said Joan.

'The new fellow near the Drovers' Arms,' continued Dotty, 'has just had one put outside their dining-room, and I had coffee there the other morning. Very good, wasn't it, Connie?'

'Very warm and light,' agreed Connie.

'I meant the coffee,' began Dotty, quite ready to embark on coffee, tea, herbal beverages of all sorts, not to mention the recipes for making them, but was forestalled by Jenny who helped her to runner beans and stopped the flow.

Conversation grew more general, much to Joan Young's relief, though she still worried about the possibility of the enlargement of the room Edward had originally designed. She was sure that he had not heard any of these rumours, and she hoped that he never would.

Joan was devoted to Edward, but knew only too well that criticism infuriated him, and that peace would vanish from their household if he felt that his work was being denigrated.

'And how is Paul?' asked Winnie, sensing tension.

'Ah, Paul!' smiled Joan. 'We had a marvellous time when he was home at half-term.'

And to Winnie's relief, she was told about a visit to an animal sanctuary which had been a day in paradise for a twelve-year-old schoolboy.

Less controversial topics than the possibility of an enlargement of Rectory Cottages were being discussed around the table. Connie enlarged on the beauty and intelligence of the new dog. Ada Lovelock told Jenny about a wonderful new cure for arthritis which Jenny might be glad to know about as time passed so quickly when you reached seventy. As Jenny was still in her forties, she might have resented this aspersion on her age, but being a good-hearted woman and quite used to the eccentricities of the Lovelock sisters, she listened with every appearance of interest.

Ella told her neighbour about the tapestry she was making for an altar kneeler, and Dimity told Bertha Lovelock that milk was supposed to be good for cleaning patent leather shoes, and Violet Lovelock told everyone within earshot about the brisk business being done at the Fuchsia Bush these days, and Jenny and Winnie exchanged contented glances at the success of the party which had been their main concern for so long.

By half past three the last of their visitors had gone. Dotty had returned for her handbag, but otherwise all had departed flushed and happy with their modest outing, and Winnie and Jenny subsided into armchairs.

'I'll stack the dishwasher,' said Jenny, attempting to get up.

'You won't yet,' said Winnie. 'And before we do that we'll have a cup of tea. But first all, Jenny, do you think there's any truth in these rumours about the old people's home? I hope it's not true. Edward would be so upset.'

'Well, let's hope it's only a rumour,' comforted Jenny.

There were other people who could have told Winnie more about the rumour.

On that February day when Charles Henstock had enjoyed lunching with Harold and Isobel, he had gone afterwards to see his old friends and parishioners at Rectory Cottages.

Jane Cartwright, one of the wardens, had welcomed him, and without preamble, the rector mentioned the matter of enlarging the room. Was it necessary, he asked?

Jane looked a little taken aback, but answered readily. 'I'm not sure how this cropped up, and in ordinary circumstances the room is quite big enough now that we have that glass annexe. If we have a party of visitors then I must say it is a bit of a squash.'

'The thing is,' said Charles, 'finding the money. We've raised an amazing amount over the last few years for Nathaniel Patten's settlement in Africa, and the Roof Fund and the Organ Repair Fund, and one or two items for the school and so on, and I really don't think we can face another large fund-raising effort if it is not needed.'

'Quite,' said Jane. 'Besides, it might upset Edward Young.'

'That is so,' agreed Charles, looking unhappy.

'Though that's his chicken,' said Jane robustly. She had no time for imagined rebuffs, and was used to coping with the day-to-day misunderstandings among her elderly charges which she privately dismissed as 'senile tantrums'.

'I must sound out one or two other people,' went on the rector, 'and you might make a few enquiries here to see if people feel the need for a larger room. Perhaps we could enlarge the conservatory? What do you think, Jane?'

Jane said that if it came to it, then adding to the conservatory would be lovely. What had put this idea into his mind?

Charles was hard put to it to tell her. Something to do with the church fête in July. Not that anything like the amount from the receipts would cover the cost of this extra glass affair, which was why he was anxious not to start another large fund-raising project so soon after the others.

Leaving matters at this unsatisfactory stage, the rector bade Jane farewell and went to visit her charges

Molly Curdle was the innocent cause of the rumour coming to the ears of Edward Young.

In Joan's kitchen one morning, she asked Joan if Mr Young would be asked to add to Rectory Cottages if the need arose.

Edward Young, who was searching in a dresser drawer for a particular old kitchen knife in constant demand by all the household, turned to confront Molly. Joan's heart sank.

'What's all this about?' he demanded.

Poor Molly recognized at once that she had made a serious gaffe. She knew the signs of wrath well enough, and had been familiar with the raised voice, red face and blazing eyes for many years.

'It was just something I heard,' she faltered.

'Who from?'

'It may have been my dad.'

Joan came to the rescue. 'Calm down, Edward. You know what John told you.'

John Lovell was Edward's brother-in-law, the local doctor, and knew Edward could be the victim of his own worries.

Edward turned away muttering to himself. 'Well, if there's any truth in these rumours, I shall find out who is spreading them.'

He strode out of the kitchen, and the two women exchanged looks.

'Oh lor'!' whispered Molly. 'That's torn it. I shan't mention *that* again.'

Nelly Piggott, bustling about in her kitchen at the Fuchsia Bush, had also heard about the possibility of the annexe to Rectory Cottages, but had given the matter scant attention.

She was quite used to hearing stray bits of gossip from Albert which he had picked up at the Two Pheasants. Half the time nothing came of these rumours, and Nelly had quite enough to do without wasting time and energy on such conjectures.

At the moment she was concerned with a certain small poster which had been pasted on the door of the Fuchsia Bush ever since the discovery of the abandoned dog in St Andrew's church porch. On that exciting morning she and Mrs Peters had decided to assist in finding the owner, and had put up the notice in the hope of finding someone who might know more about the mystery.

But now, it seemed, the dog was happily settled with Dotty, the police were no nearer solving the problem, and the notice was looking decidedly shabby. To Nelly's discriminating eye, it was detracting from the spruce appearance of their establishment. Some naughty person had written a very rude word at the foot of the poster, and Nelly felt that the time had come to remove the whole thing.

She glanced at the clock. It said half past eight. Mrs Peters was probably in the office already, she thought, for they were always early at the premises, making a start before the staff arrived.

But the office was empty, and Nelly was about to return to her duties when the telephone rang.

It was Mrs Peters, sounding weak and distraught.

'Nelly, I don't know what's hit me, but I can't come in at the moment. I'll try and make it later this morning.'

'Something you've eaten?' queried Nelly, her first thoughts, as always, on cooking.

'I just don't know. I feel so sick. Anyway, there's nothing specially urgent today, is there?'

Nelly mentioned the poster on the door.

'Yes, yes! By all means take it down, Nelly. See you before long, I sincerely hope,' she apologized.

Nelly replaced the receiver. She was full of sympathy for her suffering colleague, but quite confident about running their business on her own for a short time, for this had happened before.

She went to the door and tore off the notice. Nothing had come of it, she thought sadly, but they had done their bit.

On returning to the kitchen Nelly was annoyed to see

that the new young kitchenmaid Irena had not arrived. She was just out of school, not very bright, but was engaged to do the vegetables and wash up the cooking utensils.

'Drat the girl!' said Nelly crossly. 'Now I'll have to get Gloria to help me.' This would be extremely unpopular, for Gloria was employed as a waitress and considered herself much above helping in the kitchen.

Two minutes later the back door opened, and Irena appeared. Her right thumb was heavily bandaged, and Nelly's heart sank.

'And what, pray, have you been and done?'

The girl flushed. 'It was the bread knife. I was just testing the blade like, and my little brother 'it me on the back. It's bled awful.'

Nelly examined the clumsy bandage. It appeared to have started life as a piece of shirting, and was grubby and bloodstained.

'Well, I'm not having that in my kitchen,' said Nelly vigorously. 'Germs fair oozing out of it, and the customers flocking along to the hospital in droves by the end of the week.'

The girl drooped her head and began to fiddle with a wooden spoon on Nelly's well-scrubbed table.

'Don't you touch nothing now,' shouted Nelly. 'You'd best go straight home and tell your mum to take you to the doctor. You might need a shot of whatever-it-is to kill them germs. You can't handle food like that, my girl. We'd all end up in court, and that's the truth.'

The girl began to sniff and looked so forlorn that Nelly's heart was touched.

'There, don't take on! It'll be all right in a day or two, I don't doubt, but you stay home till it's healed.'

She rummaged in a dresser drawer, found a bar of chocolate and handed it to the tearful Irena.

'Off you go now, and let me know what the doctor says.'

She hustled the girl to the back door, and watched her cross the yard. In the outside store room stood a sack of potatoes, two dozen fresh cauliflowers and a great basket of carrots.

Gloria will have to see to that, thought Nelly, and there will be plenty of black looks flying about this morning.

What next, she wondered? It was not long before she found out.

While Nelly Piggott was busy in her kitchen, and the forlorn Irena and her mother were making their way to the surgery of one of Lulling's doctors, Dotty Harmer was busy preparing breakfast for Flossie and her new dog, which she had christened Bruce.

'Being Scotch, you know,' she told Connie. 'If it had been a bitch I should have called it Bonnie for 'Bonny Scotland', you see.'

She patted the white head of the Highland terrier, and was rewarded with a loud barking and much tail-wagging. Bruce was now thoroughly at home, and Dotty hoped that his former owners would never appear to claim him.

'It's so strange that no one has come forward,' commented Connie. 'It's obviously from a distance. I mean, anyone within six miles of Lulling and Thrush Green would recognize the dog from its description in the *Gazette*. And it was so well-cared for. I can't think why it was simply abandoned like that. After all, if some tragedy had happened surely the RSPCA would have taken care of it?'

'Maybe the owners didn't like the idea. Maybe they were religious people and thought that one of the saints would look after it if it were left on church premises. St Francis, for instance,' said Dotty brightly.

'But he's been dead for centuries,' pointed out Connie, 'and anyway he lived in Italy.'

Dotty surveyed her niece with severity. 'At times, Connie, you are far too apt to take things *literally*. I was trying to point out that some people would look upon the church as a *sanctuary*, and where anyone in need would find help. I can't help feeling that Bruce's owners might have had that in mind when they left him there. Of course, I don't think St Francis would have personal intervention in the matter.'

Connie could see that the old lady was quite prepared to launch into an interesting discussion on the intervention of

saints into contemporary life at Thrush Green, with particular reference to St Francis of Assisi who, Connie had heard her say, 'must have been a charming man'.

But Connie had lunch to prepare, and four telephone calls to make, so she gave her aunt a quick kiss, and left her with her pets.

At the Fuchsia Bush things were not going easily for Nelly Piggott. Gloria was late arriving, and decidedly sulky about having to do Irena's vegetables' preparations.

'I'm not paid for this sort of work,' she told Nelly. 'It's Irena's job. She gets above herself, that one. It's having that stuck-up name. She's always getting out of doing things.'

'Irena's granny was from Russia or Prussia, I forget which, and she was named after her. And as for shirking her jobs, I see she doesn't do that!'

Gloria flounced to the sink, muttering darkly, and Nelly hurried into the shop when she heard Willie Marchant, the local postman, shouting to inform her that he'd propped the post by the basket of rolls.

He was banging the door behind him as Nelly took the

letters to the kitchen. Almost all were for Mrs Peters, and these she put in the office, but one was addressed to Mrs Nelly Piggott, and this she took to the kitchen.

Gloria's back registered umbrage and Nelly had a pang of pity.

'I'll give you a hand in half a minute,' she promised, and sat down to read her letter. She rarely received a letter, and she took her time in studying the postmark on the envelope and then the address at the head of the flimsy lined paper inside. The letter came from someone in Leicester who signed herself as Mrs Jean Butler.

It read:

Dear Mrs Piggott,

Charlie asked me to write when he was took ill. I am sorry to say he died in hospital last week. He was a lodger here since last summer working on the roads.

We are burying him next Friday, and if you want to know more the lady I work for don't mind you phoning of a morning.

Yours truly,
Mrs Jean Butler

There was a telephone number at the foot of the page, but Nelly was too stunned by the news to notice it.

Charlie dead! Charlie so full of life and fun, cracking jokes, teasing everyone, the life and soul of every party! He couldn't be dead.

She dropped the letter on the kitchen table, staring ahead as tears began to fill her eyes.

She had loved that man. For him she had left Albert and Thrush Green and gone to share Charlie's life for over a year. For most of that time they had been riotously happy, laughing with friends at pubs, going to dances and bingo, enjoying their shared bed and board.

But towards the end Charlie had shown himself as a liar and a deceiver, sharing his affection with a woman whom Nelly had considered a friend.

There had been a violent row. Hard words had flown across the kitchen, and harder saucepans had accompanied them. Nelly had stormed out, and returned to Thrush Green, dreading Albert's wrath and possible rejection.

The wrath had certainly been in evidence, but Albert was so relieved to see her back to cook his meals and keep house that she was allowed to stay. Albert was glad to have this secret weapon of retaliation in his armoury when warfare broke out in the home, and Nelly, ebullient as ever, soon became her cheerful self, and forgot Charlie.

Only once had she seen him, and that was when he called into the Fuchsia Bush some two years before the arrival of the sad letter before her.

He had been a beaten shabby figure making his way to see an old friend in Birmingham with hopes of a job there.

Nelly had given him a meal and money, and sent him on his way saying that that was to be their last meeting.

And it was, thought Nelly.

'You going to give me a hand?' called Gloria, 'I can't do this lot alone.'

Nelly mopped her eyes and went to do her duty.

'What's up?' asked Gloria, suddenly solicitous on observing Nelly's ravaged face. 'Bad news?'

'An old friend. He's dead.'

Gloria put a wet hand on Nelly's ample back, and patted her kindly. This was as good as the telly really, and poor old Nelly wasn't such a bad old soul, although she was a bit of a slave driver.

'Local?' enquired Gloria.

'No. Though he did come here once.'

Light dawned. Gloria, and her fellow waitress Rosa, had

been greatly intrigued by that traveller who had called one snowy morning and made Nelly's heart flutter.

'That nice chap,' said Gloria diplomatically, 'who was after a job?'

Nelly nodded and attacked a carrot. She was afraid to trust her voice, and the lump in her throat was painful. They worked together in silence, until Irena appeared at the back door holding up a neatly bandaged hand.

'Two stitches, and some tablets for something called Auntie Bi-something, and I can't come to work for a week.'

She sounded proud and happy, and quite oblivious of the air of tragedy hanging over the kitchen.

'See you next week then,' said Nelly dismissively, and Irena vanished.

Mrs Peters did not arrive, but luckily the Fuchsia Bush was not too busy that morning, and there were no outside commitments.

Since Nelly had been made a partner in the business, outside catering had increased and had proved rewarding. The Fuchsia Bush had built up a reliable reputation and catered for functions such as weddings, christenings and other family occasions.

It was Nelly too who had instigated the making of a daily batch of rolls filled with ham, tongue, cheese or other delights for the local office staffs to purchase for their lunches. This venture had proved very successful and greatly added to the profits.

Her heart was heavy as she supervised the depleted staff, but the fact that she needed to be extra busy kept her from brooding over the death of dear Charlie. Later, she told herself, she would ring that Leicester number and find out more, but she had no intention of attending the funeral. Should she send flowers? She thought not. It would be best to keep all this from Albert. He had had quite enough of Charlie in the past.

During the afternoon when Nelly was helping to set the tables for tea, the telephone rang again. A neighbour of Mrs Peters told Nelly that the doctor had sent her to hospital as her stomach pains were so severe.

Mrs Peters had asked Nelly to carry on. Perhaps Mrs Jefferson could lend a hand, or knew of someone? Mrs Jefferson had worked for many year at the Fuchsia Bush and was now enjoying retirement. Mrs Peters would be in touch as soon as possible.

Nelly put down the receiver, and went to tell Gloria and Rosa.

'Never rains but it pours,' said Rosa.

'What do we do now?' asked Gloria.

'We carry on,' said Nelly, rolling up her sleeves.

A little further south in Lulling the rector was also answering the telephone.

Mrs Thurgood, a parishioner and fellow trustee of Rectory Cottages, was enquiring – one might say *demanding* – if Charles Henstock had done anything about enlarging the premises.

Trust Mrs Thurgood to push matters along with unnecessary velocity, thought poor Charles, holding the receiver some distance from his ear. Mrs Thurgood had a powerful voice.

'I have had a word with Jane Cartwright who seems to think that the present room is quite adequate for general purposes.'

'That's not how I heard things were.'

'And I've spoken to Harold Shoosmith—'

There was a snort at the other end. Mrs Thurgood did not approve of Harold. Too often he had been the victor in their clashes. Charles, she thought, was made of tenderer stuff, and it was he whom she approached first when beginning a campaign.

'And he feels as I do,' continued Charles undaunted, 'that there is no real necessity to consider the matter further.'

'Oh really?' said Mrs Thurgood, heavily sarcastic. 'And what about the old people's needs? I have their welfare very much at heart. They should be considered.'

Charles decided that he must be firm. 'It is the first thing we all think of, as I'm sure you know. But there is the matter of finance to consider as well. We have raised a great deal of money recently for Nathaniel Patten's African settlement, and helped Thrush Green school at its centenary, and there are a great many repairs due to be done on the churches of the parish. I think the enlargement of the room can wait.'

'I shall bring the matter up at the next meeting of the trustees,' said Mrs Thurgood.

'Please do,' said Charles in his gentlest voice, and put down the receiver.

Sometimes, he thought sadly, it was very hard to love one's neighbour as oneself. He escaped into the garden which always lifted his heart.

A blackbird piped from the lilac tree, and at the further end of the lawn a thrush was poised, head on one side, listening for the sound of a worm underground.

The daffodils were in bud. Some early narcissi were already flowering, filling the air around them with heady scent. The polyanthus plants turned their velvety faces to the morning sunshine, bright yellow, orange, red and a deep mauvish-blue which Charles particularly admired.

The almond tree was beginning to scatter the pink blooms which had cheered the February days, but the nearby cherry tree was in bud and soon would be in flower.

Charles remembered the words of A.E. Housman, who wrote of the wild cherry tree in Shropshire:

> *Stands about the rural ride*
> *Wearing white for Easter-tide.*

Easter-tide, thought the rector with mingled joy and alarm! Very soon now, and much to prepare for that lovely festival. Perhaps he should return to his desk?

He looked up at the blue and white sky above the nearby spire of St John's. '*From whence*,' thought Charles, '*cometh my help.*'

And went, serenity re-established, to face his tasks.

Nelly Piggott did not ring the Leicester number that morning. She did not trust her voice, for one thing, and added to that was the more pressing situation at the Fuchsia Bush.

As soon as the bustle of lunch was over, Nelly sat down in Mrs Peters' office and rang Mrs Jefferson. Could she help?

The answer was enthusiastic. Obviously the old lady was thrilled to be asked, and keen to come, but there were certain reservations. She was still under doctor's orders, and she had better ring him about the invitation. She would do so at once, she promised Nelly, and ring back.

Nelly then telephoned the hospital and was informed by a crisp voice that Mrs Peters was at that moment being examined by Mr Pedder–Bennett himself.

If she had said that the archangel Gabriel was at Mrs Peters' bedside she could not have sounded more reverential, thought Nelly crossly.

'If,' said the voice, 'you ring this evening, we shall know more.'

Within half an hour Mrs Jefferon rang again to say that Dr Lovell said that as long as she only did four hours a day, that was fine by him. Could she come from ten until two? Thankfully, Nelly agreed. Mrs Jefferson, well-versed in the ways of the Fuchsia Bush, knew just when help would be most welcome.

Nelly sat for a moment in the quiet office. She was unutterably tired, and for two pins would have put her heavy head on the desk and gone to sleep.

But there was much to be done, and she roused herself. Later she would ring the hospital at the callbox on Thrush Green. That was essential. Another telephone call must be made, for tonight was bingo night, and she could not face that at the moment. She would ring Mrs Jenner who lived along the lane from Thrush Green to Nidden, and explain matters, telling her not to bother to call on her way, as was her usual custom.

And then tomorrow morning she would ring the writer of the letter which lay crumpled in her apron pocket. She would make the call here in the privacy of the office, away from Albert and with time to compose herself before facing the world again.

Nelly had resolutely put all thoughts of Charlie from her mind since their last meeting, but the news of his death had made her realize, with sharp poignancy, just how much that damned dear deceiver had meant to her.

April

It is very well to hear the cuckoo for the
first time on Easter Sunday morning. I loitered
up the lane again gathering primroses.

Francis Kilvert

No one at Thrush Green heard the cuckoo on Easter
Sunday, for the festival came early in the month. The
Cotswolds too can be colder in spring than the Welsh
valleys which the Reverend Francis Kilvert so loved over a
hundred years ago.

But the primroses were out, and bunches of them decorated the font at St Andrew's, and in the churchyard the
daffodils swayed in the wind.

The little church of St Andrew's had been lovingly
dressed with spring flowers and leaves by the local ladies,
and very fine it looked. The larger and more venerable
church at Lulling would no doubt be more lavishly decorated, thought Winnie Bailey, as she rose with the rest of
the congregation when Charles Henstock and the choir
processed down the aisle from the west door.

St John's at Lulling, standing dignified and serene
behind its large expanse of Church Green spread before it,
had a devoted band of worshippers, many of them with far
more money than those at Thrush Green, and they made
sure that their noble church was splendidly decked at all

times, and particularly at the great festivals of the Church.

Hothouse flowers from nearby glasshouses were willingly given. Arum lilies, fuchsias, geraniums, and even orchids delighted the eyes of St John's congregation at such times, but nevertheless, thought Winnie surveying their more modest efforts, St Andrew's could hold its own on a bright Easter Sunday.

The church was fuller than usual, even though the service had been put forward by one hour to allow Charles to fit in as many attendances as possible in his four parishes.

Winnie was among many friends. She supposed she knew everyone there, she thought, sitting down to listen to Harold Shoosmith reading the first lesson behind the shining eagle which spread out its wings obligingly as a lectern.

She glanced across the aisle, recognizing with pleasure Mrs Jenner's summer straw hat which proved that winter was really over. This year it was refurbished with a navy-blue ribbon with short streamers at the back. Last year it had been encircled with imitation wild roses. Winnie felt that the ribbon this year was more dignified.

With a slight shock she realized that someone unknown to her was sitting immediately in front of Mrs Jenner.

A man with very thick blonde hair was listening attentively to the lesson. He was wearing a grey suit with a chalk stripe, and it reminded Winnie of the suits, termed 'demob suits' which had been issued to returning warriors after the Second World War. But this one was better cut and seemed to be made of very good cloth. She wished she could see his tie and shirt, for Winnie had an eye for clothes and had always taken an interest in Donald's wardrobe.

Unfortunately, she could see only the stranger's broad shoulders, but when Percy Hodge came round with the collection bag the man turned to put in his contribution and Winnie was pleased to see that his shirt was a blue-and-white striped one, and his tie was dark blue. He was certainly a very handsome fellow, and Winnie was not the only one in the congregation to speculate about the stranger in their midst that Easter morning.

After the service Charles Henstock waited in the church porch to greet his parishioners, as was his wont. The tall stranger was among the throng as they came out, but seemed to be anxious not to obtrude upon the vicar and his friends. Many eyes were turned upon him, but nothing was said.

When the last of the church members had straggled away, the rector was about to hurry to his car for the service at St John's when the man approached him.

'Could I have a word, sir?'

The accent was American, the manner almost timid, contrasting strangely with the size of the man.

Charles gave him the warm smile which had melted so many female hearts, and held out his hand. 'Of course. How can I help?'

'I'm over from the States to look up some relatives. Name of Curdle.'

'Ah! We are very proud of the Curdles in these parts,' Charles told him. 'In fact, the most famous one is buried only a few yards away.'

'I found her grave yesterday,' replied the man. 'She's the one I wanted to visit first. Now I want to find some living Curdles. Can you tell me where to go?'

'I can indeed.' The rector looked at his watch.

'I could take you over to meet them myself, but there are two things against it. I am due at my next service in a few minutes, and I know that the Curdles are away this weekend. But let me show you where they live.'

He took the stranger by the arm in a companionable way, and they stepped round the church path to the north side where Charles stopped and pointed out the fine old house belonging to the Youngs.

'My!' said the man. 'They've gone up in the world if that's their place!'

Charles explained that Ben and Molly had a more modest abode in the garden.

'But come and see me at the vicarage,' urged Charles. 'How long are you staying?'

'I want to look up friends in Edinburgh, and I have some business which may detain me there. I reckon I'll have to go there on Tuesday, or whenever it fits in with their schedule. My name by the way is Andersen, with an E, and my forename is Carl.'

'How do you do?' said Charles, shaking hands again. 'And I am Charles Henstock. Do come to the vicarage at Lulling if you can spare the time. Anyone will direct you. I am so sorry that I have to hurry away now. Perhaps I can give you a lift?'

'Thank you, sir, but I'll look around for a bit. Perhaps when I get back from Scotland?'

'That would be ideal. I shall look forward to it, Mr Andersen,' said Charles, turning back to the church.

'Mr Andersen with an E, and "skedule" not "schedule",' said Charles to himself, as he drove back to St John's. 'And what a nice fellow! I hope he comes again, and I can be of help.'

Across the road from St Andrew's church, Nelly Piggott

noticed the stranger wandering about the churchyard. He stopped every now and again, and seemed to be copying the inscriptions on some of the tombstones into a little notebook.

Nelly, who had always had an eye for male beauty, was impressed by the blonde good looks of this ambling giant, but had other matters on her mind which took precedence that morning.

For one thing, she was cooking a small turkey with all its accompaniments. For another, she had a great deal to think about the job at the Fuchsia Bush. And lastly, but by no means least, she thought about the pathetic news of Charlie's departure from this life.

She had said nothing to Albert about this matter, but had rung the Leicester number and spoken to Jean Butler. As far as Nelly could make out, that good woman had virtually looked after Charlie for the best part of a year, and though she talked of him as 'a lodger', she had evidently received no payment from him.

It was typical, thought Nelly, as the tale unfolded, that Charlie should land on his feet. Obviously, the old charm was still there. Jean Butler had been in tears, and spoke of her late lodger with true affection.

Nelly told her that it would be impossible for her to leave her job to attend the funeral, and expressed her sympathy. She almost added that they were in the same boat, but managed to resist the temptation. She was also careful not to give her address or to express the hope that they might one day meet. She rang off, glad that she had ended the affair with such discretion, but shocked by the description of Charlie's sufferings.

He had, Jean Butler told her, 'just wasted away'. He had cut his foot which had turned septic. Gangrene had set in. It had not responded to treatment, and his foot had been amputated. All through this time Jean Butler had seen him daily. According to her, he had remained brave and cheerful to the last, and had promised to take her to a dance as soon as his new foot was fitted.

It was this last flash of Charlie's spirit which particularly upset Nelly, and the poignancy of it haunted her thoughts.

It was perhaps as well that the day-to-day running of the Fuchsia Bush was now entirely in her hands, for Mrs Peters remained in hospital. Mrs Jefferson, Rosa, Gloria and the now-healed Irena backed up the establishment and two temporary girls had been taken on to help with the running of the place. There was little time for tears, and for this Nelly was grateful.

She had also found some comfort in confiding in Mrs Jenner, one of her weekly bingo companions. Mrs Jenner was much respected in the neighbourhood. For years she had been the local midwife, and was the mother of Jane Cartwright who ran Rectory Cottages with her husband Bill.

Mrs Jenner had lived all her life in the old farmhouse along the road to Nidden. Percy Hodge, her brother, still farmed there, but lived next door with his new wife Gladys. When Charles and Dimity Henstock had become homeless overnight following the fire at Thrush Green rectory, it was Mrs Jenner who had come to the rescue, and given them lodgings at the farmhouse.

As soon as Nelly had rung on that sad evening, to say that she would not be at bingo, Mrs Jenner guessed that something serious had happened.

'Come up here one evening soon,' she said to Nelly. 'Just you and me for a nice chat.'

'I'd like that,' said Nelly. 'Can we make it on Friday?'

Albert was ensconced in the Two Pheasants when Nelly walked through the dusk of evening to visit her friend.

As the tale unfolded, Mrs Jenner listened with growing

sympathy. Like most Thrush Green residents, her first impressions of Nelly had been censorious. It was generally agreed that she was noisy, pushing and 'a bit common', that damning phrase which had blighted so many villagers' characters.

Her affair with Charlie, the oilman, whose van visited the area once a week, was soon being discussed with much headshaking.

Not that Albert, as the injured husband, merited much sympathy, and when Nelly scandalized the community by going to live with Charlie, some people said openly who could blame her with that old misery Albert for a husband?

But latterly things had changed. Nelly's success at the Fuchsia Bush, her unfailing cheerfulness, and her exemplary cleanliness had made her neighbours willing to admit that there was a lot to commend Nelly Piggott.

Mrs Jenner had been one of the first to offer friendship, and her example had prompted others to welcome Nelly into Thrush Green society.

On that April evening the bond between the two women grew stronger than ever. Although Mrs Jenner deprecated Nelly's passion for the flibbertigibbet Charlie, she was wise enough to recognize that love can strike in the most uncomfortable and unpredictable ways, and that really Nelly was perhaps more sinned against than sinning.

Certainly, as Nelly poured out her tale, with her tears, sitting in Mrs Jenner's wicker armchair, her hostess was almost as moved as her sorrowful guest.

She fell back on the common panacea in times of stress. 'I shall make us a nice pot of tea, dear,' she told Nelly.

And she did.

It was about this time that Edward Young came across

Jane Cartwright, as they had both gone to post letters in the box by the wall of the Youngs' house.

'Ah!' greeted Edward. 'Just the person I wanted to see.'

Jane smiled happily. She had no inkling of what was in Edward's mind, but she had always looked upon him as a good friend.

She put her two letters in first, and Edward thrust a fat bundle of mail in after hers.

'It's about that room of yours. I hear it's considered inadequate.'

Jane's heart sank. From his tone she realized that he was annoyed, and knowing his reputation for 'touchiness' she felt dismayed.

However, she was a brave woman, and answered straight-forwardly. 'It's perfectly adequate for its purpose,' she said. 'I don't know who started these rumours. I've heard them myself, so I know they may have worried you. If we have a party, of course, which doesn't happen very often, I suppose we could do with more space.'

Edward grunted. 'So there's nothing to complain about?'

'Indeed not. We love the building and the added conservatory.'

Edward looked slightly mollified. 'Anyone else spoken to you about this affair?'

'Well, the rector asked me what I thought. I told him exactly what I have told you. He seemed relieved. He said we couldn't really afford to make any enlargements.'

'That's quite true. And I'm glad he was relieved. I am too. I did my level best to make those buildings absolutely right at the time.'

Jane was glad to see that he seemed calmer. 'You did a first-class job there,' she told him, 'and we all appreciate it.'

They parted company with relief on both sides.

*

During April the trustees of Rectory Cottages met in the Henstocks' dining-room at Lulling.

The meeting was at eight o'clock and Dimity had provided coffee and drinks for the assembled company. Having supplied her guests she retired to the vicarage sitting-room and watched a gardening programme on television. She found it very peaceful.

In the dining-room next door, the even tenor of the Usual Business had also gone its peaceful way, until Charles, as chairman, had enquired if there were any other business, and Mrs Thurgood raised her voice.

'I am greatly perturbed to hear that the communal room is too small,' she stated.

All eyes turned towards her. Charles, who had expected this matter to be raised, found that his attention was caught by Mrs Thurgood's hat.

Usually that lady's hats were high-crowned affairs with wisps of veiling or silk swathed around them, reminiscent of Queen Mary's toques of Charles's youth. But this evening she was wearing a round straw hat with an upturned brim and two streamers of ribbon hanging at the back. It seemed rather a youthful style for such a formidable figure, and Charles felt that it was vaguely familiar.

'Any comments?' he asked the assembled company, still secretly puzzling about the hat.

'I don't think,' said Harold Shoosmith, 'that the room is really too small. I had a word with Jane Cartwright and one or two of the people at Rectory Cottages, and everyone seemed quite happy with the present arrangements.'

Mrs Thurgood bridled, and the two streamers quivered. Light dawned on Charles. Of course, the hat was exactly like those worn by Edwardian children at the seaside! A sort of summer sailor's hat! He smiled with relief.

Mrs Thurgood shot him a disapproving glance. For two pins, Charles thought, she would tell him that it was 'no laughing matter'. But the lady's attention was directed to Harold.

'That is not what I heard,' she said firmly. 'It was Captain Jermyn himself who mentioned it to me.'

There was a visible relaxation of tension. Captain Jermyn, a crusty old veteran of two world wars, was known to be an inveterate troublemaker.

Charles rallied to Harold's support, making a mental note to consult Dimity about the hat when the meeting ended.

'I too have spoken to several people, and all seemed to find the room adequate.'

John Lovell also added his mite, saying mildly that he knew his brother-in-law, Edward Young, who had designed the building and the annexe, had taken infinite trouble over the dimensions of the sitting-room. He himself had always thought it pleasantly spacious. 'What's more,' he added, 'it would be horribly expensive to enlarge.'

'We've raised money before,' snapped Mrs Thurgood. 'Jumble sales, fêtes, coffee mornings, whist drives – I've helped with all of them *myself*! And I've had another idea recently. Janet, my daughter, would be quite willing to have an exhibition of her abstract paintings, and I'm sure people would flock to see it.'

From the expressions of dismay which were apparent on the committee members' faces, this hopeful vision of queues jostling to see Janet Fairbrother's incomprehensible daubs seemed unlikely.

'But where could it be held?' asked someone, playing for time.

'I thought the town hall,' said Mrs Thurgood. 'Of course, the rental of the place would have to come from our funds, but the profits should easily cover that. I propose a fund-raising effort.'

Charles took charge. 'I think we should put Mrs Thurgood's proposal to the vote. Can I have a seconder?'

There was a stony silence, whilst looks were exchanged.

'Well,' said Charles, 'it looks as though we must let the matter rest.'

'*You* may,' said Mrs Thurgood forcefully, 'but I shall not!'

And five minutes later the meeting ended.

In bed that night, Charles asked Dimity if she had noticed Mrs Thurgood's hat.

'It reminded me of the sort of thing my father wore as a boy at Walton-on-Naze, according to family photographs.'

'It's a Breton straw,' Dimity told him.

'A Breton straw?' echoed Charles mystified.

'Sailors wear them in Brittany,' yawned Dimity. 'I had one just after the war. They seemed to be in fashion after D–Day.'

'But surely there wouldn't be any sailors in Brittany wearing hats like that on D–Day,' replied Charles. 'I mean the beaches were swarming with troops, and any Breton sailors would be in uniform. Don't you think that style really goes back to earlier times?'

But Charles received no answer. Dimity had fallen asleep, and Charles shelved these sartorial problems and followed suit.

Edward Young, who was also one of the trustees, had been unable to attend the meeting, which was just as well, for he would have become extremely heated in the light of Mrs Thurgood's assertion that the sitting-room he had so carefully designed was too small. John Lovell, as Edward's doctor, felt particularly relieved that his irascible brother-in-law was absent. Such an atmosphere might well have brought on Edward's shingles again.

Nevertheless, Edward, who still found the rumour rankling, asked several local friends for their opinion. All did their best to reassure him. Most of those asked were genuinely of the opinion that the room was quite all right as it was.

One or two, including Molly Curdle who knew Edward's quick temper, kept any doubts about the adequacy of the room to themselves. Anyway, all agreed that it would cost a great deal of money.

Edward calmed down, and general relief was felt in the Youngs' household.

Edward was gazing from his drawing-room window one fine April morning, and feeling pleasantly relaxed as he surveyed Thrush Green and Rectory Cottages looking particularly fine in the spring sunshine. He admired the tubs of velvety polyanthus and wallflowers which stood each side of the Two Pheasants' doorway. Nearer at hand he saw that the lilac bushes near his own gate would soon be in fragrant bloom. There was no doubt about it. Spring took a lot of beating at Thrush Green!

As he gloried in the view before him, he noticed a small car pulling up near his gateway. A large fair-haired man got out, consulted his wrist-watch, and then went rather hesitantly across the road to stroll on the dewy grass of Thrush Green.

Edward watched him with curiosity. One did not often see strangers on Thrush Green.

Near by, Winnie Bailey and Jenny, busy changing sheets in the front bedroom, also noticed the stranger.

'Now who can that be?' wondered Winnie aloud, stuffing a pillow into a fresh pillowslip.

'Can't see properly,' said Jenny, approaching the window.

'I do hope it's not one of those *travellers*,' said Winnie. 'I believe they send out a sort of scout to find out the lie of the land. Thrush Green is just the sort of place for dozens of broken-down vehicles to park, isn't it?'

Jenny was reassuring. 'He looks too respectable to me. Might be one of those reps just stretching his legs before he goes down to Lulling to sell something to the shops there.'

'I do hope you're right. Connie was telling me a fearful tale about a friend of hers in Dorset who was absolutely surrounded by caravans and buses and tents for weeks. She couldn't get her car out of the garage.'

'She should have rung the police.'

'She did, but there's some stupid business about letting people stay for a certain length of time before action can be taken. At least, that's what Connie told me. Her friend was virtually a prisoner in her own home.'

The two women peered out of the window. The stranger was approaching the Two Pheasants, and Mr Jones emerged and engaged the man in conversation. There was a good deal of nodding and smiling, and Mr Jones pointed towards the Youngs' house.

'Well,' said Winnie after a few minutes, 'he seems to be going to see Edward and Joan.'

'Then he *must* be respectable,' said Jenny. 'Nothing to worry about.'

The two returned to their bed-making.

Edward Young opened the door.

'I'm looking for Mr and Mrs Curdle,' said the stranger. 'Have I come to the wrong house?'

'Actually, their house is over there,' replied Edward, pointing to the old stables, across the garden.

'I'm sorry to have troubled you,' said the stranger, retreating, but Edward called him back.

'There's no one there at the moment. Molly has gone across to see her father who lives over there near the pub, and Ben's at work in Lulling. Why don't you come in and wait for Molly? She'll only be a few minutes.'

'That's sure kind of you,' said the man, following Edward into the hall.

Edward was curious about his visitor. Obviously he was an American, but why did he want to see the Curdles? At least he sounded as though he had a genuine reason for being in Thrush Green. For one awful moment he had wondered, as Winnie and Jenny had, if the fellow were spying out the land for an invasion of unwanted self-styled *travellers*. The trouble with such people, Edward had thought, was that they seemed to be *settlers*, rather than *travellers*, and Thrush Green could do without them.

He saw now that his guest was well-scrubbed and his blonde hair recently washed. He was dressed in very good clothes of an informal type, a silk shirt and a cardigan which looked suspiciously like cashmere, and Edward looked at his shining shoes with envy.

At that moment, Joan came in and Edward turned to the stranger who had leapt politely to his feet.

'Oh, I didn't realize you had someone here,' said Joan.

'My wife, Joan, and I am Edward Young,' said Edward.

'And I am Carl Andersen,' said the stranger, 'with an E.'

'How do you do?' said Joan. 'With an E? Like Hans Andersen? Is he a relative, by any chance?'

'No such luck, ma'am, but my folk came from his country, Denmark, way back.'

'From "*Wonderful, wonderful Copenhagen*"?' laughed Joan, quoting from the musical.

'Nearer Odense, I'm told, where Hans Andersen was born. I was brought up on his stories.'

'Me too,' said Joan, 'and now I'll get some coffee.'

'I've been admiring the houses here,' said Carl Andersen. 'Those new ones have fitted in real well.'

Edward smiled. 'I designed them,' he said with some pride.

'Is that so? I'm in the building line myself. I take it you are an architect?'

'That's right. And you?'

'More in the way of construction. Large stuff like bridges and dams.'

Edward looked at him with greater interest. 'You're not Benn, Andersen and Webbly, by any chance?'

'That's right. At least, it was my pa that was the first Andersen. I just fell into his shoes, as it were.'

'A most prestigious firm,' said Edward reverently. 'They've done outstanding work all over the world. I've followed all they undertake with the greatest interest.'

'Well, I'm sure proud to be with them,' replied Carl. 'I've just been up to Scotland to discuss a big project up there. All pretty exciting.'

Joan appeared with the coffee, and the conversation became more general, until Edward, full of curiosity, asked directly what brought their visitor to Thrush Green.

'It's something my mother asked me to do. She's an old lady now, and an invalid, but she was born and raised at Woodstock near here, and old Mrs Curdle was her godmother.'

'Well,' cried Joan, 'this is absolutely amazing! Ben is her grandson, you know. She brought him up, but I've never heard about her godchild.'

'I expect you know that Mrs Curdle's fair used to go on to Woodstock after it had performed here. Old Mrs Curdle and my mother's mother were old friends, and Mrs Curdle took a great interest in her god-daughter. My mother has never forgotten her. She wanted me to look up her relatives in these parts.'

'Well, Ben is her grandson, as we said. Whether he remembers your mother from so long ago, I just don't know.'

'But how did your mother go to America?' Edward wanted to know. Joan, not for the first time, deplored her husband's uninhibited questioning, but said nothing.

'My pa was stationed at RAF Upper Heyford near Woodstock, during the war, and he met my ma at a dance.'

'But this is really romantic,' cried Joan. 'So he took her back with him when the war ended?'

'Not quite. This is where Mrs Curdle comes into it. My ma wrote regularly to my pa when he returned to the States, but she got no mail from him for months, and began to think he'd dropped her. Maybe even had a wife over there all the time. You know how it is.'

'So what happened?'

'She was beginning to wonder if she'd think about getting tied up with a guy from Eynsham who was pretty persistent. She told her godmother all about it, and Mrs Curdle told her to be patient because she said my pa would surely be writing soon. She told my ma she had something called 'second sight', and all would turn out fine and dandy. And it did. My pa came over, whipped her up and took her back home.'

'But why hadn't the letters got through?'

'As soon as my pa got back he took up his old job with Benn and Webbly, as it was then. He was working full steam for them, and had rooms in Chicago near the firm. The daughter of the house was sweet on him, and kept any mail from Woodstock out of sight. Burned it, no doubt.

And for weeks my pa left his mail on the hall table to be sent off, and that young good-for-nothing burned them too, I guess. Anyway, they each thought the other had stopped feeling the way they did, until my pa came to his senses, guessed what was happening and sent a cable.'

'Amazing!' said Joan. 'So dear old Mrs Curdle was right.'

The visitor looked at his wrist-watch and stood up. 'I've taken up too much of your time,' he said. 'Thank you for the coffee. I'll go and see if Molly Curdle's in now.'

They said goodbye to him at the kitchen door, and watched him approach Molly who was pegging clothes on a line near by.

'Well, I must say,' said Edward, 'I enjoyed all that. Not many of our visitors are so entertaining. I hope he comes again.'

Later that morning the Youngs saw Carl Andersen driving towards Lulling, and a few minutes later Molly Curdle came into the kitchen where Joan was making a cake.

'Isn't it exciting?' said Molly, sitting down at the table.

'And isn't he handsome? Could be a film star. I've always liked fair men.'

'I'm surprised you picked Ben then,' commented Joan, sprinkling sugar into the mixture in the bowl. 'He's a real dark beauty.'

'Oh well,' said Molly indulgently, 'that's different. Ben was always special.'

'Where is Mr Andersen staying?'

'At the Bear in Woodstock. His mother used to work there when she was a girl. She was there when she met his dad. He wants to meet Ben, and he's gone down to the garage to fix a time for a chat. I hope he'll come to supper tonight.'

'I'm sure he'd enjoy that.'

Molly looked doubtful. 'I don't know about that. It wouldn't be half as grand as dinner at the Bear, but he seems keen to come.'

'Of course he does! And Ben will be able to tell him more about Mrs Curdle than anyone else I know.'

'Dad must remember some things,' said Molly thoughtfully. 'He always said a lot on Fair Day.'

'Complimentary?' asked Joan with a smile.

Molly laughed. 'It was usually a good old moan about the noise and the mess to be cleared up next day! I don't think I'll send this nice Mr Andersen to see my dad!'

The reason for nice Mr Andersen's presence at Thrush Green was soon known and widely discussed.

Mr Jones at the Two Pheasants regretted that the handsome stranger should think the Bear at Woodstock could offer better accommodation than his own.

'Ah, but his mum used to work there,' said Albert Piggott, who had learnt a lot from Molly.

'I wonder if she was that girl young Steve Smith was so keen on just after the war,' speculated Percy Hodge. 'He used to cycle over from Eynsham every evening. Good old pull that was, on a windy night.'

'Love'll drive you anywhere,' said another customer, in a maudlin tone. There was a heavy silence while the old men contemplated their distant romantic pasts.

'Before my time,' said Mr Jones briskly. 'I was in hospital getting over working for the Japs on the Burma railway.'

Across the green Winnie Bailey and Jenny enthused about the wonderful good looks of the stranger, and tried to remember if they had ever come across his mother in days gone by.

Rosa and Gloria at the Fuchsia Bush had been intrigued by Nelly's news of this blonde giant who had excited so much interest in Thrush Green. He had not yet visited their establishment, but they had seen him walk by, and agreed that he was almost as handsome as Paul Newman and Robert Redford, though Gloria admitted to preferring dark men, preferably with a moustache and a pigtail.

But Nelly soon cut into their romantic conjectures by telling them sharply to lay up for lunch and to give the front window a bit of elbow grease.

For Nelly had enough to think about. Mrs Peters was still in hospital, and the nurses were remarkably unforthcoming about her coming out in the near future.

And if she did, Nelly told herself, it would be a long time before the poor soul would be strong enough to take up her duties again.

What would the future hold for the Fuchsia Bush?

May

But winter ling'ring chills the lap of May.

Oliver Goldsmith

The last few days of April had been bright but cold, but on the morning of May Day the skies were dark and the wind boisterous.

It was as well, thought Joan Young, gazing from her bedroom window as she dressed, that Mrs Curdle's May fair was not obliged to perform in such inhospitable surroundings.

The horse chestnut trees, in bright young leaf, tossed their tormented branches, and the puddles below shivered in the wind. The spring flowers, jonquil, daffodil and tulip, were thrown this way and that by the wind. Some had succumbed altogether and were lying broken and besmirched on the ground.

How unlike the firsts of May that she remembered! Somehow Mrs Curdle's fair had always seemed to take place in sunny weather. Was this the result of old age, wondered Joan? Was she looking back through rose-coloured spectacles at those distant days when she and her sister Ruth had swung on the swing-boats and looked down upon the roofs of the Two Pheasants and Piggott's cottage and their own house, with such heady rapture?

Nearer in time she recalled the excitement of her young

son Paul on May Day. It was the high spot of Thrush Green's year for him, just as it had been for herself and Ruth and countless other children.

She turned away from the streaming window and the lashing wind, and found comfort in times past.

Near by, Winnie Bailey was also remembering those days when Mrs Curdle's fair enlivened Thrush Green. It was many years now since that formidable figure, dressed in black, had advanced up the garden path with the enormous bunch of artificial flowers which she had made for her annual tribute to Dr Bailey and his wife.

These bouquets were received with due ceremony and greatly admired for their handiwork. Mrs Curdle carefully bound split wood with fine wire to make great mop-heads of an exotic type of chrysanthemum. The blooms were dyed in gorgeous colours, so vivid that nature had no chance here to emulate art.

Mrs Curdle herself was an honoured visitor, and sat upright and regal in the Baileys' drawing-room, graciously accepting a glass of sherry and exchanging the year's news.

No, thought Winnie, watching the rain beating down her forget-me-nots, the first of May was not what it was. How she missed dear old Mrs Curdle!

There were others who remembered her on that wild and wet morning. Dotty Harmer, turning the calendar page from April to May in her untidy kitchen, thought sadly of times past when she had hurried up the lane to see the excitement of Mrs Curdle's fair, with Flossie tugging at the lead.

Today she was worried about Flossie. The old dog wanted only to lie in her basket. Any movement seemed to pain her, and an occasional yelp and whine gave voice to Flossie's growing arthritis.

All Dotty's home-produced herbal cures seemed to be useless. Soon she must call in the vet for some professional advice, loath though she was to do so, but she was not going to let dear Flossie suffer unnecessarily.

Meanwhile, she diverted young Bruce with a ball rolled along the floor, to keep him from annoying the invalid. He was a dear little dog, thought Dotty indulgently, but like all young things, *over-active*. She would like to have let him run free in the garden, but the lashing rain deterred her, and he was still at the adventurous stage when he would rush off and get lost if he were on his own.

Perhaps the only Thrush Green resident who did not hark back to the days of Mrs Curdle was Nelly Piggott, who had braved the elements to arrive early at the Fuchsia Bush.

To be sure, Albert had made some comment about May Day in a gloomy way, but Nelly had been too busy washing up the breakfast things, and flying about the place with a duster, to take much notice. She had hardly known Mrs Curdle, and was too preoccupied with affairs at the restaurant to take much notice of Albert's meanderings.

For things at the Fuchsia Bush were worrying. Mrs Peters was still in hospital, and although the day-to-day running of the business did not daunt Nelly, and the catering was as efficient as ever, the financial side posed a serious problem.

It was Mrs Peters who kept the books in apple-pie order; she who dealt with wholesalers and discounts, with invoices and deliveries, auditors and accountants. Nelly was completely out of her depth with the office work, and she and Mrs Peters had agreed that someone must be responsible for this side of the business until the invalid was judged fit enough to return.

To Nelly's relief, one of the women from the accountant's office had been charged with the task of taking over Mrs Peters' duties. She was an elderly spinster who had been with the firm ever since leaving school. She was soon to retire, was polite, efficient and wholly respectable.

Nelly loathed her. She thought her stuck-up, bossy and condescending. Nevertheless, she realized that Miss Spooner was doing a good job which she was quite unable to tackle herself, and with her usual good sense she came to terms with this unwanted stranger in their midst. In any case, Miss Spooner only came in twice a week, which caused Nelly some relief.

She was fierce if she heard the girls criticizing the newcomer, and was careful to hide her true feelings. To staff and customers Nelly displayed complete loyalty to Miss Spooner, declaring that she 'was doing a wonderful job at the Fuchsia Bush'.

But how she prayed for Mrs Peters' early return!

*

Farther afield in Woodstock, Carl Andersen watched the
rain through the windows of the Bear. It drummed on the
flagstones of the courtyard at the rear of the hotel, and the
raindrops spun like silver coins as they hit the hard surface.

It was ten thirty in the morning. In three days' time he
would be flying back home. It had been a rewarding trip,
he told himself, both from the firm's point of view, and his
own personal search for Mrs Curdle's descendants.

Ben had been extremely helpful, supplying memories of
his redoubtable grandmother and some photographs which
Carl had had copied to take back with him to give to his
mother.

He decided that he would like a last look at the church
records, and wondered if Charles Henstock would be at home.

On impulse he rang the number at St John's vicarage
and Charles answered. He invited Carl to come as soon as
he liked.

'We have coffee about eleven,' he said hospitably, and
Carl said he would set off at once.

He found Lulling High Street awash, and very few
pedestrians about. One or two brave folk were struggling
along, heads bent against the onslaught, clutching umbrellas which threatened to blow inside out at any moment.

It was good to gain the peaceful atmosphere of the
vicarage sitting-room. He apologized for troubling Charles
again, for he had called to see him soon after Easter and in
the rector's absence he had studied the church records
which Charles had left out for him.

A slip of paper with Charles' neat writing on it lay on
the table by Carl's coffee cup. It was simply a confirmation
of the note which Carl himself had made earlier. It gave
Mrs Curdle's name and dates, and the date of her interment
in Thrush Green churchyard and the name of the officiating
clergyman.

'You see there is so little more to tell you,' said Charles apologetically. 'She had no permanent address. She was a true itinerant, and the caravan was her home. I am so glad to know that you met Ben, and have been in touch with people who remember your mother in Woodstock.'

Carl agreed that he had found a great deal which would interest and comfort his mother.

'I fear she's not long for this world, sir,' he told Charles. 'And she'd always planned to come back and see Mrs Curdle and thank her for all she did for her when things looked black. She used to tell me that I wouldn't be here at all but for Mrs Curdle, and would never have been a true American with the finest pa in all the world, if it hadn't been for Mrs Curdle.'

'She spoke the truth.'

'I might well have been an Oxfordshire boy,' went on Carl, 'perhaps living in Eynsham.'

'Well, you could have done a lot worse,' Charles told him, with a smile. 'You would probably be just as proud of your background, though if I may say so, perhaps not as handsome.'

Carl had the grace to flush. 'I'm sure you're right. As for looks, I simply take after my old man who was a real good-looker, streets ahead of me.'

'Then I can quite understand why your mother was content to wait for him,' replied Charles.

'I spent quite a time with the old folks at Rectory Cottages,' said Carl. 'Jane Cartwright gave me a lot of help, and an old lady who used to live near here, I believe, remembered Mrs Curdle, and so did Jane's mother Mrs Jenner. I've got a real bundle of notes to take back home.'

'And you've made a lot of friends too,' Charles told him, as Carl made for the door.

'I guess I have,' agreed the other. 'I'll be coming back to see them sometime.'

'We shall all look forward to it,' Charles assured him.

By nightfall the rain had ceased and the wind had dropped, much to everyone's relief.

Nelly Piggott, sitting at the kitchen table with a mug of coffee in front of her, relished the peace of the house, for Albert was next door at the Two Pheasants and all was quiet.

It had been a tiring day and a visit to Lulling Cottage Hospital to see Mrs Peters had been particularly upsetting. She had been moved from the large hospital in the county town, and as soon as she was strong enough to be discharged, she would move to her home.

Meanwhile, arrangements were being made for help in the house, home nursing and all the other matters which were necessary for the return home of the invalid.

'You let me know what I can do,' said Nelly, privately shocked by the pale face and evident weakness of her old friend.

'You're doing more than enough now,' Mrs Peters told her. 'If it weren't for you the Fuchsia Bush would have packed up long ago.'

'Rubbish!' said Nelly stoutly. 'Anyway, you'll soon be back.'

Mrs Peters remained silent, but her thin hands began to pleat the edge of the sheet. To Nelly's horror she saw a tear fall upon her work.

'I'm sorry,' sniffed the invalid.

'There, there! Don't take on. It's only weakness, my love. You'll soon pick up.'

She pulled her chair closer to the bedside, and patted one of the frail hands. The invalid raised her head and looked through her tears at Nelly.

'I don't think so, Nelly. They won't tell me anything, but I don't believe I'll ever get over this one. I'm done, Nelly. This time I'm done.'

For once, Nelly could say nothing, and after a few minutes she left the hospital and made her way home.

With infinite sadness, she perceived that her friend had spoken the truth.

It was Ben Curdle who drove Carl Andersen to Heathrow in the hired car which Ben would return to the Lulling garage.

The two men spoke little on the journey, but there was a companionable feeling between them as Ben coped with the heavy traffic and Carl considered the results of his visit.

'You're coming back soon, I hope,' said Ben as they swung into the approach to the airport.

'Sure. Later this year. And Ben, think about that trip to see us over there. You and Molly and the kids, of course.'

'We'll think about it. Of course we will.'

'It would make my old ma so happy. Don't leave it too late now.'

They drew up, and Carl got out. He seemed to have a mountain of luggage, but refused to let Ben help.

The two shook hands warmly.

'I'll write,' promised Carl. 'It's been great to find some of the family.'

'Family?' queried Ben.

'Well, I suppose we're sort of cousins in a way. What you might call god-cousins!'

Ben laughed. 'If you're sure you can manage I'll get back then,' he said, gazing at the string of cars which had formed behind him. 'Seems that folk here prefer my room to my company.'

And he turned the car in the direction of Lulling.

*

While Ben was driving homeward on the motorway, Dotty Harmer was watching the vet carrying out routine tests on poor Flossie.

The spaniel was submitting to all these attentions with very little reaction. She had wagged her plumy tail feebly when the vet had arrived, but been to weak to emerge from her basket.

Dotty had greeted him warmly and indicated a large bundle of pink rhubarb, swathed in two of its own great leaves, which lay on the kitchen table among various jars and bottles.

'I hope you like rhubarb.'

'Very much. Most kind,' said the vet, kneeling by the basket.

'So many people dislike it. My old father called it "a noxious weed", but he ate it all the same.'

The vet rolled back one of Flossie's eyelids and studied his handiwork.

'Healthy?' queried Dotty.

He grunted noncommittally, and pressed Flossie's chest. Dotty fell silent, and watched.

After some minutes he rose to his feet. 'She's pretty groggy.'

'You don't have to tell me that,' said Dotty tartly. 'That's why you're here.'

'I'd like to have her at the surgery for a day or two. Under observation, you know. I've some new tablets that I'd like to try. They've been very successful in cases like this.'

Dotty looked at him steadily. Her eyes were very bright behind her spectacles. 'Can't I give her the tablets here?'

He shifted uncomfortably under that sharp gaze. 'It would be quieter for her, and I could give her more attention,' he countered. 'I really should feel happier if I had her with me.'

There was silence as the two looked down upon the invalid.

'Very well,' said Dotty at last. 'I will give you an extra rug that she particularly likes.'

She rummaged in an untidy cupboard, and emerged with a piece of blue blanket. The vet had picked up the basket, with the unprotesting Flossie, and Dotty tucked the blanket over her.

She accompanied the vet and his load to the car, and saw the invalid comfortably settled.

The vet strapped himself in, and gave a reassuring smile. 'Don't worry. I'll take great care of her at the surgery.'

'I know you will. And I shall want the body back here for burial,' said Dotty with frightening gravity.

The car drove off. There was no pulling the wool over those sharp eyes, thought the driver, feeling unusually shaken. His father, he suddenly remembered, had been taught by Dotty's martinet of a father at the local grammar school.

It seemed that his daughter was made of the same stern stuff.

Of course, news of Flossie's removal to the vet's care was soon common knowledge at Thrush Green. The general feeling was that poor old Dotty had seen the last of Flossie, and that the vet had been humane enough to see to the spaniel's last hours away from her doting mistress.

It was Betty Bell who brought the news to Harold and Isobel Shoosmith when she blew in to set about her domestic chores. Betty also spent one morning a week at Dotty's though, as she said, it was 'love's labour lost', as the muddle which she cleared up reappeared as soon as her back was turned.

Nevertheless, she was fond of the old lady, and grieved with her over Flossie's expected demise.

'Ever such a sweet nature that dog had,' said Betty to
Harold, as she bustled about his study, snatching up books,
ornaments and any bric-à-brac that stood in the way of her
flying duster.

'Well, luckily she has the new puppy to comfort her,'
said Harold watching his pipe-rack swinging on the wall
after one of Betty's onslaughts.

'Not the same,' said she, taking a swipe at a distant
curtain rail. 'He'll be all right when he's calmed down a
bit, but to my mind he's too boisterous for an old lady like
Dotty to manage.'

'If she can cope with those devilish goats of hers,' said
Harold, who had twice been knocked to the ground by
Dulcie and her progeny, 'she can manage a puppy. But
maybe Flossie will get over this. While there's life, you
know.'

Betty stopped whirling for a moment, and shook her
head sadly. 'No, I don't think that's possible. The vet's a
good chap, but I reckon he took poor Flossie off to do her
in compassionate-like, to save Dotty's feelings.'

'Maybe,' said Harold, eyeing the clock. 'Have you finished in here, Betty? I've got a mound of letters to write.'

'Just done,' cried Betty, having a final flick at Harold's
desk. 'Got you straight, and now I'll tackle the stairs.'

She went singing from the room, and Harold straight-
ened his papers and tried to straighten his wits. Betty, he
felt, was like a strong wind. It cleared all in its path but
was dreadfully exhausting.

It seemed impossible, everyone agreed, that Flossie could
return, and the general feeling was that the vet had acted in
the kindest possible manner, and that Bruce, the new
puppy, would be some comfort to Dotty in her sad loss.

It was a great surprise, therefore, when the invalid
returned to Dotty's kitchen, amidst general rejoicing.

Whether the vet's new pills had done the trick, or the temporary respite from Bruce's boisterous attentions, or whether just a change of scene had brought about Flossie's recovery, no one could say, but everyone was delighted to hear about the reunion. Congratulations poured in and the vet's stock, always high in Thrush Green and Lulling, grew higher still.

Albert Piggott, who had secretly been surveying Dotty's garden for the best plot in which to inter her spaniel, now set aside his spade, comforting himself with the thought that his labours had been only postponed. The preparation of final resting places had always given Albert gloomy satisfaction.

Meanwhile, the invalid enjoyed her cosseting and the loving attention of Dotty and Bruce.

On sunny days, her basket was put in a sheltered spot and she dozed or simply gazed about her old haunts, at the apple blossom above her, and the daisies starring the grass by her bed.

Sometimes she took a gentle walk down the path, and pottered about in the meadow beyond, sniffing the old familiar scents and returning, splendidly gilded, from the yellow buttercups which had engulfed her.

Flossie had returned to life, and found it sweet.

By the middle of May, 'that loveliest month' was living up to its name. The cold winds and heavy rain which had marred its advent had given way to sunshine and all the heady promise of early summer in the Cotswolds.

The gardens of Thrush Green were bright with tulips, forget-me-nots and wallflowers. The roses were showing plump buds, and the wisteria on the southern walls drooped massive tassels against the Cotswold stone. The hawthorn hedges along the road to Nidden were spattered with white flowers, and here and there a briar rose added its pink frailty.

Winnie Bailey had decided to take a morning walk along her favourite lane, cow parsley frothing each side as far as the eye could see, and was delighted to come across Ella Bembridge, her friend and neighbour, resting her elbows on a farm gate and gazing across the little valley to Lulling Woods.

'Well met!' called Winnie. 'Are you playing truant like me?'

'I'm testing my vision,' replied Ella.

'Testing your vision?' echoed Winnie, joining her at the gate. 'Do you think you need glasses?'

'I have them already for close work, but it's my long sight I'm worried about. I saw the eye chap at Oxford yesterday.'

'And what did he say?'

'I've got something which goes under the pretty name of Senile Macular Degeneration.'

'My word! That sounds rather depressing. Does it hurt?'

'Not a bit, but the retina is not doing its stuff. The worst bit for me is that I can't see colours as keenly as I did. Maddening with my embroidery work.'

'It must be,' agreed Winnie sympathetically. 'So what can be done?'

'Not much. Extra bright light, large-print books, that sort of thing.'

They resumed their walk together, passing Percy Hodge's farm, and patting his collie dog which bounded out to greet them.

'The worst of getting old,' said Winnie, 'is the time one has to spend in patching oneself up. I have to go to the chiropodist tomorrow and the dentist on Thursday.'

'I notice you say "kyropodist",' said Ella. 'I do too, but so many people say "shiropodist". I don't know which is right.'

'I say "kyro" because I imagine it comes from the Greek, but I'm open to correction.'

'I've been meaning to look it up,' said Ella, 'but as soon as I go to find the dictionary, the telephone rings or something boils over on the stove.'

Winnie nodded her agreement at this cussed aspect of life, and the two paced along together enjoying the May morning and each other's company.

They paused by a small copse of beech and hazel on the left of the lane. A mist of bluebells covered its floor, giving off an unforgettable scent, the very essence, thought Winnie, of a sunny May morning.

Above the bluebells arched long tentacles of bramble, just putting out young leaves and stretching prickly arms to catch at the hazel boughs above. The two women gazed in silence at this timeless scene until, with sighs of content, they turned to make their way back to their duties.

They stopped at Winnie's gate to admire the splendid copper beech tree in the Youngs' garden. The young leaves were now auburn, and thick enough to hide the noble frame of the tree which had been displayed throughout its naked winter form.

'You know it was quite pink a fortnight ago,' said Ella. 'Just a pink haze with all the branches and the trunk showing through. A marvellous sight.'

'I'm glad your sight was up to it,' said Winnie. 'And don't forget, if you want needles threaded or wool or silk matched bring the things to me and I'll help.'

'Thanks a lot, Win,' said Ella gruffly. 'Always does me good to see you. Let's have another potter together before long.'

'Willingly,' agreed Winnie.

Mrs Peters was now at home in her house near Church Green at the farther end of Lulling from Thrush Green. She was glad to be back, and the return to her own surroundings seemed to give her renewed strength and will to live.

A widowed cousin had offered to come and help. She was no nurse, she explained from the outset, but she could run a house, and shop and cook, and be alert for any needs that her patient might require.

The local nurse came in daily, and many friends called for short visits so that the day passed as pleasantly as was possible for one so ill.

Despite her weakness, she was avid for news of her

beloved Fuchsia Bush and Nelly was a regular visitor. She was glad to be able to report that all was running smoothly, as indeed it was, despite the absence of the senior partner.

One evening in May, when Nelly was at the patient's bedside, she was surprised to be asked to get in touch with Mrs Peters' solicitor.

'I particularly want to see him about my will,' she said. 'Ask him to come here one morning, whenever he can manage it. And with my will, please.'

'But can't you ring him?'

'I could, but there always seems to be someone about, and if you make the appointment from the office I'd feel happier. He can ring me to confirm his time for calling. Young Mr Venables is always so obliging.'

'Young Mr Venables', as opposed to 'Old Mr Venables', who had been dead for fifty years, was himself in his seventies and officially had retired from the family business some years before.

However, Justin Venables was a man of habit and life did not seem quite right without regular attendances at his Victorian furnished office in Lulling High Street, so twice a week he called in to do a little business with carefully selected and honoured clients. This, incidentally, was a great relief to Mrs Justin Venables who found his presence in the house, after eight-thirty in the morning, the time at which he had departed for years to his office, a great encumbrance to her own domestic timetable.

Nelly walked back to Thrush Green that evening much perturbed. She did not like this talk of wills. To her it sounded ominous. Had poor Mrs Peters been told something by the doctor? Was she in a weaker state than she appeared to be? Did she know, as a fact, that recovery was impossible?

It was all very upsetting, and Nelly was too worried to notice the lilacs and syringas which scented the evening air, or to hear the rooks clattering about the trees by St Andrew's church as they fed their clamorous young.

The house was empty, and Nelly was thankful to sit in its silence recovering from the walk up the steep hill from the town, and trying to come to terms with her worries.

At least one thing was plain. She had promised to ring young Mr Venables, and that she would do as soon as she went into the Fuchsia Bush next morning.

The visit of Carl Andersen which had occasioned so much interest in Thrush Green was soon forgotten by most of the residents. Other excitements had arisen. There was talk of an invasion by the nomadic 'travellers' planned for the last weekend of May. There was an Open Day, later that term, at Thrush Green school, and Miss Watson and Miss Fogerty, who had taught there for many years, were going to attend, leaving their retirement home at Barton-on-Sea for an extended visit.

Two new babies were expected in the Cooke family at Nidden. One was supposed to be Mrs Cooke's, but as she was in her mid-forties there was some argument about this. Most of the Thrush Green gossips thought it unlikely. The more cynical pointed out that the fecundity of the Cooke females was exceptional, and that Mrs Cooke might well be capable of producing healthy infants for years to come.

Nevertheless, the Youngs and the Curdles often spoke of their American friend, and when Willie Marchant, the postman, delivered a fat packet of photographs covered in exciting stamps, they gathered round the kitchen table to pore over them.

They were all splendid specimens. Carl Andersen was obviously an expert photographer, and the usual sloping landscapes, tilting churches and the like, so common among a batch of amateur snaps, were nowhere to be seen.

His portraits of the Youngs and the Curdles were particularly attractive, and even Edward, who was usually highly critical of any work of art, agreed that they were a splendid record of Carl's visit.

Edward had troubles of his own at this time. He was a compulsive worrier. The doubt put into his mind about the size of the existing common room at Rectory Cottages still niggled him. Reason told him that it was perfectly adequate as it was. Reason also pointed out that there was no money available anyway for an enlargement of the premises. Reason also told him that he had the assurance of a great many sensible people, such as Jane Cartwright and Charles Henstock, that his original plan together with the glass annexe added later suited everyone perfectly.

But reason did not entirely comfort Edward Young. Just as a nervous woman will fidget with her necklace, or a fretful child will pick relentlessly at a scab on its hand, so Edward worried about the possibility of having made a mistake in his designs.

The subject had been brought painfully to his mind a week or two earlier, when he had attended the funeral of one of the elderly residents, and had returned with other mourners for a cup of tea in the communal sitting room at the home.

The man whose funeral he had attended had helped Edward in the garden for many years. It was Edward who had helped to find him a place at Rectory Cottages when his wife had died and it was apparent that he was unable to cope alone.

Edward would miss him. He took his tea cup to the window and gazed across at the churchyard where one of the Cooke boys, helped occasionally by Albert Piggott, was patting turves into place, and arranging the funeral flowers upon them.

Nearer at hand, immediately beyond the window at which he stood, his architect's eye noted the level expanse of flag stones on which one or two seats were arranged with some tubs of late hyacinths. There would certainly be room for an extension of the conservatory should it ever be needed.

He turned back to the room, and felt slight panic. It *was* overcrowded. It *was* stuffy. It *was* short of seating.

Jane Cartwright came up to him, offering tomato sandwiches.

'No, thank you, Jane. Rather a crush in here.'

Jane intuitively knew what was worrying him. 'Well, there are nearly thirty people here today. Usually there are a dozen or so at the most.'

She spoke comfortingly, but Edward was not comforted.

'Maybe I should have allowed more space when I drew up the plans. It is so difficult to envisage numbers in a space.'

Jane laughed.

'Numbers vary, as you know. One can only plan for the average number of bodies, and they vary in size too, as you can see if you look around you.'

'You're right, of course,' agreed Edward. But he was not happy, and he took his doubts with him when he crossed the green later to his own home. He should have made that annexe larger, he told himself.

On the day when Carl Andersen's photographs and letter arrived at the Youngs, and Edward was still tormenting himself about Rectory Cottages, Charles Henstock was listening most unwillingly to Mrs Thurgood on the telephone.

His heart had sunk as soon as she had announced herself in the booming voice which so many had learnt to dread.

His dismay grew as he listened to the matter she was explaining, and he sat down on the hall chair in preparation for a long monologue on her side, and a fighting response on his own.

'I have been thinking about that extension at Rectory Cottages,' she began.

'That was settled at the meeting,' replied Charles.

'And it seems to me,' went on Mrs Thurgood, ignoring the interruption, 'that something must be done at some time, and why not now?'

'We can't afford it,' said Charles firmly.

'And what really brought it to my mind again was a lucky meeting with an old friend of ours, a charming fellow who was at school with my late husband. He was having lunch at the Randolph when I was there last week. I always lunch there after visiting the dentist in Beaumont Street. As it happens, he is the director of a well-known firm which specializes in garden-room-conservatories. He could easily extend for us.'

'We abandoned the idea,' broke in Charles.

'I mentioned our little problem,' she continued remorselessly, 'and he said he was sure that they could give us very favourable terms, under the circumstances. He was kind enough to say how much he appreciated our friendship of so many years, and he would be delighted to help when the time came.'

A providential huskiness came into the lady's delivery, and Charles took advantage of it.

'The time will *not* be coming,' said Charles loudly. 'As you are aware, the trustees voted to put the matter aside. There is *no money* available, and the room is considered quite adequate for its needs.

There was the sound of indrawn breath at the other end of the line, but whether it meant that the lady was recovering her full vocal powers or simply preparing for another onslaught, no one could say.

'You are turning down this wonderful offer?'

'Yes, I am.'

'You realize that you may be giving offence to a valued friend of my family?'

'I am sorry.'

'My daughter's offer to exhibit her pictures at the Town Hall to raise funds is also open. No one has had the courtesy to let her know about the arrangements.'

A lesser man than Charles could have been forgiven if he had broken into frustrated screams and banged his head on the vicarage hall wall, but Charles, despite his gentle demeanour, had an inner steel when it was required, and it was certainly needed now.

'Mrs Thurgood,' he said flatly, 'you know as well as I do that it was agreed to let the matter rest. If you have led your daughter and your old friend into thinking that we have plans for a further extension, then it is up to you to disabuse them of the idea which you yourself have encouraged. I refuse to discuss it further.'

'Well,' began an outraged voice.

But Charles put down the receiver, just as the front door opened and Harold Shoosmith arrived.

'Hallo, Charles! You look a bit tired.'

'I've just had Mrs Thurgood on the phone. She's still pressing me about the extension.'

'Leave her to me,' said Harold ominously.

June

Busy in making alterations in my Kitchen
Garden cutting down an Old Hedge by my
Fir Plantation.

James Woodforde

The gardeners of Thrush Green were equally busy. The
hedges and grass were under daily onslaught from
clippers and mowers, as the sun grew stronger and the days
longer.

Harold Shoosmith, attacking his privet hedge, was glad
to break off his labours when Betty Bell summoned him
indoors for mid-morning coffee.

'It's a pity we didn't grub out all the privet when we
came here, and plant yew instead.'

'Gloomy old stuff, yew,' commented Betty. 'Churchyards
and that. Gives you the creeps.'

'Why yew?' queried Isobel.

'Only needs one clip a year,' said the labourer. 'This
dam' privet wants three to keep it tidy.'

'Heard about Dotty's – I mean Miss Harmer's – Bruce?'

'Don't say he's ill,' exclaimed Isobel in alarm.

'No, no. I called in on my way here and he's full of
beans. He'd just broken a jar full of rhubarb juice Dotty'd
put on the floor to cool. All over everywhere.'

'On the floor?' echoed Harold. 'What was it doing on

the floor?'

'No room on the table. She was going to make some medicine. She stirs it up with ginger, and then bottles it.'

'It sounds pretty grim.'

'It is. Very *opening*.'

Isobel hastened to change the subject. 'Well, tell us about Bruce.'

'They've found his owners.'

'Good heavens! Where?'

'South America. They done a moonlight flit when they left Bruce in the church porch.'

Harold and Isobel exchanged glances.

'Are you sure about this?'

'Young Darwin the policeman was telling them down the pub yesterday.'

'Young Darwin,' said Harold sternly, 'has no business to be chattering about police matters at the pub.'

'Well, you asked me, so I told you,' retorted Betty. 'They're all that chuffed at the police station. Been working at it for months now. It's going to be in the paper this week.'

She put her empty mug aside, and rose to continue her duties.

'This won't buy the baby a new frock,' she announced. 'I'll go and give that bath a good doing over.'

'I wonder if there's anything in this story,' said Harold to Isobel.

'We shall have to wait and see what the local paper tells us,' replied Isobel. 'I must say it sounds rather sensational.'

'And it still doesn't explain why the dog was dumped here,' agreed Harold. 'Ah well! Back to the privet.'

Of course, Betty Bell was not the only one to have heard the news. Tongues wagged freely at the Two Pheasants, and the mystery of the dog being left in St Andrew's porch was the chief aspect of local conjecture.

'I heard,' said Percy Hodge the farmer, 'as this couple was fond of making trips up this way. Didn't they come in here for a pub lunch now and then?'

Mr Jones the landlord fidgeted uneasily with his beer mugs. 'Blowed if I know. I get all sorts in here in the summer stopping off for ploughman's lunch and that, before going on to Minster Lovell or Oxford. Can't say I've any particular memory of this pair. They hadn't got a dog or I might have remembered.'

'Well, they wouldn't have,' pointed out Albert. 'That Bruce was only a pup when we found him. Bet they hadn't had him more'n a few weeks.'

'What they doing in America then?'

'Done a bunk. With a pile of money evidently. Been up to a bit of no good somewhere. Fiddling the books, they say.'

'You can't fiddle books these days,' said some wiseacre. 'It's all on the computer.'

'And that can go wrong,' pointed out Percy Hodge. 'You only need to get a power cut and – fizz – it's all up.'

Heads were shaken in agreement, and the gossip about the felons, now allegedly in South America, changed to the unreliability of modern inventions and the superiority of earlier equipment.

While her father was enjoying the company of his cronies at the Two Pheasants, Molly Curdle was writing a letter of thanks to Carl Andersen for the set of photographs.

She also enclosed a separate letter for his mother and some more photographs which had turned up after Carl had departed. They were sepia in colour and rather faded, but a long-dead hand had clicked the camera and caught three or four splendid shots of Mrs Curdle near her caravan, with St Andrew's church in the background.

Ben took the bulky letter into Lulling to post and was appalled when he found how expensive it was to post anything by air mail. However, he did not grudge the money, as his father-in-law certainly would have done, for he knew that Molly and Carl's mother would get enormous pleasure from the transaction.

He had become very fond of Carl, his 'god-cousin', during the few weeks that he had been in Thrush Green, and he looked forward eagerly to seeing him again before long. There was an easy friendliness about the American, a warm freshness of outlook which touched Ben deeply. He had always been shy. The fact that his life had been always on the move with Mrs Curdle's fair had meant that his schooling was sketchy. It was Molly who had taught him to become proficient in reading and writing, and after acquiring those elementary skills he had become more confident.

But the early experience of being a 'gypsy boy', and mocked by some of the crueller children he had met in his youth, had left Ben very vulnerable and still inclined to think of himself as less competent than most men.

His mechanical skills were outstanding, and his honesty and his gentle nature were appreciated by all who knew him, but innate modesty made Ben deprecate his own qualities.

In Carl he had found a warm-hearted companion with whom he was instantly at ease. He had been touched by the enthusiastic invitation to visit him in the States, but did not think that he and Molly would be able to accept it. It would be too expensive. The children's schooling might be disrupted. His employer would not relish parting with his labours for any length of time.

No, all in all, it would be more sensible to wait for Carl's next visit. He hoped that it might be soon, and that he would not have to hurry away.

Who knows? Perhaps next year, thought Ben, things might favour a visit to Carl's home. Somehow, he felt sure, the bond between the two families would grow stronger with the years.

Thrush Green was at its best in early June. To be sure, the horse chestnuts' pyramids of flowers were almost over, and their pink and white confetti spattered the grass. In the garden too, the still-green daffodil leaves lolled, annoying tidy gardeners who were anxious to put out their bedding plants. The rapture with which the golden flowers had been greeted earlier had now changed to exasperation. All very well for the poet to say, '*Fair daffodils we weep to see thee haste away so soon,*' thought Winnie Bailey, surveying her overcrowded border, but the trouble was that they did not haste away quickly enough. One was forced to wait until the leaves had sent down their nourishment to the bulbs below, and very frustrating it was.

Nevertheless, there was comfort to be found in the shaggy scented pinks, the bobbing columbines and the great blowsy crimson peonies which came year after year with unfailing cheerfulness.

The wisteria cascaded in mauve profusion down the front of the house, and by the gate two laburnums dangled their golden chains. Winnie loved all these faithful old friends which appeared regularly every year, and demanded little attention. She was no great gardener. New strains of plants did not excite her. She was not interested in such things as topiary, old-fashioned roses, water plants, or exotic lilies or orchids, as many of her friends were.

But she relished her own modest patch which she and

Donald had largely created when they first moved into the house they shared for many years.

She looked across Thrush Green to the dusky beauty of the Youngs' copper beech tree, and thought of her promise to Ella about another shared walk. She must get in touch with her before this spell of sunny weather deserted the Cotswolds, she told herself.

It so happened that Ella was at Dotty Harmer's while Winnie was enjoying her garden stroll.

She found Dotty by the chicken run, flinging armfuls of fresh greenery to the hens.

'So nutritious!' she shouted to Ella, as she hurled leaves of all descriptions to the squawking fowl. Ella bent to collect a mound of chicken salad to assist the operation.

'Not *too* much cow parsley, dear,' puffed Dotty, 'but any amount of dandelions, shepherd's purse and chickweed. They all clear the blood, you know.'

Ella obediently plucked at some fine clumps of dandelion leaves, and remembered ruefully that they stained hands pretty fiercely. Would it come off on the white cushion cover she was in the throes of embroidering? Too late to worry now, she told herself philosophically.

After a few minutes Dotty called a halt and invited her friend into the kitchen. Bruce, who had been shut in there, went wild with excitement, leaping upon Ella's lap and licking her face rapturously.

'He's a fine fellow,' said Ella. 'Does you credit, Dotty.'

She was wondering if Dotty had heard the rumour about Bruce's former owners, and turning over in her mind the wisdom of broaching such a delicate subject.

She need not have worried.

'Betty Bell tells me that the wretches who abandoned

him have been found. I only hope they are brought to justice,' said Dotty.

'I gather that they left the country owing a great deal of money,' replied Ella. 'The police will want them for that.'

'To my mind,' said Dotty sternly, 'the money is of secondary importance. Cruelly abandoning a young dog is *far worse!*'

She began to fill the kettle.

'Lime tea or peppermint?' she enquired. 'Both homemade.'

Ella hesitated. Like the rest of Dotty's friends, anything homemade by Dotty could have a devastating effect on even the most robust alimentary canal.

'Well,' began Ella.

'You can have instant coffee, dear, if you prefer it. I have a private fear that it can give some people peptic ulcers, though Dr Lovell assures me that I am quite mistaken.'

Ella clutched at this straw. 'Coffee then, please, Dotty. And I'm sure John Lovell would know about such things.'

'He didn't know about the healing properties of wound-wort,' Dotty replied. 'I lent him my *Gerard's Herbal* to put him right.'

She brought two steaming mugs to the table, and returned to the subject of Bruce's owners.

'One thing I'm sure of,' she announced. 'I shall *refuse*, absolutely *refuse*, to return Bruce to such callous people. They are not fit to have animals in their charge.'

'Oh, come now, Dotty! He was obviously well cared for, and in a splendid basket, with food and drink. They were just desperate to get away, but they did leave him in a sheltered place – one might almost say a sanctuary – where he'd soon be found.'

Dotty brushed this aside. 'How did they know he would

be found? And they doped him to keep him quiet. Quite unforgivable! My father would have horsewhipped them on the spot! And quite right too!'

Two red spots glowed on Dotty's wrinkled cheeks, and Ella hastened to calm her.

'Well, no doubt they'll get their just deserts when they are picked up,' said Ella. 'And I'm sure no one will expect you to part with Bruce.'

'I should hope not. Where are they, anyway?'

'South America, I heard.'

'America?' cried Dotty, spilling her peppermint drink as she thumped the mug on the table. 'And *South* America too? Why, that's even worse than *North* America, and you know how badly *they* behaved, rebelling in the naughtiest way, and wasting all that good tea in Boston Harbor! I doubt if we shall ever see those miscreants if they have hidden themselves in *South America*.'

'We'll have to wait and see,' said Ella, rising. 'Many thanks for the coffee, Dotty, and can I have the goats' milk while I'm here?'

'Of course, of course,' said Dotty, bustling to the larder, 'and I've put up a bottle of rhubarb and ginger cordial for you. It's wonderfully effective.'

Ella thanked her civilly and put the bottle in her basket.

Walking home she wondered whether it would be a good thing to pour it down the sink. Would it block the pipes, she wondered? On the other hand, it might clear out the drain effectively. It would make an interesting experiment.

Edward Young was restless.

Joan Young was used to these periodic upsets. They often coincided, as in the present case, with some hold-up in his work, and she did her best to calm him, although she

knew, from experience, that only the resumption of the job in hand would cure his frustration.

Work on a splendid Regency house in Cheltenham had kept him engaged for some time, but the builders had been held up by a shortage of vital material and work had stopped for almost a week.

In his present state of impatience, Edward had turned again to the unresolved problem of Rectory Cottages' communal room. His doubts remained, and it was particularly unfortunate that it was at this time that he came across Mrs Thurgood in Lulling High Street.

She seized him by the arm so violently that he spun in his tracks.

'Just the man I wanted to see,' she trumpeted. Edward's

heart sank at these ominous words. 'I should like a word in your ear about Rectory Cottages.'

'I'm afraid I can't stop now,' began Edward, but was ignored, just as poor Charles Henstock's protests had been.

'I shan't keep you a minute,' replied Mrs Thurgood, hemming him into a corner between the steps leading up to the Lovelock sisters' front door, and the Fuchsia Bush. She pushed her tartan-covered shopping trolley across Edward's line of escape, and started to hold forth to her captive.

'It seems,' she began, 'that the sitting-room is proving rather small, and as you designed it I wondered if you felt it should be enlarged. I gather that is the general opinion.'

Taken aback as he was, and literally hemmed in on all sides, Edward did his best to fight back.

'I stand by my original work,' he began, but was interrupted by his persecutor, who had now raised her voice to a remarkable pitch to overcome the din of a large and slow vehicle which was sweeping the gutters at enormous expense to the Lulling rate-payers.

'Times change!' she shouted. 'It may have seemed adequate at the time, but it now appears to be too small.'

'No one else thinks so,' retorted Edward. 'As I understand it, the matter was discussed at a meeting of the trustees, which unfortunately I had to miss, and it was found perfectly adequate.'

'That's not what I hear,' bawled Mrs Thurgood. The driver of the giant sweeper had now paused to greet a friend near by and their voices added to the bedlam.

'In any case,' responded Edward fortissimo, 'there is *no money!*'

Half a dozen people now appeared and began to push their way towards the Fuchsia Bush, chattering noisily. One person shoved Mrs Thurgood's trolley aside and Edward escaped.

Mrs Thurgood, greatly disgruntled, continued on her way.

Inside the Lovelocks' house, Miss Ada said to Miss Violet: 'I don't know what the High Street is coming to. There was a dreadful brawl going on right outside our front door.'

'Oh, it was only Mrs Thurgood,' said Violet. 'She was talking to someone I couldn't see who was pinned against our wall.'

'Humph!' snorted Ada, 'that Mrs Thurgood gets more vulgar every week. Short of deporting her, I cannot think what can be done about her.'

'Just ignore her,' said Violet.

'I do that already,' said Ada tartly.

Edward Young was profoundly disturbed by this encounter. Reason told him that he should ignore the whole incident, that Mrs Thurgood was nothing but a trouble-maker and that this wretched business of the communal room should be set aside.

Reason, however, was being overwhelmed by agitation for poor Edward as he mounted the steep hill to Thrush Green in time for lunch.

The schoolchildren were already at play. Their midday dinner had been demolished, and now, replete with shepherd's pie and rhubarb crumble, they were cowboys, aeroplanes, spacemen or, in the case of the infants, simply mothers and fathers in the quietest corner of the playground.

Alan Lester was talking to his neighbour Harold Shoosmith just outside the school gate. Edward went to join them.

'The sun has brought us all out,' said Alan, waving to the children. 'Hope it's like this on Open Day.'

'When's that?'

'Early July. That's if we're ready. I live in hope.'

'It's often perfect then,' said Harold, 'but in any case you won't have everything outside, will you?'

'In this climate?' replied Alan. 'Not likely! We've a couple of things planned for outdoors but only if the weather's fine.'

'At least you have the school to shelter in if it pours,' observed Edward. 'When it has teemed down on fête days we've had to invite everyone into the house. This year we shall be away, so Harold here had better be warned. He's nobly taken over my duties, as you probably know.'

'We'll keep our fingers crossed,' promised Alan.

Betty Bell appeared wheeling her bicycle. She was making her way home after her morning's work.

'There's a steak and kidney pie just being dished up,' she informed Harold. 'Smells a dream!'

'Then I'd better go and see about it,' agreed Harold, and the three friends parted.

It was in this week that Ella and Winnie took their promised walk. They were both early risers, and agreed that the country was at its best in the first hours of daylight.

They set off, sticks in hand, soon after nine o'clock, two sturdy middle-aged ladies in coats and stout shoes, for although it was June the morning was fresh despite the sunshine.

The lane to Nidden was as peaceful as ever. People who worked in Lulling or Woodstock or Oxford had already gone. The schoolchildren were safely at assembly, and Winnie and Ella had the quiet road to themselves.

One of Percy Hodge's black-and-white Friesian cows put her head over the hedge and gazed speculatively at them.

Her eyelashes were fringed with mist. She chewed the cud slowly, ropes of saliva dripping from the great pink tongue. She looked infinitely content.

'It's funny how soothing cows are,' observed Ella. 'All that milk, I suppose, comes to mind.'

'I think it's the smell of their breath,' said Winnie. 'So soporific. Very calming. And so completely the opposite of bulls which frighten the life out of me.'

The mist of early morning had now cleared, and the view to Lulling Woods lay spread before them, a gentle rolling patchwork of varying greens, here and there enlivened by a vivid yellow field of rape. The two friends propped their arms on a convenient field gate, and gazed their fill in companionable silence.

A blackbird flew past, its yellow bill stuffed with squirming insects. It vanished into the hawthorn hedge beside them, and the air was instantly aquiver with the cries of young birds greeting their meal.

The brambles and goosegrass at the base of the hedge glistened with dew in the shadow, but already the shiny hawthorn leaves and may blossom in the sun were lightly steaming in the growing warmth.

'It's going to be a scorcher,' said Winnie, stirring at last.

'And about time too,' said Ella. 'I like summer to *be* summer.'

The cow parsley was now over. The froth of white flowers had turned to green seed heads, but among the luxuriant leaves the crane's-bill was appearing, its startling blue flowers giving colour to the verge. Pink campion, starry marguerites and the rusty spires of dock added their portion, and low on the ground, among the dusty edges of the road, spread the grey leaves of silverweed.

They strode past the cottages where the Cootes lived. Even here, among the derelict cars, mowers and wheelbarrows and building materials, there were signs of summer. An elder tree leant from the hedge, showing its great creamy blossoms to the sun, and some exuberant crimson peonies had found their way through the detritus to flaunt their beauty.

The two friends walked on, past the copse where the bluebells had so stirred them on their earlier walk, and on towards the scatter of cottages which comprised Nidden. A tabby cat sat on a stone gatepost, and responded to Ella's stroking by opening a pink triangle of mouth and giving little purrs of appreciation. A toddler stumbled down the path to the gate, and gazed, thumb in mouth, at the two strangers, but refused to speak.

Ella looked at her watch. 'I'm supposed to be back for the laundry man,' she said. 'Do you mind turning back now?'

'Not a bit. I'm mightily refreshed in body and spirit.'

They waved goodbye to the unresponsive child and the friendly cat, and turned for home.

At Thrush Green school preparations were well ahead for Open Day towards the end of term.

Alan Lester had already sent out invitations to parents, governors and other friends of the school, including one to his predecessors Miss Watson and Miss Fogerty, now enjoying retirement at Barton-on-Sea.

'Really,' commented Miss Watson at the breakfast table, 'it is most gratifying to be kept in touch with school affairs. But it seems a pity to me to see that the children have not written the invitations in their own handwriting. I suppose they have a copier now. It no doubt cost a fortune.'

Little Miss Fogerty, at the other side of the table, rallied to Alan Lester's defence. She knew how much dear

Dorothy missed her position as a respected headmistress, but she saw no reason why she should find fault with her excellent successor.

'You must admit, Dorothy, that the invitations are easier to read. And I believe that the parents raised the money for the copier. I think it is a good idea.'

'Would you pass the marmalade?' enquired Dorothy somewhat coldly.

There was silence for a few minutes, broken only by the crunching of toast.

'You're quite right, dear,' said Miss Watson at last. 'I must say I am looking forward so much to our visit. Isobel asked if I would be willing to judge the children's fancy dress competition at the fête. Alan Lester had broached the subject.'

Miss Fogerty recognized this speech as an overture of reconciliation and forbore to tell her friend that Isobel had already mentioned the matter to her in a recent telephone conversation. The two had been friends since college days, and the fact that they had been neighbours at Thrush Green had strengthened the tie.

'I do hope you will do it,' said Miss Fogerty. 'You are quite the right person to appreciate the work and ingenuity that goes into these affairs.'

'I don't know about that,' replied Dorothy, with unusual modesty, 'but I shall do my best, and hope that Thrush Green will forgive any shortcomings.'

'I'm just going to have a look at some cuttings in the cold frame,' said Agnes Fogerty folding her napkin. 'I promised Isobel some slips from our shrubs, and I must say they are looking very perky.'

'You have green fingers, Agnes,' said Dorothy kindly, propping up the invitation on the mantelpiece. 'And a much more generous nature than I have.'

But the second comment, though strongly felt, she kept to herself.

Willie Marchant, the postman, dropped three letters through Albert Piggott's door one sunny morning and, as usual, it was Nelly who bent to pick them up.

Two were addressed to Albert, and looked like run-of-the-mill circulars, but the third was addressed to Nelly, in a hand she did not recognize immediately.

It was quite heavy and bulky, and Nelly saw that the postmark bore the stamp of Leicester. She slipped it into her apron pocket, out of sight of Albert, and handed him the two which were addressed to him. He gave them scant attention.

'More rubbish!' was his only comment.

Nelly did not open her letter until she was safely in the office at the Fuchsia Bush. To her surprise, a cellophane bag containing a gold chain was enclosed with a letter from Mrs Butler, Charlie's landlady.

The letter read:

Dear Mrs Piggott,
   Charlie asked me to send you this as a little keepsake. It belonged to his mother, and it is real gold. He hoped you would like it to remind you of happy times past.

The letter was signed with Mrs Butler's shaky scrawl, and Nelly undid the present with mixed emotions.

The long necklace slid out of its wrapping. Nelly knew gold when she saw it, and this was certainly the real thing. It was of Victorian design, quite heavy, and well over two feet in length.

Her first feeling was that it was too valuable for her to accept. Her second was that it was typical of Charlie's generosity, and that she was overwhelmed by it.

Remembering her last glimpse of Charlie, shabby and almost destitute, she wondered that he had not sold such a valuable object. But it was also typical of him to have kept something of his mother's which he prized on her account.

Nelly sat alone in the quiet office, remembering those days with Charlie. They had ended in Brighton with the deepest humiliation and hurt that she had ever suffered. Even now, the remembrance made her shudder and feel sick.

When he had thrown her over for another woman, and Nelly had no alternative but to return to Thrush Green and the recriminations, and probably rejection of Albert, she would never forget that long miserable journey home, shaken by Charlie's treachery and fearful for what lay ahead. Although Albert was remarkably forbearing, contenting himself with a few wounding words now and again, the general disapproval of her neighbours was harder to bear. Nelly knew that in such a close-knit community her shame would never be completely forgotten. But her natural exuberance and hard work gradually overcame the censure of her neighbours, and as the years had passed, Nelly's back-slidings, if not quite forgotten, were almost quite forgiven.

Nelly picked up the beautiful chain. Dear Charlie, she thought fondly! She still had a soft spot in her heart for the scamp, and she would treasure this generous gesture from her dead lover.

She slipped it over her head, tucking it under her blouse so that it was hidden. It slid down between her ample breasts, cold but strangely comforting.

News of the apprehension of the owners of the dog Bruce was annoyingly short. The local paper, which all had expected to give exciting accounts of the miscreants, had let down its avid public badly.

Normally, any mention of Lulling or its surrounding villages and their inhabitants merited a paragraph or two. In fact, one of its endearing qualities was the ability to find some local connection, however remote.

Harold Shoosmith always enjoyed this aspect of the local paper. Having read the obituary of a bishop one morning in *The Times*, he was delighted to find half a column in the local paper claiming that the bishop's younger brother had once been mayor of Lulling.

On another occasion a famous but fickle actress, whose latest peccadilloes were making headlines in the national press, was given prominence and a photograph in the local paper because she had opened a church bazaar in Lulling some three years earlier.

So it was even more galling to its faithful readers to find that there was next to nothing about those dreadful people who had pinched masses of money, done a bunk to Bolivia or Peru or one of those fancy places where criminals went and, worse still, had left a poor starving dog tied up in their church porch.

Instead of a half-page of juicy reading, there was a meagre paragraph stating that the police were investigating certain allegations about the appropriation of missing funds from a number of companies in the area.

'Never a word about Bruce and Miss Dotty,' cried Betty Bell indignantly. 'I've half a mind to give up having it, except you have to look down the deaths every week to keep upsides with things. My mum never got over meeting an old school friend in Lulling one market day and asking her, jolly-like, if her Fred still liked his pint, and the woman burst into tears and said he'd died the week before. She didn't tell my mum at the time, but he'd choked on a mouthful of rum. Since then I've always had a quick quiz at the deaths. No point in upsetting people.'

'Quite,' agreed Harold, moving three letters he was trying to answer from the path of Betty's duster flailing round his desk.

'Tell you what, though,' said Betty, suddenly still, 'I'm going over to my sister's at the weekend, and she has that Hampshire paper. Maybe it's got something in it as those bounders lived that way, didn't they? Time they was caught and strung up, leaving that poor animal like that.'

Harold was then left in peace as Betty continued her duties in the hall. It seemed, he thought with some amusement, that the fugitives were already condemned before trial, and that by far the greatest of the charges they might have to face in the future was the abandonment of the dog Bruce, which was of paramount importance in the eyes of Thrush Green.

He returned to his letter-writing, putting Betty's indignation against unsatisfactory local papers and callous dog owners out of his mind until she arrived some days later waving another local paper triumphantly.

'Here you are! A lovely bit in it, page three, and a photo too. You can keep it, as I've had a good read of it. For two pins I'd show it to our lot so they could see how a proper paper should be.'

Harold thanked her and put it aside to read later. Certainly some enterprising editor had sent his reporter to the place where the missing couple had lived, and the result had been most satisfactory from the readers' point of view.

A garrulous old lady, of formidable appearance according to the accompanying photograph, had kept the key of the missing pair's house and generally looked after affairs in their absence.

'Mrs Ivy Potts, 74' began the account, causing Harold to wonder, yet again, why newspaper editors imagined that the ages of those mentioned in their columns were of the slightest interest to readers.

Carrying on, after this momentary mental pause, Harold discovered that the aged Mrs Potts had been struck dumb when she found the place deserted. A note had been left on the kitchen table with a week's wages, and she had been told to carry on as usual until further notice.

After a week with no word ('not even on the telephone') she became worried. For one thing, the milk was getting too much for reasonable consumption and it seemed a wicked waste to pour it down the sink with all those starving people in Africa you saw on the telly, and there was a stack of papers, the sort you couldn't really read, especially that pink one which was all figures, which her employers seemed to read most of all.

But she was worried most about the dog, she told the reporter. (Thrush Green would like Mrs Potts, thought Harold, reading avidly.) Of course, they might have taken it with them. On the other hand, it might have run off and got killed. She felt she ought to tell the police, and they said she had been quite right when she went to the police station. From now on it was up to them, concluded Mrs Ivy Potts, 74.

Harold agreed, as he folded the newspaper with satisfaction.

Albert Piggott was normally the most unobservant of men when it came to the appearance of womenfolk. He did, however, notice the gold chain which Nelly had hung over her best blouse before going out with Mrs Jenner and Mrs Hodge, formerly Mrs Lilly, to spend an evening at bingo.

'Where'd you get that thing?' enquired Albert suspiciously.

'What, this?' exclaimed Nelly, with assumed casualness. 'Why, it was sent with that mail order as come last week. Free gift, you know.'

'Trumpery stuff!' grunted Albert. 'A sprat to catch a mackerel. Just hopin' you'd spend good money buying more fal-de-lals.'

'Well, I don't ask you to pay for 'em,' said Nelly tartly. 'So I'll wear what I like!'

There was a knock at the door, and her two friends were outside, waiting for her to join them.

Halfway through the evening there was a break for refreshments, and Mrs Jenner admired Nelly's chain as they drank coffee.

Nelly repeated the tale she had told Albert, but was beginning to wonder if she should ever display Charlie's last gift in public. Until this evening she had kept it hidden under her clothes, relishing its secret comfort. Tonight she had felt a desire to wear it openly before her friends, proud of its beauty. But Albert's questioning, and now Mrs Jenner's interest, made her uneasy, and she resolved that this would be the last time she would display it.

'They make things really marvellously these days,' commented Mrs Jenner. 'That necklace could pass for real gold anywhere, I do declare. And how,' she went on, leaving the subject, 'is poor Mrs Peters?'

'A sad sight,' said Nelly. 'I dread what I might find every time I go in.'

'Would she like me to pay her a visit?' asked Mrs Jenner. 'Not professionally, of course. I wouldn't want to be in the way of her proper nurse, but just a short friendly visit, say.'

Nelly said that she was sure the invalid would enjoy a visit. They were called back to their tables, and hopes of fortune to come put the matter of Nelly's new necklace to one side.

But later that night, after Mrs Jenner and Mrs Hodge

had seen Nelly into her home and were continuing along the dark Nidden road to their own abodes, the subject of Nelly's chain cropped up again.

'I've never had a free gift like that,' said Gladys Hodge. 'Most I've ever had was those things you find stuck on the cover of your women's magazines like a phial of scent or a nail file.'

'It certainly looked very nice on Nelly,' said Mrs Jenner diplomatically. She was almost sure that the chain was made of gold, for she had one very like it, of Victorian design, which she had inherited from her mother.

'Yes,' agreed Gladys, still sounding puzzled. 'It looked so real, didn't it? But where would Nelly get a valuable necklace like that if it was real?'

Mrs Jenner, who had learnt to be discreet during her years as the local midwife, was not prepared to pursue the matter further. Her own conjectures she intended to keep to herself. However Nelly acquired the chain was her own affair, and that was that. She had no intention of starting a rumour which might upset her friend Nelly.

The two stopped at the Hodges' gate.

'Care to come in for a drink?' invited Gladys.

But Mrs Jenner declined, pleading tiredness and a longing for her bed.

'I've just thought,' said Gladys excitedly, as she was about to open her gate. 'That necklace of Nelly's might have come from Mrs Peters. They tell me she's been giving away one or two keepsakes to friends and relations, poor soul. Knows she hasn't got much longer, I hear. She'd want Nelly to have something, wouldn't she?'

'It's a possibility,' agreed Mrs Jenner, glad that her friend had found some answer to her queries.

'Well, goodnight then,' cried Gladys. 'See you soon.'

She vanished up the path to the back door of the farmhouse, and Mrs Jenner, keeping her own counsel, went thankfully to her bed.

July

We were greatly amused by a Country Dancing
School. They kickit and jumpit with mettle
extraordinary, and whiskit and friskit, and toed
it and go'd it, tattooing the floor like mad.

John Keats

Alan Lester, the headmaster of Thrush Green primary
school, was a fair-minded man and believed in letting
his staff have as much freedom as was compatible with the
good running of the school.

But during the preparations for the school's Open Day
his toleration was being sorely tried by the noise from the
infants' room.

Miss Robinson, who had begun her teaching career under
Miss Watson's tutelage, was an enthusiastic dancer, and
encouraged her young charges to excel in bending and
stretching, pointing toes, waving arms and legs, and generally pursuing all those exercises which would add grace
and beauty to youthful deportment.

She soon realized that she would have to modify her
aims. Young children, particularly sturdy country ones, are
apt to fall over when asked to stand on one leg with the
other stretched gracefully behind. Ballet-like arm move-
ments, in a confined space, can lead to clashes with neighbouring bodies followed by recriminations.

Very sensibly Miss Robinson accepted that her pupils' dancing ability was limited, but she turned her attention to the type of dancing which they enjoyed and which, she hoped, would lead them to more artistic heights.

The simpler rhythm and movement of country dancing suited her aims perfectly. The clapping, the stamping, the twirling and the whirling were greatly enjoyed by her class, and she had spent the last few weeks of the summer term rehearsing three particularly noisy and energetic examples of such dancing.

These dances had originated in middle Europe, and poor harassed Alan Lester in a neighbouring classroom began to wonder if perennial troubles in the Balkans and the surrounding areas might not have their roots in the aggressive expression of the inhabitants' infant years. There was a ruthless militarism about the sounds which caused the classrooms' flimsy partitions to shudder under the onslaught, and Alan did his best to encourage Miss Robinson to rehearse her charges in the playground, at the end farthest from the school, whenever the weather allowed.

The whole school looked forward to showing parents and friends the results of its yearly labours, and Alan was secretly very proud of its achievements. He knew the school was doing well under his guidance, and hoped that Miss Watson and Miss Fogerty, in the company of parents and old pupils, would approve of their school in its present form.

This inner confidence gave Alan the ability to suffer the infants' zealous endeavours with mitigated pain.

In any case, he told himself, it would soon be the end of term, and he and his wife and family could relax in Wales.

Two postmen delivered letters and packets to Thrush Green and both were called Willie. It was Willie Marchant who liked to test his own and his bicycle's strength on the steep hill from Lulling to Thrush Green. Willie Bond preferred to dismount and push his bicycle up the hill, as did most of his fellows.

Willie Marchant liked to tack from one side to the other, puffing heavily, and causing great alarm to any traffic on the road. The screeching of brakes, the horrified faces looking through car windows, perturbed Willie Marchant not at all.

'I bin doing it all me time,' he was wont to say. 'They knows my ways, and it's up to folks to look out for me. I ain't gettin' off for nobody. I got enough right to be on the highway as the next.'

It was Willie Marchant who delivered an air-mail letter to Ben and Molly Curdle one bright summer morning, and they settled down to read it in their kitchen. They knew it was from Carl, and both hoped that it would give news of his arrival in time for the fête, which he hoped to attend.

But the news was sad.

Dear Molly and Ben,

I am sorry to have to tell you that my mother died last week. She had a severe heart attack and was rushed to hospital, but died that night. I am badly shaken, and don't mind admitting it.

She was delighted with your letter and photos, Molly dear. So glad she was well enough to enjoy them.

My visit to Thrush Green must be postponed as I have a mass of my mother's affairs to attend to, but I will keep you informed about plans, and you can guess how much I look forward to seeing you both again.

As ever,
Carl.

'Poor old lady,' sighed Molly, putting down the letter.

'Poor old Carl,' commented Ben. He remembered his own devastation when his grandmother, old Mrs Curdle, had died. He sympathized deeply with Carl's grief at such a time, and wished that he and Molly could be with him.

'Well, there it is,' said Ben, rising to prepare for work. 'We must just hope things are simpler to clear up than he seems to think.'

'He won't be at the fête, though, will he?' said Molly sadly. 'He would have liked that.'

Ben patted her shoulder.

'Well, anyway, she enjoyed your letter and the snaps. Good thing you wrote when you did.'

He left Molly looking slightly comforted.

Although Carl was scarcely known in the neighbourhood, and his mother had left Woodstock some fifty years earlier, nevertheless the news of her death was soon common knowledge in the little world of Thrush Green and Lulling.

Much sympathy was felt for Carl, and those who knew him comparatively well, such as the Youngs and Charles Henstock, wrote immediately to their new friend.

Charles Henstock even wondered if there were relatives still in Woodstock who should be informed, and mentioned this to Dimity, as she sat topping and tailing gooseberries in the kitchen.

She, knowing Charles's soft heart and his selfless concern for those in trouble, could see that he was quite capable of scouring the streets of Woodstock, whatever the weather, if he felt that he could be of any use to any of Carl's mother's bereaved relations.

'It is really a matter for Woodstock's vicar,' she pointed out. 'He would know if there are any relations who should

be told. But I doubt if anyone would really be interested in the death of someone who left the parish so long ago.'

Charles's brow cleared. 'You are quite right, of course. I'm glad you mentioned it. I should have been sorry to meddle in a matter which is a neighbouring vicar's concern. As it is, I don't think Carl had any close relations here in Lulling, so we must let the matter rest.'

He stood for a moment or two watching Dimity's scissors snipping busily at the gooseberries.

'That seems a very tedious job,' he observed. 'Is it necessary to take the ends off?'

'Quite necessary, dear. And I quite enjoy it. I think of how much you will relish a gooseberry pie when I cook these in the winter. It's a labour of love.'

'I am a very lucky man,' replied Charles, and went back to his study in a happy mood.

Down at Barton-on-Sea Miss Watson and Miss Fogerty were busy with their preparations for their visit to Thrush Green.

As always, Dorothy Watson's first worry was about her wardrobe. She was fond of her clothes and critical of her appearance. Agnes, who had always put decency and economy before sartorial grandeur, could do little to calm her friend's agitation. Shortage of money had always limited Agnes's scope, and as the years passed she found it rather restful to have so few clothes to choose from.

Dorothy called from her bedroom one morning, just as Agnes was wondering about that day's pudding. Should it be the raspberries left from yesterday? (Hardly enough to cover the bottom of a fruit dish.) Or open a tin of apricots? (Surely rather extravagant with fresh fruit in abundance in July.)

She hastened to obey Dorothy's summons, and found her surveying a pile of clothes spread out on the bed.

'It's so difficult to decide,' cried Dorothy. 'If it were *winter* I should definitely take my black for evenings, but one likes to look more festive in *summer*. On the other hand, the evenings may be chilly and I really don't want to drag any old cardigan over my summer dresses.'

Agnes, who relied heavily on 'any old cardigan' to supply extra warmth whatever the occasion, pointed out that a silk dress with long sleeves might be the best answer to the problem.

'This green always looks well,' she ventured, lifting up the garment in question.

'Thrush Green must be sick and tired of that old thing,' responded Dorothy. 'I bought it for a party at Ella and Dimity's years ago.'

'Well, what about the blue?'

'Waist's too high. Right under the bust. Most uncomfortable.'

'I always liked you in this pink one.'

'Too youthful. Mutton dressed as lamb, and no shoes to go with it.'

A less patient woman than Agnes might have suggested that it had been a mistake to buy these things in the first place, and that a jumble sale was the best place to dispose of such problems, but Agnes held her peace.

'I still think the green would be best,' she said diplomatically. 'You can wear black or brown shoes with that, and different silk scarves if the weather is chilly. It has a most becoming neckline.'

Dorothy's agitation was subsiding, she saw with relief.

'You are such a help,' said Dorothy. 'I might pack that light stole I bought in Prouts' sale one year. It goes with everything, and dear Anthony Bull once said I looked distinguished in it.'

With the blessing of the Reverend Anthony Bull, Charles Henstock's predecessor at Lulling, it was quite apparent to Agnes that most of Dorothy's worries were over.

She returned thankfully to eking out the raspberries with some chopped banana.

Barton-on-Sea, with the rest of southern England, was enjoying a long hot spell of summer weather.

Holidaymakers rejoiced. Weddings, carnivals, cricket matches and meals out of doors all thrived in the glorious sunshine. Even the farmers were comparatively happy, for the winter barley had ripened early, and harvesting could begin. Of course, they complained that the lack of rain meant that the ears of corn were not as heavy as they should be, and that the pests which attacked their crops were particularly virulent in hot dry weather, but no one took much notice of their grumbles. The majority basked and felt thankful.

The roses were at their best, and the delphiniums, penstemons and lilies made a glory in the cottage gardens. The scent of pinks and honeysuckle sweetened every breeze, and in the warm dusk of evening the tobacco plants sent out waves of heady fragrance.

The lime trees round St Andrew's church at Thrush Green and the avenue of limes leading to the splendour of St John's at Lulling were massed with pale scented flowers, above the clover-spattered grass. Wherever one looked there were flowers, below, above and all around. Summer had come in true splendour this year, after the dark months of winter and spring.

In the cottage gardens, black, red and white currants were ripe under their protective coverings of old lace curtains or, in more sophisticated places, secure in large fruit cages.

Cherries were being eyed appreciatively by the birds, and the apple trees displayed green marbles of embryo fruit.

Amidst the glory of summer these signs of autumn were manifest, and none was so obvious as the waving rosebay willowherb which rioted in the verges of the lanes, tossing pink heads in the breeze above the dried grass below.

But the prolonged spell of sunshine had its darker side. Good gardeners were having to water night and morning to keep their flowers and vegetables alive. Lawns were scorched, bird baths were dry, and many trees were beginning to shed their leaves far too early.

But these were minor worries. On the whole, life was sweet in such a summer, and Alan Lester looked forward with growing confidence to fine weather when the school had its Open Day, and Joan and Edward Young, getting ready for their holiday, told each other that Harold Shoosmith looked like having fair weather for the fête for which he had nobly undertaken Edward's responsibilities.

'Fingers crossed,' said Joan. 'There's plenty of time for it to change.'

'Well, if it does decide to rain on the great day,' responded Edward, 'to quote the Duke of Norfolk about the Coronation, "We get wet", and that's happened before. But somehow, this year, I think we're going to be lucky.'

And Joan, thankful to see him in a cheerful mood, hoped that he was right.

Near by, Harold and Isobel Shoosmith were getting ready to welcome Dorothy Watson and Agnes Fogerty. Dorothy would be driving, for she had become an intrepid driver since her retirement.

Ben Curdle had been her instructor when she had bought her first car in her last few years at Thrush Green, and she could not have had a more competent and reassuring tutor.

As usual, it was Agnes who was ready first. Always an early riser, and with only half the amount of packing to do, compared with her friend's luggage, Agnes was ready to go by nine o'clock, but Dorothy was still fussing with last-minute affairs.

At twenty past nine Dorothy staggered to the car with two suitcases which she put into the boot.

'Don't shut it, dear,' she called to Agnes who was sitting patiently on the hall chair, handbag on lap. 'I've one or two little odds and ends to put in, and I'm just popping down to see Teddy and Eileen. I promised them some magazines.'

'Can't they wait until we come back?' protested Agnes.

'No, no! It won't take me a jiffy,' shouted Dorothy, vanishing through the back door.

Agnes put down her handbag and paced up and down the hall with growing irritation. Teddy again! That everlasting Teddy!

Some years earlier, when the two ladies had settled at Barton, they found that one of their neighbours had recently lost his wife. As the poor man was also blind, good friends did what they could to help, and Dorothy practically took charge and caused Agnes acute embarrassment.

To be frank, Dorothy had fallen in love with the man. He was charming, intelligent and bore his afflictions bravely, Agnes was the first to concede, but Dorothy's ruthless pursuit of their neighbour was not only absurd, in Agnes's opinion, but also dangerously disruptive to the life which she had set out to share with her friend and former headmistress.

She had confided her fears to Isobel Shoosmith, who found the news equally dismaying. However, she cautioned patience and hoped that time would bring Dorothy to her senses.

It was a great relief to Agnes and Isobel when another friend of Teddy's, named Eileen, had married the man, and all seemed set for a trouble-free future. Even Dorothy had accepted the situation cheerfully at the time, but lately, it seemed to Agnes, her attentions to Teddy were growing again.

It was all so frustrating and pointless, thought Agnes, looking at the hall clock, which said twenty five to ten. And Eileen must notice, and probably feel very hurt.

'Never come between husband and wife,' Agnes's mother had often said to her, and although little Miss Fogerty, with her mouse-like looks and timid ways, was not likely to become a *femme fatale* she had remembered her mother's words, together with such dicta as: 'Let your underclothes be as neat and clean as those that are seen,' and 'Look after the pence and the pounds will look after themselves.'

The situation was quite dangerous, thought Agnes with some agitation. Dorothy should have more sense than to meddle in this way.

At a quarter to ten Dorothy bustled back, looking very happy, and apologized to Agnes for keeping her waiting.

'You get in, dear, while I lock up. I'll bring my raincoat and walking shoes, and then everything's done.'

Five minutes later they were leaving Barton-on-Sea and heading through Hampshire to Thrush Green.

'Isn't this lovely?' cried Dorothy. 'It will do us good to get away for a bit.'

Agnes fervently agreed. Pehaps Teddy would be forgotten, she thought, surveying the countryside as it flashed past.

But her hopes were dashed a few minutes later when Dorothy spoke.

'You'll hardly credit this, Agnes, but Eileen is going away for a few days.'

'So are we.'

'But leaving Teddy! In his condition! Alone in the house!'

'He lived alone long before he married Eileen,' Agnes pointed out.

'He could stumble over something, and hurt himself dreadfully,' went on Dorothy, ignoring the interruption.

'So could anybody.'

'I think it is quite heartless of Eileen. She, of all people, must know how helpless he is.'

Agnes felt that the time had come for a little plain speaking.

'Teddy is well able to look after himself. He managed perfectly when he lived alone, and I'm sure he realizes that Eileen needs a change now and again.'

'I daresay. Teddy is always thinking of others. I only know that I couldn't leave him, if I were in Eileen's shoes.'

'I think,' said Agnes slowly, 'that you sometimes let your kind heart overrule your head. It is not really your place to worry about Teddy. He probably finds it embarrassing, and Eileen must see how things are.'

Dorothy swerved to avoid a child who was see-sawing along the side of the road on a bicycle much too big for him.

'How do you mean?' demanded Dorothy, 'when you say that Eileen must see how things are?'

'You show your feelings too readily.'

Agnes noticed that her friend's neck and face were becoming red, a sure sign of danger ahead. Nevertheless, she stuck to her guns.

'Of course I do,' replied Dorothy shortly. 'I'm fond of Teddy.'

'So am I,' said Agnes. 'And so are all his friends. But he is a married man, and one has to be careful not to upset his wife, and through her, to hurt him.'

She was also wondering if she could quote her mother's warning verbatim about 'coming between husband and wife', but held her tongue. Already she felt she might have gone too far.

Silence fell for a few minutes, and then Agnes saw a welcome sign.

'Oh look, Dorothy! We're just coming to a Little Chef café and it's coffee-time. How fortunate! And their toasted tea cakes are so good. Shall we call in? My treat this time.'

'What a good idea,' said Dorothy cheerfully.

Agnes was relieved to see that Dorothy's flush was fading.

Two days after their arrival at Thrush Green, the long-awaited Open Day dawned.

To everyone's relief it was calm and sunny. The children were unnaturally spruce and tidy, Alan Lester was in his new summer suit, and Miss Robinson in an ankle-length cotton frock of drab colouring which was fashionable at the time, and which made her look like a refugee. As this was exactly what she wanted, she was blissfully happy.

The school too was unnaturally spruce, and the walls were adorned with children's paintings, maps and charts and samples of needlework and handiwork. On every desk was displayed the work in progress, the exercise books lying open at the neatest page.

The children welcomed their parents and friends with a summer song, chosen and accompanied by Miss Robinson.

> *Summer is icumen in*
> *Lhude sing cuccu!*
> *Groweth sed, and bloweth med,*
> *And springth the wude nu –*
> *Sing cuccu!*

Although the words were largely incomprehensible to the listeners, the applause was hearty, for the children looked so angelic, and coped with the thirteenth-century vocabulary so well, that the audience was enchanted.

Then Alan Lester gave a short address of welcome, taking care to mention the two distinguished guests Miss Watson and Miss Fogerty in the front row, and to thank everyone who had contributed to the occasion in one way or another.

The programme went ahead smoothly. The infants clapped and stamped – almost together – through their much-rehearsed folk dance, and Alan Lester led the applause, privately thinking that this would be the last time he would have to endure such noise.

Work was inspected and much admired in the school itself, and tea was set out under the lime trees in the playground which gave parents, friends and staff a chance to mingle over the tea cups.

Margaret Lester, Alan's wife, was in charge here, looking prettier than ever, and Dorothy Watson observed quietly to Agnes, 'When you *think*, dear,' and needed to say no more, for nearly all those present remembered that Margaret Lester had arrived at Thrush Green with a serious drink problem that had threatened their family happiness. She had overcome it bravely, and Thrush Green had rejoiced.

Alan Lester was buttonholed by an earnest parent who told him all about her child's dyslexia, with which he was already acquainted, and how the doctor had told her that it was often the sign of a particularly brilliant mind. With commendable courtesy, Alan nodded agreement but kept his thoughts to himself.

Miss Robinson was less lucky. Mrs Cooke, mother and grandmother to many of her pupils over the years, sat firmly beside her and described, in appalling detail, the facts of her sister's hysterectomy.

Poor Miss Robinson found herself now violently opposed to the state of matrimony, and quite unequal to eating the jam tart in her hand. She hastily shrouded its red stickiness in a paper napkin, excused herself by saying her class needed her, and fled.

It was almost six o'clock by the time the school and playground had emptied. Parents and children had trickled away. Margaret Lester and her helpers were busy with the last of the washing up, and Alan said goodbye to young Miss Robinson.

'It went splendidly,' he said. 'I thought your class danced very well indeed.'

Her face lit up. 'Miss Watson said the same. She thought it would be a good idea to repeat it at the Christmas concert.'

'That's quite a thought,' said Alan Lester.

*

Nothing had been said about Teddy, between the two ladies, since the conversation on their journey to Thrush Green.

Agnes secretly wondered if she should have spoken at all, and hoped that she had not hurt Dorothy. Although she had not been affected by love in her sheltered and limited life, she realized how important a part it played in the affairs of most people.

The fact that Dorothy was now in her sixties, and might have been considered able to withstand Cupid's darts, had nothing to do with the case, Agnes realized. She had known several mature people, of both sexes, who had formed attachments, some disastrously, with as much passion as those half their age. It was an unaccountable phenomenon which Agnes could not understand, but it undoubtedly existed.

She felt extremely sorry for Dorothy, and decided to say no more on the subject. She would do her best to make Dorothy's stay at Thrush Green as pleasant as she could.

With this laudable aim in mind, little Miss Fogerty had no difficulty in enjoying her day and sleeping peacefully at night in the dear familiar surroundings of Thrush Green.

But for Dorothy in an adjoining bed in Isobel's spare bedroom, matters were not as easily dismissed. Agnes had given her much to ponder.

In many ways she was superior to Agnes, better educated, stronger in health, more travelled and well read. It was no surprise that she had become a respected headmistress while little Miss Fogerty remained an assistant, and in the same school, for many years.

She was a well-balanced and energetic woman, willing to play her part in local affairs and zealous in keeping up with modern ideas, particularly in education. She also had the ability to reject any trends which she shrewdly recognized as silly and short-sighted, and to support others which, although new and debatable, had a sound basis of practicality for teaching.

In her younger days she had enjoyed many friendships with young men, and had been engaged to be married twice. One man had been killed in the last days of the war. The other, Dorothy soon discovered, was bombastic, a bully and mean with money. If he was like that in his twenties, Dorothy thought, what on earth would he be like in his sixties? She dismissed him, much to his surprise, and never regretted it.

She had enjoyed her teaching career. She had found retirement a little disconcerting with so much time to organize. Perhaps it was this, combined with pity for Teddy's plight, which had sparked this attachment to him? Perhaps he took the place of all the children she had cared for over the years? Perhaps some latent and unsuspected maternal instinct had manifested itself? Who knew?

Dorothy had been surprised by the strength of her feelings for Teddy, but gave them full rein. It had never occurred to her, until Agnes spoke, that there was an element of silliness and possible embarrassment in this relationship.

Looking at it soberly Dorothy began to see that Agnes was right. She could be causing Eileen pain. She could be embarrassing Teddy. She could be a laughing-stock to their friends in Barton-on-Sea. It was something she had never considered before, and she lay awake, listening to Agnes's small genteel snores, and studied the position carefully.

Agnes was so often right. Her life might have been more confined and narrow than her own, but those very limitations had made Agnes know the difference between right

and wrong, with no blurring of lines which a more sophisticated mind might allow.

She must mend her ways, she decided. She would say
nothing to Agnes, for 'Least said, soonest mended' was a
motto which she favoured. She would not be able to feel
any less warmly towards dear Teddy, he meant too much
to her, but she would cut down her visits, remember that
he was Eileen's husband, and generally behave with more
decorum, as befitted a retired headmistress of mature years.

What really hurt, she was honest enough to admit, was
the fact that she was making a fool of herself before her
friends.

Somewhere, years earlier, she remembered reading a
great truth which had stayed with her. Was it written by
that discerning literary man Bonamy Dobrée? It was to the
effect that no one minded being thought *wicked*, but one
hated to appear *ridiculous*.

Perhaps she had been both, thought Dorothy? Well,
there was always tomorrow and, thanks to dear Agnes, she
would do her best to reform.

Joan and Edward Young, with their son Paul, departed the
next day for their holiday. Ben Curdle drove them to
Heathrow in their car, and would drive it home, and lock
it safely in the garage for a fortnight.

Harold Shoosmith had been left with a sheaf of notes
about the arrangements for the fête, for Edward was a
conscientious man and felt slightly guilty at leaving his
usual post on fête day.

It was to take place on the Saturday after the school's
Open Day, and everyone hoped that the weather would
hold.

The programme proudly displayed on the door of the
Two Pheasants, on trees in Thrush Green and Lulling, and

in various shop windows, announced such excitements as a Bouncy Castle for the very young, a visit from the morris dancers, pony rides, innumerable stalls and competitions and a fancy-dress display.

The last, of course, was the one which particularly affected Dorothy Watson as judge. She had no fears about her competence to be discriminating and fair, but *what to wear herself* was her main concern.

Luckily, the day dawned as fine and warm as those which had preceded it, and Agnes and Isobel were soon able to assure Dorothy that the pink frock, which she thought too youthful, was exactly right for the occasion, and most becoming to her.

Dorothy allowed herself to be persuaded, and on remembering that Thrush Green had never seen it before, as it had been bought in Barton-on-Sea a year earlier, she donned her pink splendour immediately after the cold buffet lunch provided by her hostess.

The fête was to be opened by Lady Penge, who lived near Lulling and was often called upon to perform such duties. She was noted for her good works in the area, sat on innumerable committees, and was patron to a host of charities and a local magistrate.

But apart from all these qualifications, it was her distinguished appearance which gave the occasions she graced such style. She was six feet in height and as slim as a poplar tree. From her silver hair to her triple-A handmade shoes she oozed fine breeding. Some thought her supercilious, but others maintained that her highly arched eyebrows gave her this air, and it had nothing to do with her innate kindness.

Her clothes were expensive and impeccable, her smile sweet if a trifle vague. She had no memory for faces, and frequently cut dead old friends, and even her own family, in Lulling High Street, but was readily forgiven.

'Well, she's *gentry*,' one would say indulgently to his neighbour.

'Too much inbreeding,' one farmer would comment to another.

'But she do look a real lady,' the women would tell each other, admiring the picture hats, the silk dresses, or the furs and tweeds, according to the season.

Lady Penge was due at ten minutes to two for the opening at two o'clock, and everyone rested assured that she would be on time. A welcoming committee headed by Harold Shoosmith were to assemble in his drawing-room before making their way to the dais.

But before opening time, activity at Thrush Green was hectic. The firm engaged to install the electrical equipment which was needed for the relay of Lady Penge's speech, not to mention the announcements by Harold and his helpers during the afternoon, and the general racket of so-called music which would provide a background to the afternoon's amusements, was having difficulty with the cables which snaked everywhere about the green.

Flustered women set out their wares on half-a-dozen stalls. Pudding basins, Oxo tins and handleless cups rattled with loose change. Bunches of garden flowers stood in buckets of water in the shade, and inside the tea tent the activity was frantic as wobbly card tables were draped in the very best cloths with edgings crocheted by long-dead hands. Urns were being inspected, teaspoons counted, sandwiches and homemade cakes shrouded in polythene against inquisitive wasps, and all was bustle.

This excitement was echoed in the houses around Thrush Green, and nowhere was the fever more acute than in Molly Curdle's living-room where she and two other young mothers were getting their children ready for the fancy-dress parade which would be one of the first items on the programme.

It was a full-time job. Lunch had been demoted from the usual sit-down meal to a hasty snatching of a sandwich or sausage roll from a large pile in the kitchen, which Molly had prepared beforehand.

Young George Curdle had insisted on being an Egyptian mummy, adequately swaddled, as seen on television, and reclining in a sarcophagus. Molly and Ben had done their best to dissuade him from this project, and had suggested more practical roles such as a highwayman, a pirate or even a pierrot, as Joan Young had offered a costume from her own young days. But George was adamant. Highwaymen and pirates were old-fashioned, and the pierrot costume was just plain sissy. He was going to be an Egyptian mummy or nothing at all!

His little sister Anne was quite content to wear a fairy costume, complete with wobbly wings, a silver crown made of oven foil, and a wand with a star at the top.

The two other mothers, having turned their docile daughters into a gypsy and a teddy bear, were helping Molly in the difficult task of wrapping George's limbs, torso and finally head in yards and yards of toilet paper stuck here and there with inches of Scotch tape. Already they were using the second roll, and no doubt, thought Molly agitatedly, a third would have to be found. George was an anxious victim.

'You sure that box is like a real carsophagus?' he enquired, nodding towards an enormous dress box supplied by Winnie Bailey the day before.

'*Sarcophagus*,' corrected Molly, 'and it's as big as you'll need. And *ftand ftill*,' she added, holding the end of the sticky tape between her teeth.

The job was interminable. The toilet paper kept breaking. George complained that he was hot, that there were gaps in the wrappings and how would he go to the lavatory?

'You don't,' said one of the helpers shortly. 'Egyptian mummies have to wait.'

'I'd better have a sausage roll before you do my face,' he announced, and his sister fetched him a couple as his neck was being swathed.

By a quarter to two the mammoth task was complete, and George was told to lodge himself carefully on a kitchen chair, and to hold his coffin in readiness.

'And what are you?' enquired a neighbour, looking in to borrow tea towels.

'I'm a mummy. And this is my carsophagus,' said George's muffled voice.

'Well, well,' said the woman, mystified. 'Fancy that!'

Everyone agreed that it was wonderful to have fine weather for the fête. It was bound to hold, and that dark cloud to the west was nothing to worry about.

Lady Penge, accompanied by the welcoming dignitaries, emerged from Harold Shoosmith's house and they made their way to the dais set up near the lime trees by St Andrew's church.

Promptly at two o'clock, Harold approached the microphone and introduced Lady Penge to the waiting crowd.

'Does this thing go up and down?' were the first words heard by the attendant populace, as Lady Penge fingered the microphone.

There were some ear-splitting crackles as the instrument was adjusted, and one of the electricians leapt forward to see to it.

'A friend of my dad's was electrocuted with one of them,' remarked an elderly woman to her neighbour. 'The power was off for three hours. Couldn't boil the kettle.'

'Shush! Shush!' said someone on the platform, as Lady Penge's dulcet tones began to reach her audience. Her speech was received with the usual deference and a hearty round of applause, and the youngest and cleanest of the Cooke grandchildren presented a bouquet of what the locals called 'boughten carnations', with a commendable curtsy, and everyone was free to visit the stalls and part with their money.

The cake stall, as always, was the one which was first besieged. Nelly Piggott had supplied a generous amount of sponges, shortbread, gingerbread and the like, and would have loved to have been present. Duty at the Fuchsia Bush on a busy Saturday forbade this, but she had done her part nobly beforehand.

Dorothy and Agnes were in their element, meeting old friends and pupils, and relishing the tit-bits of news which would furnish them with many happy memories when they returned to Barton.

Many people complimented Dorothy on her pink dress, and Agnes, in her grey silk shirtwaister, now four years old, was glad to see how Dorothy glowed with pleasure. If only, she thought, with a sudden spasm of pain, they could stay at Thrush Green far from Teddy's insidious presence!

The microphone came into use again. Above the alarming crackles and explosive noises, Harold announced the fancy-dress competition which was to be judged by 'their old friend Miss Watson'.

'I don't care for "old",' said Dorothy, 'and surely there are others to help me judge?'

Charles Henstock who was near by assured her that everyone would have complete confidence in her choice.

But Dorothy was not to be persuaded. 'You must help,' she said firmly, grasping his arm. 'I might choose all from the same family. You know the dangers. Come to my aid!'

'Of course, of course,' said Charles soothingly, and the two stood side by side as the children assembled.

There was the usual hubbub.

'Mind my wings!'

'My shoe's come off!'

'Where's Miss Muffet's spider?'

And over all, the stentorian if somewhat muffled yells from George Curdle. 'Lay me in my carsophagus!'

At last the three age groups were sorted out by Miss Watson, to whom this sort of chaos was nothing.

'Under fives first!' she announced, and half-a-dozen small rabbits, fairies, a tramp and a crawling green object which represented a dinosaur lined up self-consciously.

'Walk round in a circle,' commanded Dorothy. 'We want to see backs as well as fronts.'

She turned to her fellow judge. 'Well?'

'I think the fairy is the prettiest,' said Charles.

'But we must consider other things,' pointed out Dorothy. 'Has *ingenuity* been used? Is the *workmanship* adequate? On the other hand, is the costume *hired* or something already made for another occasion?'

'Well,' said Charles, somewhat deflated by all the apparent criteria needed for judging fancy-dress competitions, 'I think I must rely on your judgement.'

By this time, the dinosaur's costume was falling to pieces. Wailing came from its wearer.

'I do hope,' said Dorothy to Harold who had appeared, 'that *every* child will be given something for entering.'

'Indeed,' Harold assured her, showing her a pile of tickets. 'This gives them a free ice-cream at the stall.'

Satisfied, Dorothy returned to her task.

'I rather like the tramp,' she said to Charles. 'That tin cup tied with string round his waist, and the beard. A lot of thought has gone into that.'

'I agree,' said Charles, and the tramp was awarded first place, amidst general applause. Rabbits, fairies and dinosaurs seemed content to rush off to the ice-cream stall, and the next group, containing George Curdle and his dress-box, took the stage.

'And what are you, George?' enquired Dorothy.

'I'm an Egyptian mummy, and this is my carsophagus.'

'*Sarcophagus!*' corrected Dorothy, ever the teacher. 'Well, you obviously can't walk round with the others if you're dead, so the rector will help you to lie down.'

George was lowered gingerly into his coffin, and lay looking skyward as his companions circled round the two judges.

A few minutes later they looked down upon his supine body, and retired a few paces.

'Definitely!' said Dorothy.

'Without question!' agreed Charles.

The outcome was announced. George was helped to his feet, his bandages fast disentegrating, ice-cream tickets were handed out amidst general rejoicing, and Dorothy and Charles prepared to judge the last entries.

The winner of the final group was a fourteen-year-old Cooke girl, dressed as a Bright Young Thing of the twenties, complete with a long cigarette holder and knee-length strings of pearls. As she also did an extremely competent Charleston as she paraded round the judges, everyone agreed that she was 'quite something', and Charles was obviously enchanted.

After this, the morris dancers were the centre of attraction, clapping and thumping, twirling and frisking, reminding Alan Lester, who was selling raffle tickets, of his infants' recent efforts, and the unwelcome possibility of suffering, yet again, before the Christmas concert.

By half past five the crowds were thinning, and the black cloud had moved over the sun. The stalls were almost cleared, and the ladies in the tea tent were stowing away plates and cutlery and folding the tablecloths, now far less pristine than when they were first spread.

Lady Penge had departed after her duty round of the stalls, bearing her bouquet, some homegrown beetroots, four pots of jam and a knitted tea cosy. As she had also left a ten-pound note with Harold Shoosmith 'for the funds', everyone agreed that she had performed her duties with honour, as always.

At six o'clock the first drops of rain pattered on to the chestnut trees and began to darken the trestle tables. There was a mad rush to get everything under cover. Mackintoshes were put on, head scarves tied, children exhorted 'to run home', and Thrush Green, scattered with pieces of paper, ice-cream wrappers and all the debris of the day's activity, emptied rapidly.

'We really ought to get this cleared up,' said Charles anxiously to Harold, as they sheltered under the lime trees by the church.

At that moment, a flash of lightning tore the black cloud apart, thunder shook the earth and the heavens opened.

'It'll keep till morning,' shouted Harold above the din. 'Let's make a run for it!'

The two men, clutching the cash boxes which held the proceeds of the day's work inside their jackets, ran with their heads down to the sanctuary of Harold's house.

Isobel threw open the front door. 'Quickly, quickly! I've put on the kettle for a cup of tea.'

'Always welcome,' gasped Charles, mopping his wet face.

August

In working well, if travail you sustain,
Into the wind shall lightly pass the pain.

Nicholas Grimald

Work was everywhere evident in Thrush Green in August. The winter barley had been harvested, and golden bales stood in the fields awaiting collection. Soon the great combines would be chugging round the wheat crops and the farmers were praying for a dry spell over the harvest period.

In the gardens the strawberries had given way to raspberries, and red and white currants dangled from the bushes, much to the delight of the marauding birds. Apples and plums were filling out on the trees, and prudent housewives were tidying their freezers and looking out ancient kilner jars, ready for the winter stores.

Gardeners were busy collecting seeds or taking cuttings. In most homes the gardening catalogues were in evidence, and bulbs were being ordered for the garden and for the adornment of the house during the dark days of winter.

Everywhere, it seemed, crops of some sort were being collected and preparations made for the months ahead. What the poet called 'sustained travail' which was happening in Thrush Green and, for that matter, everywhere else, was going on busily and giving a great deal of satisfaction in the process.

It certainly provided some of Thrush Green's inhabitants with some comfort amidst their troubles. Nelly Piggott was one who was glad to busy herself with preparations for winter, and particularly for Christmas, as she went about her duties at the Fuchsia Bush.

They kept her from dwelling too painfully upon her partner's rapid decline. Mrs Peters seemed to be more wraith-like at every visit paid by Nelly to her bedside. She greeted Nelly with the same warm smile and little cries of welcome, but day by day her face grew paler and her arms more stick-like. When Nelly put her own fat arms round her friend, she felt as if she were embracing a child, so small and fragile was the little figure.

But the mind within that gaunt head was as clear as ever, and Mrs Peters continued to question Nelly about the state of affairs at her much-loved business. It was, thought

Nelly privately, about the only thing which kept that small bright flame fluttering in its frail container.

Edward Young too was glad to have such jobs as mowing, hedge-trimming and fruit-picking to take his mind from other matters. The question of the extension to the communal room at Rectory Cottages still worried him. During the holiday abroad he had been able to dismiss his secret unease. 'Out of sight was out of mind,' to a certain extent, and he had thrown himself into the joys of a strange land and the company of Joan and Paul, and put his cares aside.

But now that he was back in his home, with Rectory Cottages within constant view, his old doubts had come back to torment him. Joan had discovered him standing by his work table, pencil in hand, studying a diagram before him which was plainly a plan of enlargement of the present premises.

Joan had said nothing, but worried secretly. It was one thing to be married to a gifted and conscientious architect, but being married to a dedicated perfectionist who was capable of worrying himself into another attack of shingles or, even worse, a nervous breakdown, was something which Joan found most alarming.

It was she who made sure that he did his share of harvesting and tidying-up in the garden, trusting that, as the poet said so long ago: '*The wind shall lightly pass the pain.*'

At Barton-on-Sea Dorothy and Agnes were equally busy.

They had returned much refreshed from Thrush Green, with a great many pieces of news which would keep them happy for weeks to come.

Agnes wondered if the return to their own surroundings would rekindle the fire for Teddy which, it seemed, had quite died away in the alien air of Thrush Green.

She sat in the little garden shelling peas. Dorothy had gone shopping, and it was very quiet in the sunshine. Agnes let her hands rest for a moment and lay back in the wicker garden chair.

Every now and then some thistledown floated across her line of vision. She thought how pretty it looked, silvery miniature umbrellas drifting in the warm air. Her neighbours, and Dorothy too if she were present, would be adversely critical of these airy seeds, for a neglected garden near by produced a fine crop of weeds, including thistles, and the good gardeners of the neighbourhood were highly censorious. Secretly, Agnes found great pleasure in a rampant white convolvulus which had draped itself along the wire fence, but she was alone in her admiration.

The old lady who had lived there had died some months earlier. Her children lived overseas, and although it was said that the agent had been told to keep the garden tidy, nothing had been done.

Only Eileen, it seemed, had struck a happy note among all the disapproval for she claimed that she had seen goldfinches feeding on the thistledown.

'A *charm* of goldfinches,' murmured Agnes aloud, returning to her task. What a pretty group name, she thought! So much nicer than a *school* of porpoises or a *flock* of sheep.

As the fat green peas rolled into her basin, Agnes wondered about Eileen. Had she noticed that Dorothy was calling less frequently? Was she aware of Dorothy's unfortunate infatuation for Teddy?

Agnes remembered how shocked she had been when she realized that Dorothy used to make a point of visiting Teddy on the afternoons when Eileen was pushing the book trolley round the local hospital. Certainly the book service happened only once a fortnight, but surely Eileen must have noticed?

Or perhaps Teddy did not tell his wife? Was he embarrassed? Or was he just flattered? It seemed to Agnes that males, even those of six years old, with whom she had been familiar for many years, found it necessary to have attention, preferably from doting mothers or older sisters, and later, of course, from their wives.

It was hardly surprising, thought Agnes, removing a piece of thistledown from the shelled peas, that widowers were so much more helpless than widows.

Women were used to coping with a variety of activities – shopping, cooking, cleaning, caring for children and writing letters. When their husbands died, they buckled to and did their best to cope with the jobs which formerly had been their husbands' department. They learnt to mend a fuse, to change a bulb, to understand the bank statements, and if they could not manage one of their husbands' jobs they soon found someone who would do it for them, if suitably reimbursed.

Men seemed to go to pieces without a partner. Teddy, she had to admit, was an exception. He had managed admirably as a widower, but then his innate courage in coping with his lack of sight had no doubt given him extra strength in adversity. But Agnes recalled other bereaved men who had had no idea how to cook the simplest meal, or how to wash and iron clothes. Sad souls indeed, thought Agnes, and no wonder so many married again!

She popped open the last pea pod. What a blessing it was to be single, she mused happily. She was free and as footloose as the thistledown which floated by her in the sunshine.

Very content Agnes carried the peas into the kitchen.

In the kitchen at Lulling Woods Dotty was as busy as her neighbours. She was stringing runner beans at the kitchen table. The door into the garden was open, and outside in the sunshine young Bruce was happily worrying a bone.

'He looks fighting fit,' said Ella, who had called to see her old friend and to collect her goat's milk.

'He's a very healthy little dog,' agreed Dotty, knife poised.

'No news of his owners, I suppose?'

'I am his owner!' said Dotty forcefully. 'They have forfeited all right to him.'

She looked quite fierce with the knife in her grip. Ella hastily changed the subject.

'And Flossie?'

The old dog lay in her basket near by, and wagged her tail when she heard her name.

'Rather pianissimo,' said Dotty. 'I don't think it is worth getting the vet in, but she is rather up and down these days. Still, she eats quite well, and seems happy enough. Like us, Ella, she's getting old.'

Ella nodded her agreement. 'I hear Mrs Peters is in a bad way,' she said. 'I imagine the Fuchsia Bush will be on the market before long. It's sad, I think. She spent years building it up.'

'Piggott tells me that Prouts may buy the premises. Some talk of specializing in expensive blouses and jewellery and stuff, and calling it a *boutique*.' Dotty's tone was scornful.

'Nelly will miss the work. She's an absolute wizard at cooking. She'll soon get a job elsewhere, probably in one of the hotels.'

'She won't stay at home,' agreed Dotty, putting the last shredded bean into the colander. 'Now, what about a nice cup of mint tea before I get your milk?'

'No, no, Dotty,' said Ella hastily. 'I'm off to the dentist very soon, and I'm afraid I can't spare the time.'

'Ah well! I shall look forward to seeing you very soon, and meanwhile you must take a pot of my beetroot preserve. I've put in some rather special herbs for flavouring. You must tell me what you think of it.'

Ella thanked her, making a mental note to concoct a comment which combined truth with civility for a future occasion.

She knew, from experience, that it would not be easy.

Before long the dry spell of weather broke with a spectacular thunderstorm one hot August night.

In their beds, gardeners listened happily to the patter of rain on thirsty soil, and farmers listened less happily, wondering if the downpour would flatten the wheat.

Lightning flickered over Thrush Green, thunder roared and rumbled, babies woke and screamed, dogs barked and Nelly Piggott, who had been unable to sleep, rose from her bed and covered the mirror, as her mother had advised years before, and returned to her tousled sheets to go over, yet again, the amazing and upsetting scene in Mrs Peters' bedroom earlier that evening.

She had found her old employer lying listlessly against the pillows. She smiled weakly at Nelly.

'I can't sit up,' she apologized. 'My neck has no strength in it.'

Nelly drew a chair close to the bedside and held the thin hand lying on the counterpane.

'It's about the Fuchsia Bush,' whispered the invalid. 'Young Mr Venables knows about it.' She began to cough.

'Don't worry then,' said Nelly, alarmed. 'I'll find out what you want done from him.'

The coughing eased.

'It's done,' she breathed. 'I'm leaving it to you, Nelly.'

Nelly was stunned. She was also deeply unhappy. She

recognized the outstanding generosity of the frail woman before her, but the thought of taking over the responsibility of the business filled her with horror.

'But I'm not up to it! You know I love the place, and I've been pleased to keep it ticking over while you've been laid up. But to own it!'

Mrs Peters smiled. 'Nelly, it's like this. I've no one close to me to leave it to. It's been my whole life. I put into the Fuchsia Bush all my money and youth and energy. I want it to go on. And you're the one who knows how to do it.'

The thin hand gripped Nelly's plump one desperately.

Nelly took a deep breath. 'It's a wonderful thing to hear,' she said shakily, 'and don't think I'm not grateful for what you've arranged, but I've no head for business. I'm just a good cook, no more than that.'

'The business side can be looked after, just as it has been for the last few months, and Justin Venables will advise you about that. I wasn't going to tell you, but lying here I suddenly thought that it wasn't really fair to spring it on you when I'd gone.'

A tear rolled down the pale cheek, and Nelly too found that she was crying, and did not attempt to mop her tears away.

'You see, Nelly, everyone loves you, and the customers and staff will rally round, you'll see. The thought of leaving the Fuchsia Bush is the only thing that I regret. I shan't be sorry to leave this pain and all the other problems. But if I know my life's work is going on under your care, I'll be happy.'

Nelly was unable to speak. Pity for her employer, the overwhelming news and the knowledge that there was no choice for her, but only one course to take, as well as the choking pain in her throat, kept Nelly silent.

'Say you will,' pleaded the invalid. 'Nelly, say you will!'

Nelly swallowed the lump in her throat. 'I'll do my best. That's a promise. I'll keep your Fuchsia Bush going as you'd like it to be, to the best of my ability. And I'll never cease to be thankful for such a wonderful present. You know that!'

She bent forward to kiss the invalid, and realized how exhausted she looked. This interview had been too much for her. It was obvious that she had summoned up all that remained of her strength to tell Nelly her plans.

Nelly herself felt exhausted, and stirred herself to go.

'You must rest now,' she said. 'Is nurse coming in this evening?'

'She's due any minute.'

'Then I'm going to leave you, my dear. Sleep well, and I'll see you tomorrow.'

Mrs Peters nodded, closed her eyes, and Nelly tiptoed away.

It was beginning to get dark when Nelly emerged at last on to Church Green. The noble bulk of St John's church was casting a long shadow, and Nelly sat down on a seat against a drystone Cotswold wall, and did her best to come to terms with the astounding news she had just heard.

There was nothing to be done about the offer. It was the wish of a dying woman, a plea from one she loved, and it was her duty to accept the situation. It was an honour to be asked to carry on the Fuchsia Bush, and the most generous gift that anyone could bestow.

Nevertheless, the outlook struck despair into Nelly's heart. She could rule her kitchen. She could rule the front of the house, the customers, the counter trade and the organization of the mobile van which trundled round Lulling with delectable fare for the office staffs. She was beginning to understand the ordering from wholesalers, the timing of deliveries, those she could trust absolutely and those who needed watching.

But the overall business arrangements were beyond her. The maintenance of the premises, the insurance of the staff and the property, the tax returns, the round of incomprehensible forms, all these things confused her, and she knew that she would never be able to understand them. If any unscrupulous persons wanted to steal from the firm by 'fiddling the books', Nelly knew she would be powerless to thwart them.

She sat there in the gathering twilight, deeply unhappy and oblivious to the growing chill in the air. Across the green, she saw the rotund figure of the rector making his way to the distant post box. She felt an overpowering desire to hurry after him, to pour out her worries and to be comforted.

She knew that such comfort would be freely given. No one appealed to Charles Henstock in vain, but Nelly remained seated, the tears returning.

This was something she must face alone. Not even Charles Henstock could provide complete satisfaction. Certainly, Albert could not even begin to understand how she felt.

Her fingers strayed to the gold chain which hung round her neck and was hidden under her clothes. If only Charlie were here! He would provide comfort and cheering advice. His first reaction would be a disbelieving whistle at such a stroke of fortune, but that done he would bring a shrewd streetwise mind to the practical difficulties and give Nelly generous support and sympathy. He was a scamp, Nelly was the first to admit. He had hurt her badly, but in a matter like this he would have been able to offer good advice.

She fingered the chain lovingly, remembering the giver,

and became conscious of inner comfort. Something would
turn up. People would help her. She would go to see
young Mr Venables, if need be, and the rector, two good
men who would give sound advice.

She began to feel chilly and rose from the seat. As she
bent down to retrieve her shopping bag, she heard a man's
voice.

'Want a lift home?'

It was Percy Hodge, who farmed along the Nidden
road, the husband of her bingo companion.

'Thank you,' said Nelly. 'I'd be glad of a lift.'

He held out his hand for the shopping bag, and peered
at her face. 'You all right? You look upset.'

Nelly decided that the plain truth was needed. 'I've just
come from Mrs Peters. She's not long for this world,
Percy.'

'I'm sorry. No wonder you're upset.'

He led the way to his ancient Land-Rover across the road.

'I had to come down to the police station,' he explained,
'about my gun licence.'

He opened the door, and Nelly heaved herself up to sit
beside him.

They drove slowly down Lulling High Street. There
were very few people about in the dusk. The street lights
were beginning to flicker into life, and some of the shops
had lighted windows.

The Fuchsia Bush was shut, and there were no lights
there. Nelly could hardly bear to look at it.

'That's real sad about Mrs Peters,' said Percy, slowing
down as they met the Oxford road. 'She was a real nice
woman. A good worker too.'

Nelly nodded, not trusting her voice.

Percy changed gears and the Land-Rover began to grind
noisily up the steep hill to Thrush Green.

'I wonder what'll become of the Fuchsia Bush?' queried Percy when they reached the top.

'I've been wondering about that too,' said Nelly tremulously.

The nurse had called in while Nelly was sitting unhappily on Church Green. She knew at once that her patient was dead, and rang the doctor.

By morning, it seemed, all Lulling knew the sad news. At Thrush Green it was Betty Bell who told the Shoosmiths as they were clearing the breakfast table.

'Mind you,' said Betty, after sincere tributes had been paid to the late owner of the Fuchsia Bush, 'it was a happy release really. Poor thing had no hope of getting better. I wonder who'll be the third?'

She looked speculatively at her employers.

'Third what?' asked Harold.

'Death.'

'Does there have to be a third?'

'Oh yes! Haven't you heard that? Why, deaths always go in threes.'

'But Mrs Peters' death is the first I've heard.'

'There was that nice Mr Andersen's mother,' Betty pointed out. She went to the dresser drawer for a clean duster to start her morning's work.

Harold addressed her back. 'But she was in *America*, for heaven's sake. She wasn't *local*.'

'Don't have to be *local*,' responded Betty, inspecting the duster. 'It's deaths what you hear about. Well, we've heard about Mrs Andersen, and now Mrs Peters, and soon we'll hear about a third.'

'Really, Betty,' broke in Isobel. 'You are positively ghoulish!'

'If that means bilious you're right. I had some of

Dotty's – I mean Miss Harmer's – marmalade for breakfast. Don't worry though. I'll work it off!'

She vanished upstairs, and soon they heard her singing.

Later that morning, the news was being spread at the Two Pheasants.

Percy Hodge was in a position of some importance as he had had first-hand news from Nelly the previous evening.

'Your Nelly was proper upset,' he told Albert. 'I could see she'd been crying.'

'Ah!' agreed Albert. 'My Nelly's real soft-hearted. She's been working overtime to keep things up together at the café for Mrs Peters.'

'I suppose it'll be up for sale,' ventured someone.

'It's got a good position in the High Street,' commented another.

'Will Nelly be looking for another job?' queried a third to Albert.

'I don't know nothing about it,' said Albert crossly, slamming his empty beer mug on the counter. 'I don't much like all this talk when that poor woman ain't been dead for less than a day.'

He thrust his way between his cronies and went out of the door, slamming it behind him.

'What's bitten old Albert?' said Percy to Mr Jones, the landlord.

'Well,' he replied, 'I don't think Nelly tells him much, and that rankles. And besides that, I think he's wondering if Nelly will be out of a job.'

'Then he'll just have to do a bit more himself,' said one of the men with malicious satisfaction. 'Won't hurt him!'

His hearers agreed with him.

Mrs Peters' funeral took place on a Friday morning, and St

John's church was almost full, for she had been a popular figure in the little town and its environs.

Towards the front of the church sat the three Lovelock sisters, much to the surprise of most of those present, who had only heard about some of the complaints made about the Fuchsia Bush in early days.

Now, they realized, the frail and querulous old ladies knew that they had lost a friend, ever ready to provide practical support, and to forgive any little upsets. Their mourning was sincere for their departed neighbour.

Charles Henstock took the service, and the sincerity and simple grace of his short address summed up the feelings of the congregation.

The Fuchsia Bush was closed for the day, and Nelly and the staff were among the chief mourners.

Nelly was outwardly calm now, but still inwardly in turmoil. In her handbag was a letter from Justin Venables, asking her to call at his office on Tuesday morning next 'in connection with her late employer's Last Will and Testament'.

Somehow, those capital letters had increased her fears. She would be glad to get the interview over, to have some guidance, to be given some support in this alarming situation.

Since Mrs Peters' death Nelly had kept her own counsel. It was useless to confide in Albert, she realized. Most women, she thought, with some bitterness, have a husband, or a son, or a brother to rely on, at such times.

Fingering Charlie's gold chain she thought sadly that her only support came from a fickle lover long dead. What lay before her must be tackled singlehanded. It was going to be a lone furrow to plough, and an uphill one.

Speculation about the future of the Fuchsia Bush was rife.

The general opinion was that the property would be sold, perhaps as a going concern, and if so the new owner would surely have the sense to keep Nelly in charge of the kitchen.

Some thought that such a prime site in Lulling High Street might attract one of the supermarket giants, but as there was not much space for loading and unloading it seemed doubtful.

However, this issue made a pleasant source of interest, and with the death of Carl's mother, as well as the possibility of catching the criminals who had absconded with thousands of pounds, and worse still, abandoned Dotty's dog, kept tongues happily wagging during the month of August.

Charles Henstock had his own worries, for Mrs Thurgood had renewed her attack about the '*gross inadequacy*', as she put it, of the common room at Rectory Cottages, and to add to his discomfort he had met Edward Young, whilst walking in the High Street, and was surprised to find him reviewing the possibility of an enlargement to the existing annexe.

'But, Edward,' Charles had protested, 'you were quite satisfied with it before. You know we took a vote on it.'

'I wasn't there,' Edward reminded him. 'Since then I've been in there once or twice, and I must admit it does seem a bit cramped.'

'Well, cramped or not,' said Charles, raising his hat politely to a passing parishioner, 'you know we have no money to take on such work. We must cut our coats according to the cloth. I keep telling Mrs Thurgood so.'

Edward looked alarmed. 'Is she still being a nuisance? I find her absolutely appalling.'

'So do I,' agreed Charles ruefully. It was so unusual to hear Charles uttering anything that was detrimental about his flock that Edward realized that he had suffered much.

'Far be it from me to join forces with that awful woman,' he told Charles, 'but I do just wonder . . .'

He paused to let a perambulator pass him.

'We ought to get Harold to tackle her,' he continued. 'He'll settle her hash!'

'He does,' sighed Charles. 'Frequently. But she bounces back!'

On the following Tuesday Nelly awoke feeling that something unpleasant was about to happen, and remembered that she had to pay the dreaded visit to young Mr Venables' office that morning.

She lay in bed, watching the sunshine wavering across the ceiling, and wondering what would be the appropriate wear for a visit to a solicitor. Something, she decided, between funeral garments and the sort of formal dress one would put on for a business lunch.

Mentally she surveyed her wardrobe and settled on a lightweight grey suit, rather tight to be sure, and a white silk blouse. The ensemble, she hoped, would be suitably ladylike, and yet not too smart to invite speculation from Rosa and Gloria. In any case, a voluminous overall could hide her unusual morning splendour before she left for her appointment.

That settled, Nelly rose, washed and dressed, and went downstairs, where Albert was shaving at the kitchen sink.

He caught sight of her in the mirror. 'You're all dolled up,' he grunted, razor poised. 'Where are you off?'

'I've had this years,' said Nelly truthfully. 'And I'm off to work, where you should be. The weeds round that churchyard of yours would keep a couple of Percy Hodge's cows going for a month.'

Silenced, Albert continued to scrape his face, while Nelly dashed about her duties in her usual early-morning fashion.

By eight thirty she was at the Fuchsia Bush, and at a quarter to eleven she told the staff, and Miss Spooner, the visiting accountant's assistant, that she would be back in about an hour. She had some of Mrs Peters' business to discuss with young Mr Venables, she explained. It was as well, she knew from experience, to give people some little nugget of information, preferably truthful, to chew on, rather than leave them to speculate.

Justin Venables' office was little changed from the time when he had first entered it. To be sure, the black gauze which had shadowed the lower half of the sash window looking out into the High Street had been replaced with a white net curtain, so the room was much lighter, but still screened from public gaze.

Justin did not smoke, and did not encourage his clients to indulge by offering them cigarettes, but a hideous cast-iron ashtray had stood on the desk for almost a century, and still remained there for those who were addicted to tobacco. It bore the legend, 'Long Live Victoria 1837-97' and would no doubt be snapped up, at great expense, by any collector of Victoriana, if given half a chance.

Nelly sat nervously opposite Justin at his enormous desk.

'Would you care for some coffee?' asked Justin.

'Thank you,' said Nelly, and Justin struck a bell sharply on his desk, and Miss Giles, much the same age, it seemed, as her master, appeared at the door.

'Just two cups,' nodded Justin, and in silence Miss Giles vanished, only to return two minutes later with a tray containing two steaming cups, sugar and a plate of digestive biscuits.

She must have had the kettle at the boil, thought Nelly, and felt somehow comforted by this little domestic interlude.

'I wonder if you have any inkling of how Mrs Peters left her affairs?' queried Justin spreading out a document before him.

Nelly put down her cup. The coffee was rather nasty, and she hoped that Justin was not paying the full price for good quality instant coffee when obviously he was getting the cheapest.

She wrenched her mind from this to reply to Justin's question. It seemed right to answer him truthfully.

'Just before she died,' she answered, 'Mrs Peters told me she was leaving the business to me, but I don't know if that's correct.'

'Quite correct. I hope it pleases you. It shows how much she thought of your ability.'

Nelly shook her head. 'I was knocked sideways. I still am. It's too big a job for me to do, Mr Venables. I've no head for the money side.'

Justin nodded understandingly. 'I know exactly how you feel, Mrs Piggott. Now, I propose to read this Last Will and Testament, and then I will explain anything which puzzles you, and try to advise you about steps to take for the future running of the business.'

He cleared his throat and began, while Nelly did her best to follow the incomprehensible legal vocabulary, and failed after five minutes.

Justin still had a musical voice, and while the sonorous phrases droned round the room Nelly let her attention wander to the rows of envelopes bound with pink tape that stood along the shelves, and the black tin boxes stacked higher still bearing white-painted names. The wooden cupboards could have done with a good polish, mused Nelly, and the windows had not been cleaned for weeks. It was a pity too that the Turkish carpet was so dusty. Nelly would have liked half a day in the room to put it to rights.

After a time, Justin put down the will, and bent towards his client.

'Now, to business! I believe Miss Spooner still calls twice a week to attend to the office side.'

Nelly agreed.

'She is excellent, of course, but I should see if you could get someone younger, perhaps trained by her, and able to cope with modern office equipment and make things more manageable for you. Let me suggest one or two other things.'

The large clock on the wall ticked the hour away, while

Justin talked and made a few notes for Nelly to consider later.

It was chiming the half hour after midday when Nelly made her farewells, still bemused but much comforted, as she returned to the bustle of the Fuchsia Bush.

The latter part of August was unusually hot. The verges along the lanes were dusty and crowned with dry grass and dead flowers.

The grass on Thrush Green was crisp and brown, the earth like iron, and all the gardeners were tired of daily watering and asking each other how soon hosepipes would be banned.

Winnie Bailey and Jenny took their mugs of coffee into the garden, and sat under the shade of an ancient plum tree.

'It's as hot as Africa,' commented Jenny. 'Or America, according to the telly. People are dropping down dead with the heat.'

'Really? I missed that.'

'I wonder if that nice Mr Andersen's all right?' continued Jenny. 'Is he coming back soon?'

'He wants to. I believe Molly has heard from him.'

'I expect he'll stay in Woodstock again, if he gets over. My cousin's a chambermaid at the Bear. She seems to think he'll be coming back there.'

'Did he say so?'

'I'm not sure, but he got very friendly with a nice woman who was there for a few months.'

Winnie digested this interesting morsel of gossip. 'What does this woman do? Is she on holiday?'

'No, she works in the big houses. Tells people what curtains to buy and how to change their wallpaper and that. She goes up to London getting great samples of

material and wallpaper books. Sometimes she's got three
or four houses in the neighbourhood, and then she takes
one of the biggest bedrooms at the Bear with a great desk
in it, and works there.'

'It must be rather expensive,' commented Winnie.

'I expect the people who employ her pay for that,' said
Jenny, 'and maybe the Bear gives her a special rate as she
stays quite a time. Shall I ask my cousin?'

'Good heavens, no!' replied Winnie. 'Her affairs are her
own business. Is she nice? She sounds very busy. An
interior designer, I suppose we would call her.'

'They all like her there. She tips very generously, and
don't give any trouble. She and Mr Andersen sometimes
shared a table in the evenings. Both a bit lonely I expect.'

Winnie was intrigued by this news, but forbore to ask
further. Could romance be in the air? If so, Winnie knew
from experience that the good news would reach Thrush
Green before very long. Jenny's cousin, or one of her
friends, would see to that.

It was later in the week that she came across Joan
Young. They were both shopping in Lulling High Street,
and met at the greengrocer's.

'Are you good at melons?' queried Joan. 'I believe
you're supposed to smell them to see if they're ripe.'

'I press the top,' replied Winnie, trying her luck on a
nicely mottled one. 'I should think this is about right.'

'Edward can't bear them when they're still hard. He says
he'd just as soon eat raw marrow.'

'I sympathize,' said Winnie. 'It's nectarines I can't
fathom. The reddest ones are often the least ripe. All very
tricky.'

They entered the shop to pay for their purchases, and
while they were waiting Joan told Winnie that they had
heard from Carl Andersen.

'He's coming over in September, and hoping to be here for several weeks. He *telephoned* last night,' she added. 'Think of that! I hope he won't be ruined when his bill comes in.'

'I'm sure he can manage that,' said Winnie. 'I gather that he is a prosperous businessman. Where's he staying?'

'At the Bear again. They made him very comfortable, and although we wanted to put him up, I can understand that he likes to be free. I gather he's following up that business venture in Scotland that he's interested in. It will be lovely to see him again.'

'Indeed it will,' agreed Winnie. She also wondered, as she added a fine cucumber to her purchases, if the gifted interior designer would be pleased too. But of this she said nothing.

After lunch that day, Winnie took her rest in a deckchair in the shadiest part of the garden. Jenny had boarded the two o'clock bus to Oxford to do some shopping for clothes, and it was very peaceful under the trees.

The bees were busy among the lavender flowers, and forcing their way between the velvety lips of the snap-dragons. Somewhere nearby a young bird was piping for attention, and high above the swallows swooped and soared. Soon they would be gathering together to chatter about their plans for migration. Then, thought Winnie sadly, it really would begin to feel like autumn.

In the distance, somewhere along the Nidden road, she could hear the throbbing of a combine, bringing ever closer the thought of cleared fields soon to be ploughed for next year's crop. Yes, autumn would soon be here.

She remembered inconsequently an English lesson at her school. The class had been asked to provide adjectives describing autumn, and she had proffered 'wistful' and 'mellow'. The English mistress had said rather brusquely that they had already put 'yellow' on the blackboard, and the young Winnie, somewhat piqued, had pointed out that *her* adjective was 'mellow' and not 'yellow'.

The mistress had looked at her with fresh interest, and enquired if she had learnt any poems by John Keats, who had written 'To Autumn'.

Winnie had replied truthfully that she had never heard of John Keats, and 'mellow' was written below 'wistful', and justice had been done.

She leant back and closed her eyes. How extraordinary one's memory was! She had not thought of that school for years, and yet that memory was vivid. So, suddenly, was the vision of her first paintbox with the fascinating names printed neatly below each bright square of paint. Crimson Lake, Bice Green, Prussian Blue, Viridian Green, Chinese White, Gamboge and a dozen more which she would have in tubes as she grew older and more expert, but that first paintbox was the one she remembered most clearly.

She recalled her attempt to paint a cabbage in an early art class, when an arrangement of vegetables, carrots, young turnips and pea pods – some closed, and others open displaying a row of glistening peas – had been that day's still life subject.

She had found, with a thrill of discovery, that Viridian, Chinese White, and then a touch of Crimson Lake, had produced the most satisfactory soft green wash which had gained her a gold star on the finished picture. Such idle memories, mused Winnie, half asleep.

A yellow leaf fluttered from the plum tree and landed on her lap. Soon, thought Winnie, there would be mushrooms, those magical pearls thrusting up overnight through the dewy grass.

She held the dead leaf between her thumb and finger, enjoying its roughness, and closed her eyes again.

September

Read Boswell in the house in the morning,
and after dinner under the bright yellow
leaves of the orchard. The pear trees a
bright yellow. The apple trees green still.
A sweet lovely afternoon.

Dorothy Wordsworth

The trees of Thrush Green were also beginning to have a golden tinge. The lime trees round St Andrew's church were a paler sunnier green than at the time of the July fête.

The sturdy chestnut trees still boasted dark green foliage, but on the grass beneath there were a number of wrinkled palmate leaves which presaged the coming of autumn.

There was a definite chill in the morning and evening air. Thoughts turned to stocks of coal and logs, of bulbs to be planted for Christmas flowering, and the thud of catalogues about the festive season, still months away, was heard on many a doormat in the area. Sensible people refused to be hustled into panic buying, and preferred to enjoy the mellow sunshine and the last of the summer flowers which made September one of the loveliest months at Thrush Green.

The news of Nelly's inheritance was soon common knowledge, and occasioned much speculation.

Nelly, well versed in the reactions to news in small communities, decided to tell Albert the day after she had visited Justin·Venables' office. She was quite prepared for his usual disgruntled response to her pieces of news, although she felt sure that the prospect of money might mitigate the gloom.

They had finished their evening meal, and were sitting at the kitchen table, stirring the cups of tea with which they liked to finish their repast.

'I had some good news today,' ventured Nelly.

'Oh ah!'

'I went to see young Mr Venables.'

Albert looked up in alarm. 'What you bin up to? You don't want to get muddled up with them legal blokes.'

'It was about Mrs Peters' will. She left me the Fuchsia Bush.'

Albert dropped his teaspoon with a clatter into the saucer.

'Left you the Fuchsia Bush?' he echoed with astonishment. 'What for?'

Nelly surveyed his unusually animated countenance. 'What for? For me to run, of course.'

There was silence while Albert tried to come to terms with this staggering piece of news. His voice was husky when he at last found words.

'You'd never be able to run the Fuchsia Bush, girl. You ain't got the brain.'

Although this was exactly Nelly's own private opinion, and had been so since that sad evening of Mrs Peters' death, to hear it put into such disparaging words, and by Albert of all people, brought out all Nelly's fighting spirit.

'You don't know nothing about it! Mrs Peters wouldn't have left it to me if she hadn't thought I'd be able to cope.'

'She was wandering, poor soul. Must've bin. Why, you gets in a muddle with the grocer's bill! You ain't no businesswoman.'

'I'll soon learn,' said Nelly shortly, taking the tea cups to the sink. 'And don't go blabbing about it in the Two Pheasants. Time enough when the news gets out later.'

'You'd best by far sell the place,' shouted Albert, above the noise of clashing crockery. 'Bring us in a tidy bit. We could move somewhere bigger.'

Nelly turned off the taps, left the sink, and resumed her place at the table. Albert surveyed her stern face with some trepidation.

'There's no "us" and "we" about this, Albert Piggott! Mrs Peters left it to *me alone*, and I'm the one as will say what happens to the Fuchsia Bush.'

'All right, all right,' muttered Albert. 'Keep your hair on. I was only suggesting –'

'Then you can keep your suggestions to yourself. I'm going to keep the Fuchsia Bush running as Mrs Peters wanted. It was her dying wish.'

'Maybe. But she'd never know if you sold it,' said Albert rallying. 'I wonder as Mr Venables didn't tell you to! Best all round, I'd say.'

'Say what you like,' retorted Nelly. 'I'm the one that has the last word, and the last word is that I'm not selling!'

'You could have one of them new houses up towards

Nidden. Fitted kitchen, bathroom and all that. And never need to go out to work. Me neither!'

Nelly looked at him with utter contempt. '*I am not selling!* And work is what I like. You'd be a happier man, Albert Piggott, if you took the same pride in your job.'

Silenced, Albert rose to make his way next door to the public house. He knew when he was beaten.

'And watch your tongue,' shouted Nelly after him. 'No need to broadcast the news to your good-for-nothing pals. It'll get round soon enough, if I know anything about gossip.'

Nelly was right, of course. The news flashed round Thrush Green and Lulling, and the general feeling was that Nelly was lucky to have dropped into a fortune.

'Of course, she'll sell it,' was the comment most frequently heard. 'I just hope whoever buys it will keep it going as it is. The Fuchsia Bush is an important place in Lulling High Street.'

People began to stop Nelly as she went to and fro to her work.

'Aren't you lucky?'

'What a windfall!'

'You've certainly hit the jackpot this time, Nelly.'

These remarks irritated Nelly beyond measure.

In the first place, she resented the envy which prompted these comments. She was the first to recognize her indebtedness to her late partner. She grieved for her daily, missing her companionship and steady good sense.

But she did not consider herself unadulteratedly *lucky*. The responsibility of owning the business quite overshadowed her feelings of pleasure and gratitude. It was a burden she could well do without, and only the fact that Mrs Peters had shown such faith in her gave Nelly some comfort.

She replied civilly to all who commented, telling them that she hoped to continue Mrs Peters' work to the best of her ability, and with advice from Mr Venables. And, she always added with some emphasis, she was definitely *not selling the property*.

That, at least, was greeted everywhere with relief. Violet, Ada and Bertha Lovelock made a point of calling at the Fuchsia Bush for coffee one morning, and expressing their pleasure at the news. It was a changed attitude on the part of the old ladies, thought Nelly, from the days when she had been maid, cook and general dogsbody for a short time at the house next door.

There, she recalled, the doling out of minuscule amounts of the cheapest margarine, a handful of currants, a half teacupful of sugar with the request to make 'a good fruit cake for tea'. She remembered too the dab of metal polish, in an old saucer, which was deemed adequate for polishing the vast amounts of silver knick-knacks covering several tables in the drawing-room.

Then she was treated as 'a skivvy', thought Nelly, receiving her former employers graciously. Now she was being acknowledged as a property owner and a sound businesswoman in her own right.

It was such encounters which began to give Nelly the confidence to tackle the sacred trust which had been thrust so dauntingly upon her.

News of Carl Andersen's return was welcomed by everyone who had met him on his first visit. But it was Edward Young who was particularly pleased at the news.

He had been greatly impressed by Carl Andersen, and even more stirred by the fact that Carl was one of the directors of the world-famous company of Benn, Andersen and Webbly whose work was respected in both hemispheres.

The firm had been much in the news over its bold and inspired work on such projects as dam-building, bridge-making and the laying-out of airports in the vast areas of Africa and Asia. Edward had followed the fortunes of the company in a number of articles in his architectural journals, and marvelled at the massive concept needed to visualize these mighty schemes.

His own architectural skills were confined to domestic work. He had a flair for designing modern houses which would fit well into their settings, and an equally strong feeling for the modernization of the small stone cottages which were scattered within a few miles of his own home. He had built up a reputation for this type of work, and as he had some domestic talents himself he was alert to the difficulties of planning kitchens for families or bathrooms for the disabled.

He relished his work, and was at pains to get every detail correct as well as pleasing to the eye. It was this anxiety for perfection which sometimes made him short-tempered, and which Joan understood and readily forgave.

It was she who shared his pleasure at the thought of Carl's return. Molly and Ben were also delighted, but Joan's feelings went further. Edward would have a companion with whom he could discuss all kinds of architectural matters. He would have a friend whose accomplishments he respected and whose work he found absorbing.

With any luck, thought Joan, he would put this wretched business of enlarging the sitting-room at Rectory Cottages to one side, and find the peace of mind he so needed to do work of his own.

All in all, the coming of Carl Andersen was awaited by everyone in Thrush Green with the greatest pleasure.

Dotty Harmer had heard the news of the American's

expected visit, and of Nelly Piggott's inheritance, but had
more pressing matters to engage her attention.

Flossie was not well. She had certainly rallied after the
vet's attentions earlier, and had pottered about her domain
and endured the boisterous attentions of Bruce with commendable tolerance.

But now she was listless. She could not be bothered to
eat, and Dotty kept her going with a dribble of evaporated
milk now and again which was all, it seemed, that would
tempt the patient.

'She can't go on like this,' said Kit, who had come to
Dotty's kitchen with Connie to confer with her. 'I should
get the vet again.'

Connie, more worried about Dotty than Flossie, heartily
agreed. At this rate, she could see, she would have two
invalids to care for.

'I'm sure you're right,' she said at last. 'It's just that I
dread him saying that he can do no more for poor Flossie.'

'I'll ring him at once,' said Kit, making for the door. He
was as anxious as his wife to get some knowledgeable
support in the situation.

Dotty squatted down beside Flossie's basket and fondled
her ears.

'In theory, of course, I am entirely in favour of the vet
putting Flossie out of her misery, if misery it is,' she said
to Connie when Kit had vanished. 'If only doctors would
do the same for us!'

'Now come!' protested Connie. 'You know they have to
take the Hypocrites Oath —'

'*Hippocratic!*' interrupted Dotty.

'Well, whatever it is. And they have to swear to try and
save life, not terminate it.'

'I know that! I know that,' snapped Dotty. 'All I'm
saying is that if you are human you are caught all ways.

No one will help us out, no matter how bad the pain. As Hamlet very sensibly said,

> *When he himself might his quietus make*
> *With a bare bodkin*

we still have to go on suffering! I shan't let Flossie suffer, and that's flat, but I just hope the vet can give her another few months of happy living.'

Connie was alarmed at Dotty's ferocity, and the pink patches which had flared in the old lady's face. She bent down and helped her to her feet.

'I think you could do with a drink,' she said gently. 'Shall I get you a little brandy?'

'No, no, I should much prefer a cup of lime tea.'

'Very well,' agreed Connie, 'and I will have one too.'

She filled the kettle, thinking that lime tea, at least, was fairly harmless. There was agitation enough in the household at the moment, without adding alimentary complications into the present climate.

While Dotty awaited the vet's visit with some trepidation, Albert Piggott had put aside his broom in the church porch, and crossed the road to the open door of the Two Pheasants.

The news about the Fuchsia Bush had been widely discussed in both bars during the last few days, and Albert was heartily sick of the heavy-handed teasing he had to endure.

But nothing, he told himself sturdily, was going to make him change the habits of a lifetime, and when the doors of the pub opened he intended to enter and refresh himself, as was his wont.

There was only one other customer in the bar, and that was Percy Hodge. He looked up as Albert entered.

'How's the millionaire this morning?' he greeted Albert, grinning at his own wit.

'You shut up!' growled Albert. 'You're asking for a thick ear, and that's flat.'

'Now, now, gentlemen,' cried Mr Jones, who was never free from the possibility of getting a name for 'a disorderly house', as the licensing justices put it. 'My old mother used to say: "Little birds in their nest agree, or else they will fall out."'

Both customers found themselves wholeheartedly disliking Mr Jones' long-dead mother and her platitudes, but had the grace to remain silent.

'Bit parky in the morning now,' continued Mr Jones cheerfully. 'Have to think about getting the coal stocks in.'

'When we had a station at Lulling,' said Percy, accepting the olive branch offered by this change in conversation, 'my old dad used to buy a wagonload and share it out with his neighbours. Much cheaper that way.'

'Not many people nowadays to share in a wagonload,' commented Albert. 'They mostly has gas or electric.'

'Dr Bailey had some,' reminisced Percy, 'and old Mr Harmer, Dotty's father. By the way, I hear her Flossie's in a bad way.'

Albert was alarmed. He was as fond of Flossie as Dotty was. He made up his mind to visit them both later in the day.

'What's up then?'

'Just old age, I should think. Betty Bell told my wife when she was at bingo. Dotty was on about getting the vet. She'd tried all her own homemade remedies.'

'Humph!' said Mr Jones, but said no more. A publican learns to be discreet in a small community.

'I'll pop down later,' said Albert, putting down his glass. 'Same again, please. Perce, d'you want another?'

Surprised at this unusual generosity, Percy pushed his glass forward.

'Don't mind if I do,' he said, and was careful not to make any wisecracks about the *nouveaux riches*.

Later that morning the vet arrived at Dotty's to examine the patient.

He took a long time over the job while Dotty and Connie watched him anxiously. Flossie had waved a languid tail to show that there was no ill-feeling over past indignities she had suffered at his hands, but otherwise had stirred little.

'There's nothing really nasty to worry about,' he assured the watchers. 'It's simply a case of general ageing. Most of the vital organs, lungs, heart and so on are just getting less able to do the job. I could take her back with me, if you agree, and try that new remedy, or I can give her an injection here and now, and leave some pills with you.'

'I'll keep her here,' decided Dotty. They watched the syringe being carefully filled, the injection given and Flossie gently massaged with an experienced hand.

'Looking like autumn,' said the vet, as he washed his hands at the kitchen sink, and gazed through the window. A flurry of yellow leaves had fluttered from Dotty's old plum tree, as a gust of wind stirred the branches.

'Plenty of sloes about,' he went on, as he dried his hands. 'I shall have to get on with my sloe gin.'

'Do you still prick them?' asked Dotty. 'I used to use a silver hatpin of my mother's until Connie told me of a much better way.'

'And what's that?' enquired the vet. 'Never too late to learn, you know.'

'Spread them on a dish and put them in the freezer,' Connie told him, 'then they burst when you take them out, and are all ready for the gin when they've thawed.'

'Now that's worth knowing,' agreed the vet, shrugging himself into his jacket.

'Don't worry about the old lady,' he added. 'She's in no pain, and got plenty of mileage in her yet.'

Connie thought privately, as they watched him make his way to the car, that his comments would be applicable to Dotty as well as her pet.

September was running true to form. It was chilly in the early morning and evening, and summer clothes were being put away, and warm woollens were donned thankfully.

But by mid-morning the early mists had usually cleared, giving way to pellucid blue skies and the particularly mellow sunshine of early autumn.

In the gardens at Thrush Green the dahlias blazed supreme, making the most of their brief flamboyance before the frosts turned their glory to brown death. The summer flowers of such hardy types as penstemon, phlox and geraniums still showed colour, and gardeners were reluctant to cut them down, clinging to these last brave vestiges of summer beauty.

Blackberries, as well as sloes, were in abundance, and in Lulling Woods there were some exotic-looking fungi, some with shiny red-spotted caps reminiscent of the country-man's red-spotted handkerchiefs, which most people, even Dotty Harmer, rejected as fodder.

But there were mushrooms in the field behind Dotty's house, and these were quickly garnered by the knowledge-able inhabitants of Thrush Green, and relished with their breakfast bacon.

At the village school the nature table was crammed with the bounty of the hedges and trees, and strings of shiny conkers accompanied the boys whenever they were in the playground. Early apples, such as Beauty of Bath, or the early purple plums, took the place of biscuits or cake at elevenses time. Soon, Alan Lester knew, the school heating system would need to be stirred, and winter would be upon everyone with preparations for the joyous celebration of Christmas at the end of term.

He recalled the dreadful threat of mid-European dances all over again. He put the thought firmly behind him, and decided to concentrate instead on these last few golden days of a Cotswold summer.

It was during this halcyon spell that Carl Andersen arrived.

Ben Curdle went to Heathrow to meet him. It was a welcoming sort of morning, he thought happily, as he took the car from the garage. Gossamer threads and spiders' cobwebs spangled the garden hedge, and the sun was dispersing the mist and promising a fine day ahead.

As he approached the airport the traffic slowed to a halt. On one side of him loomed an enormous lorry with a radio going full blast in the cab, and a fat young man nodding his head in time to the racket. He seemed to be quite at home in these conditions.

On the other side was another fat man, somewhat older, balder and better dressed. He was obviously in a state of some agitation, drumming his fingers on the steering wheel, looking at his watch, and picking at a scab on the back of his hand.

Ben felt sorry for him. No doubt he had an important appointment to keep. Maybe it involved a lot of money, he speculated. He was thankful that he had no such pressing worries.

If he was late, Carl would know that he had been held up and would be content to wait, just as he himself would be patient if the flight was delayed.

Perhaps he was too submissive to what Fate threw at him, mused Ben, watching his unhappy neighbour getting more and more agitated? But what good did it do to get steamed up like that? You took life as it came in the country. Thrush Green folk were used to waiting, waiting for crops to ripen, for lambs to be born, for pheasants to hatch. It all came right in the end, thought Ben philosophically as he saw that the traffic had begun to inch along again.

As it happened, Carl's flight was delayed by almost an hour, but Ben enjoyed a cup of coffee and surveyed his companions as he waited.

They certainly seemed a jumpy lot on the whole, was his opinion, as he slowly stirred his coffee. He was the first to admit that flying somewhere must be a worrying business, what with tickets and luggage and excitable children and confused elderly relations, but he felt sure that if the proposed visit to America ever took place, he and Molly would be a lot calmer than most of those about him.

In one of his rare periods at school, an irate teacher had called him 'thick, boneheaded and a country bumpkin'. Ben thought he was probably right. He knew that he was also patient and obedient. Rebellion would never occur to him. At times like the present, mused Ben, it was a good thing to be 'a thick, boneheaded country bumpkin'.

As the passengers on Carl's flight gradually emerged, it was easy to spot Carl himself by his great height and the thatch of fair hair which overtopped his neighbours.

Both men beamed with delight as they saw each other, and Ben held out a welcoming hand. But Carl dropped both his bags and enveloped Ben in a muscular bear-hug of joy.

'Good to see you,' he cried. 'Sorry I'm late.'

'No bother,' said Ben, stooping for a bag. 'The car's this way.'

Halfway home Ben uttered the words he felt must be said. 'Molly and I were real upset to hear about your mother.'

'I know, I know,' replied Carl, his voice suddenly husky. 'I can't believe it myself. Still expect to get a phone call or a letter. Somehow I can't believe she's really gone. She sent all sorts of loving messages to you both.'

There was silence as they sped westward, until Ben spoke again. 'Bill and Jane Cartwright were saying that there are a couple of old people in the home who remember your mother. I'm sure they'd like to tell you about her, if you felt like it.'

Carl's face lit up. 'That's good news! I want to find out all I can about her connections with Thrush Green and Mrs Curdle.'

'If only Gran were still alive,' said Ben, 'she'd be able to tell you so much. She had a memory as sharp as a razor. A tongue to match too, at times!'

The men laughed, as Ben raised a hand from the wheel and pointed to a distant church tower.

'In ten minutes' time we'll be home!'

The arrival of Carl Andersen was one item of news at Thrush Green, but a more dramatic one was centred on Dotty Harmer.

Flossie was a trifle stronger after her injection, and although Dotty was still anxious about her, the general feeling was one of relief.

As Betty Bell told Isobel and Harold one morning, 'They're all breathing again at Lulling Woods.'

But three days later there was more sensational news.

It appeared that Connie had made her usual morning visit to Dotty's bedroom and found it empty. It was seven o'clock, just getting light on a misty September morning.

Connie quickly searched Dotty's bathroom, sitting-room and kitchen. All were empty.

Clad only in her nightgown and slippers she ran into the damp garden. Sometimes Dotty wandered down to see her beloved hens and goats, no matter how skimpily clad.

But all was quiet, and the garden deserted. However, the gate to the fields beyond stood open, and Connie went through to survey the scene.

No one was in sight.

She ran back to tell Kit. Dotty could not have gone far, she felt sure. These days she only wandered a few hundred yards from her home, but she had been known to get as far as Lulling Woods that summer, stopping to rest every now and again. That time Connie had been with her, and very worried too about their distance from home. Dotty, however, had been adamant that she could easily get back, and was so violent in her reaction to Connie's anxiety that Connie had fallen silent, and simply supported her strong-willed aunt on the return journey whenever the old lady seemed to flag.

On her return to Dotty's kitchen, Connie noticed that Flossie was comfortably ensconced in her basket, but Bruce was nowhere to be seen. Could Dotty have taken him for a run? Could he have escaped and Dotty had gone to look for him?

Kit was shaving when Connie returned with her troubles.

'I'll ring the Shoosmiths first,' he said. 'They would spot her if she has wandered towards the green. Then we'll try to get Betty Bell on the phone. She'll keep a look-out in the Lulling Woods area. I'll be with you in a tick.'

Within a few minutes the calls had been made, and the two had dressed and were out on their mission.

At Betty Bell's house, hard by Lulling Woods, no sooner

had she replaced the receiver when she heard joyous barking at her kitchen door, and was almost floored by the exuberance of an excited Bruce who was delighted to come across a dear friend.

Betty shut him in her scullery, with a handful of biscuits, and rang Connie's number but, as she feared, they were already out. Shrugging on an old coat, she went to seach for Bruce's mistress.

Harold and Isobel were greatly perturbed at the news, and both dressed quickly and set out, one towards Nidden and the other towards the hill which led to the town. It was Harold who decided, as he set off, to call at the Piggotts', for their cottage had a good view of the field path from Lulling Woods which Dotty used when making her way to Thrush Green.

The couple were at breakfast, and the delicious smell of fried bacon and tomatoes made Harold realize how hungry he was.

Albert pushed aside his half-finished repast and got to his feet with surprising speed.

'I'll have a look now,' he said, and Harold suddenly realized that beneath Albert's crusty exterior there was a genuinely soft spot for Dotty.

Albert set off along the lane towards Lulling Woods, while Harold descended the short hill, made sure that Dotty was not wandering in the road at the bottom, returned to Thrush Green and made a systematic tour all round it.

Early morning traffic was beginning to stir. A school bus was waiting for older children at a corner of the green. There were a few lights in upstairs windows where people were only just stirring, for the morning was chilly and overcast.

There were lights downstairs at the Two Pheasants, for
Mr Jones was an early riser, and was clearing up the
night's debris from the bar, ready for the day's business.

A few dogs were straying around the green, let out for
their early morning run, but Harold noticed that Bruce was
not among them. Kit had warned him that Dotty's dog
was missing as well as his mistress.

Harold met his wife not far from the Youngs' house
near the turning to Nidden.

'Not a sign,' said Isobel.

'No luck with me, either,' said Harold. 'I'll try Kit on
the phone. It looks as though the police will have to be
called.'

'Dotty will be *furious*!' said Isobel.

'Better furious than run over,' responded Harold, as
they made their way back to the warmth of their home.

Kit and Connie had just returned when Harold rang to
report from his end. All were now in a state of extreme
anxiety, and Kit was particularly alarmed at his wife's
distress. Connie, usually sturdily calm in any situation, was
in tears and beside herself with worry.

'Definitely time to get the police,' agreed Kit, speaking
to Harold, as he watched Connie mopping her eyes. 'I'll be
in touch immediately, if she turns up, but meanwhile I'm
getting on to the police station.'

By this time, Betty Bell had made her way into Lulling
Woods. It was murky and rather frighteningly silent. In
the open fields leading to the wood things were stirring. A
rabbit had lolloped away at her approach. A lark was
singing above, and small birds were twittering in the
hedges.

But there was something sinister about Lulling Woods
in its early morning stillness, and Betty was filled with

foreboding. She had set off so hurriedly that she was still in her bedroom slippers, and their shiny soles skidded on the carpet of pine needles.

As a child, she remembered, she had always been frightened if she was alone in this wood, and had always hurried along the main path. When she was with her friends she was happy to play in the little side paths or the bracken, but occasionally her mother had sent her with a message to the Drovers' Arms which was situated at the further end of the woods, and then young Betty had fairly scampered between the tall trees which bordered the main path in order to get to open country again, and the haven of the remote public house.

Today, worried as she was, the wood seemed doubly menacing. Trees dripped, brittle sticks broke beneath her tread making frightening cracks of sound among the silence. There was no sign of movement anywhere, no birds, no beasts and, above all, no comforting human presence.

She stopped for a moment to get her breath. Her heart seemed to be the only thing in motion, and then she heard a distant sound. It was a high-pitched voice. It might have been a child crying, but with a flood of relief Betty realized that it was Dotty calling for the truant Bruce.

Almost in tears, she began to run through the wet bracken, calling as she went.

She found Dotty on her hands and knees at the entrance to what was probably a fox's hide-out. She was scrabbling with her hands at the opening, and peering shortsightedly into the aperture.

Betty knelt to help her up, but the old lady pushed her aside.

'There may be a trap there, you see. Bruce has run off and I'm so afraid he may have been caught in a trap.'

'He's with me,' Betty cried, 'he's quite safe. He's in my scullery.'

She was appalled at the state Dotty was in. Her dressing-gown and the nightgown protruding at its hem were soaking wet and covered in mud. One slipper had vanished, and blood was oozing from a scratch on her ankle. Her hands too were bleeding where she had been trying to scrape away the loose earth. She was trembling with cold and exhaustion, but made no effort to cease her labours.

'Those wretched Cooke boys set traps,' she told Betty. 'They go down at night. I've seen them myself, and spoken to them too pretty sharply, but they take no notice. I wish my father were alive, he would—'

She broke off, and turned to Betty. Suddenly, she looked as if she had returned to this hostile frightening world from one of her own. Pathetically, like a hurt child, she began to cry, and put her muddied arms round Betty's neck.

'I wish he were alive,' she whimpered. 'I do wish my father were alive.'

'There, there,' cooed Betty, patting the trembling back. 'You come home with me, and see old Bruce. You'd like to see Bruce, wouldn't you?'

Dotty nodded, tears still coursing down her cheeks. Slowly Betty led her back to the path, and even more slowly to the warmth of her kitchen, and Bruce's rapturous welcome.

Some half an hour later, Kit made a second call to the police station, telling the sergeant on duty that all was well, and that the missing, both human and animal, were now safely at home.

'That's good news, sir,' said the police officer heartily. 'We can't have anything happening to Miss Harmer, she's a bit special.'

'She certainly is to us,' agreed Kit.

Carl Andersen's tall figure was soon a familiar sight in Thrush Green and Lulling. He seemed very happy to be back, and greeted his friends warmly.

One morning he called at Rectory Cottages to see Bill and Jane Cartwright. As it happened, they were both outside the conservatory, attending to the geraniums which flourished in the sunshine.

They welcomed him enthusiastically and all three sat on a garden seat near by to catch up with the news from each side of the Atlantic.

Jane said how sorry they had been to hear about his mother's death, and added, 'A very nice couple have come to make their home here. They knew your mother when they were working near by, and I'm sure they would love to tell you about the old days, if you've time.'

Carl assured them that he would look forward to meeting them.

'No time like the present,' said Jane, consulting her watch. 'Let's see if they're around now.'

The three went inside, and Jane tapped at a door which was immediately opened.

Introductions were made, and Bill and Jane returned to their duties, leaving Carl to talk to the Millers.

He was thin and tall, and she was short and plump. Both, it appeared, had been in service at Nidden Hall, a large estate between Thrush Green and Woodstock, when they were young, and that was when they had been acquainted with Carl's mother.

'She was a lovely girl,' enthused Mrs Miller. 'She could have had anyone. There was a young fellow at Eynsham who was very keen, wasn't he, Dad?'

'I've heard about him,' said Carl, with a smile. 'I gather

that if Mrs Curdle hadn't persuaded my mother to wait for
a letter from my father, I might have been a local boy.'

'So you know about Mrs Curdle?' cried her husband.
'Now she was a character, and no mistake.'

Carl explained that she had been godmother to his
mother, and that he owed his existence and his American
citizenship to her wise counselling long ago.

'We lost touch, of course, when your mother left Woodstock, and then when we retired we came to live at the foot
of the hill here, in one of the old cottages. They had to be
pulled down, and though we were offered a council flat,
we didn't really fancy it, and the rector suggested we
might like to come here. He's a good man.'

'I heartily agree. I hope to call on him soon.'

'Come and have a cup of tea one afternoon, and I'll look
out any old photos I can find. I believe there are one or
two groups with your mother in them, and we'll see what
we can remember between us.'

And so it was left, Carl making his way a little later to
the Youngs' house, where he had been invited to lunch.

One or two children were straggling across the grass
from Thrush Green school, and among them were George
and Anne Curdle.

Shrieking with excitement they rushed to the tall figure
and threw their arms around his legs.

'And what are you two up to? Playing hookey?'

'No, going home to dinner. Mum likes us home midday
as we live so close. Most of the others stay to school dinner.'

'It's not half as good as mum's!' pronounced Anne.

'And you get more,' asserted George. 'You coming to
see her?'

'Later on. The Youngs are giving me lunch.'

'That'll be good too,' George assured him. 'Mrs Young
makes smashing jam tarts.'

They parted at the gate, and within minutes Carl was ensconced in the Youngs' sitting-room with a glass of sherry.

'I've just been meeting some old folk who remembered my mother,' he volunteered.

Edward was instantly alert. 'Did you go into the sitting-room?'

Carl looked a little surprised. 'No. Jane and Bill were in the garden, so we sat there. Come to think of it, it was just outside that communal room.'

'I'd like your opinion of it sometime,' said Edward. 'Some of us are wondering if it is too small.'

'Sure. Any time,' agreed Carl.

Joan, veering away from controversial matters, asked about his flight, and soon the conversation became more general.

'I've invited Winnie Bailey to join us,' said Joan, 'and Harold and Isobel. They are just arriving, I see.'

During lunch Carl found himself answering a good many questions from Winnie who sat beside him. Was he well looked after at the Bear? Was the food good?

He was able to assure her that he was thoroughly spoilt, and much enjoying his stay.

'Is it busy at the moment?'

'Not as busy as the manager would like, I gather,' responded Carl. 'A party came in last night, but they haven't a great many regulars just now.'

'What a pity,' said Winnie, still hoping for news of that mysterious interior designer who sometimes shared a table with this handsome American.

'So there's no one there whom you met last time?' persisted Winnie.

'Not at the moment,' agreed Carl. Winnie thought that he looked faintly amused, and wondered if he had guessed what was behind her enquiries. The man was no fool, and no doubt knew as well as she did how quickly rumours fly about.

'I believe you knew Mrs Curdle as well as anybody here,' said Carl, carrying the conversation into her own territory. 'Do tell me, was she as formidable as photos make her look? My mother adored her, but was also very respectful, and Ben tells me that it didn't do to cross her in any way.'

'That's right,' said Winnie warmly. 'She was a woman in a thousand, and we were lucky to be counted among her friends. If you've got time later, I will show you the bouquets she made for us every year, and find some photographs too.'

'And I believe Dotty Harmer's father wrote a piece about her for the local paper,' Harold added. 'I came across it when I was looking up some facts about Nathaniel Patten some time ago.'

The mention of Dotty at once changed the topic of conversation to the recent worry about the old lady, and her lucky rescue by Betty Bell.

'It seems to me,' observed Carl, 'that life in Thrush Green is pretty exciting.'

'We find it so,' said Edward, smiling at his wife.

October

Busy most part of the Afternoon in
making some Mead Wine, to fourteen Pounds
of Honey, I put four Gallons of Water,
boiled it more than an hour with Ginger and
two handfulls of dried Elder–Flower in it,
and skimmed it well.

James Woodforde

Dotty Harmer took some time to recover from her
ordeal, but once she began to feel stronger she chafed
at the delay in getting on with her usual autumn collections
of fruit and herbs for the winter ahead.

'I'm missing the sloes and those nice crab-apples on the
way to Nidden, and I intended to make a really large
amount of rose-hip syrup this autumn. It really is most
frustrating.'

Connie promised to gather all that she needed for the
store cupboard, and did her best to support the doctor's
ruling that the patient must have a few days in bed.

At first, Dotty had been too exhausted to argue, and lay
back on her pillows dozing or reading. Flossie was glad to
be allowed at the foot of the bed, and the two old ladies
rested together.

As the days passed, Flossie was the more amenable
invalid, while Dotty grew more vociferous about all she

had to do, and more anxious about the welfare of the hens and goats at the end of the garden.

'We're managing quite well,' Connie assured her, 'and Albert comes down regularly night and morning, so you've nothing to worry about.'

But the climax came when Winnie Bailey arrived one misty afternoon, bearing a freshly made pot of bramble jelly for the invalid.

'It's a wonderful year for blackberries,' Winnie told her.

'And I'm going to go out and pick some for myself,' said Dotty firmly. 'No matter what John Lovell says. *I'm all right!*'

She looked so fierce as she said this that Winnie felt some alarm. She said so to Connie when she was making her farewells out of Dotty's hearing.

'If she says she's going out then she will,' said Connie resignedly. 'We've been lucky to keep her in bed for these few days. You know Aunt Dotty.'

'Indeed I do,' responded Winnie.

Betty Bell, quite rightly, was acclaimed as a heroine for her double rescue effort, and the finest azalea to be had in Lulling was given to her by Kit and Connie.

She was modest about her achievement. 'Well, if it hadn't been me then someone else would have found her, I've no doubt. Willie Marchant would have been along pretty soon, on his way to the Drovers' Arms.'

At the bingo session that week in Lulling, Nelly, her friend Mrs Jenner and Gladys Hodge all agreed that Dotty might well have succumbed to exposure if she had remained any longer in the chilly wood clad in little more than her nightgown.

'Hypothermia,' Mrs Jenner told them, 'is the biggest enemy of the aged. Jane is always alert to it at the home.'

As Mrs Jenner herself was a retired nurse, and Jane Cartwright, her daughter, was the equally well qualified and competent warden at Rectory Cottages, her words were accepted with respect.

'I'm a great believer in long-legged knickers myself,' said Gladys.

'And a nice woolly jumper that pulls down well over the kidneys,' agreed Nelly.

'It's a great pity, I think,' put in Mrs Jenner, 'that shawls have gone out. My old grandma always had one hanging on the back of her chair, ready to throw round her shoulders if she had to go out, or if she felt a draught. But then she was Yorkshire born and bred, and had plenty of sense.'

There was general agreement among her hearers that Yorkshire folk certainly knew what was what, and took sensible steps to combat their chilly climate.

The loud voice of the master of ceremonies recalled them to their tables, and Betty Bell, Dotty and hypothermia were put aside in the pursuit of fortune.

The news had even reached Miss Watson and Miss Fogerty at Barton-on-Sea.

'Sometimes I wonder if Dotty should be in a home,' said Dorothy Watson, putting down her crossword puzzle to hear the news from Agnes.

It was Isobel Shoosmith who had imparted the news in her weekly telephone conversation with her old friend.

'Oh, Dorothy,' protested Agnes, 'you know she couldn't be better looked after than she is now.'

'It's a great responsibility for Connie and Kit,' pronounced Dorothy, who was in one of her headmistressy moods, and finding the crossword somewhat difficult. She was ready for a mild argument with Agnes to add some excitement to the evening.

'And Dotty would hate to live with a lot of other old people,' continued Agnes.

'She would have to learn to make the best of it,' said Dorothy, at her most magisterial. 'We all have to come to terms with old age and disability. Look at Teddy! What an example to us all!'

Agnes felt no desire to 'look at Teddy', admirable fellow though he was, and was somewhat alarmed at his sudden introduction into the discussion. Dorothy had been so reticent about Teddy since their last visit to Thrush Green that she had earnestly hoped that Dorothy's passions had waned. But had they?

'Why, only this morning,' went on Dorothy, unaware of Agnes's reaction to Teddy's name, 'I had a terrible shooting pain under the ball of my left foot. I could hardly walk.'

'You must let me have a look when we go to bed,' said Agnes, glad to be on safer ground. 'You may have a thorn in it.'

'No, I think it's something called "Morton's Toe", or "Morton's Fork" perhaps.'

'Wasn't that something to do with taxes in Tudor times?'

'Which, dear? The Toe or the Fork?'

'Oh, the Fork without question,' said Agnes firmly.

'How erudite you are,' exclaimed Dorothy. 'Now, tell me why BAIL I has something to do with the law. Five letters.'

'ALIBI,' said little Miss Fogerty promptly.

And peace reigned again.

Carl Andersen soon set about his pleasant task of learning more about Mrs Curdle and her times.

He enjoyed meeting people, and although the serious business of the present trip was to go ahead with the great project in Scotland in which the firm of Benn, Andersen and Webbly was engaged, he found the atmosphere at Thrush Green relaxing, and his new-found friends much to his liking.

The lady with whom he had shared a table at the Bear on his earlier visit was also engaging his attention, but he had no intention of discussing that matter with anyone at Thrush Green.

He had been amused at Winnie's attempts to find out more. As she had surmised, he knew quite well how rumours fly around, and he was determined not to cause any embarrassment to the lady in question.

At the moment, she was back at her base in Chelsea, the jobs in the Woodstock area having been completed. Carl had lost no time in finding her, but found that she was now engaged on the designing of a mews flat for an up-and-coming pop star whose tastes in furnishing and general decor needed some guidance.

It was a formidable undertaking, almost as difficult as the Scottish problem was for Carl. He respected her desire for privacy whilst she was struggling, but pointed out that a little relaxation now and again, in the form of a meal out or a visit to the theatre, would assist her efforts, and she seemed glad to agree.

Meanwhile, he made another visit to the Millers at Rectory Cottages and spent a happy hour hearing about Woodstock over half a century ago, and the influx of American servicemen during the war, including of course, the handsome man who had become Carl's father. Mrs Miller's wrinkled face lit up at the remembrance.

'He was easily the best-looking man I ever saw,' she said rapturously. 'Your colouring, Carl, but even better-looking.'

'Well, thank you for the compliment,' laughed Carl, 'but

I know my limitations. I remember him as a fine father as well as a potential heartbreaker. Luckily for us, he never looked at anyone other than my ma, and she was a bit of a glamour-puss herself.'

Later he went to see the Henstocks, and found that Charles was in the churchyard of St John's overseeing the arrival of a load of gravel to renew the paths. His chubby face broke into a beam on seeing Carl.

'Dimity told me you were here,' said Carl. He gazed up at the impressive spire, outlined against a clear October sky.

'Do you know, I've not been inside yet,' he told Charles.

'That must be rectified as soon as possible. But not today, I fear. I have a funeral later this morning, and we want to get this gravel laid before then.'

'Did Mrs Curdle ever come here?' Carl asked, as they watched the gravel rushing from the tip-up lorry with a mighty roar.

'I don't think so. She did have a little to do with the church at Thrush Green, and as you know, is buried there, but her fair only spent one complete day there before it moved on.'

'But surely you had a fair here too?'

'Oh, yes indeed! We have our bigger Mop Fair, and of course there are other great local fairs like St Giles' at Oxford, and the one at Abingdon. But they are held in the autumn and last for several days. Mrs Curdle's was a family affair, and much more modest.'

He turned to speak to the men, and then invited Carl to the vicarage, but he said that he had promised to call at the Fuchsia Bush for Molly Curdle.

'I've always thought,' said the rector, as they walked away from the scene of activity, 'that it would be interesting to write a history of English fairs. Have you ever thought of it?'

Carl laughed. 'I shouldn't know where to start! I'm no literary gent, you know. Steel and concrete are more in my line.'

But Charles Henstock's attention was drawn to an approaching figure, and he seemed somewhat agitated.

'Oh dear! Mrs Thurgood!' he exclaimed. 'I do so hope she isn't going to the vicarage.'

But the lady veered aside to enter the porch of one of the adjacent almshouses, and relief relaxed the vicar's countenance.

'A worthy soul,' he said hastily, 'but a troublemaker.' He looked suddenly at his companion. 'You said you called at Rectory Cottages the other day. Did you sit in the communal room?'

'I suppose so. The sitting-room place, with a conservatory.'

'Did you think it too small?'

Carl began to feel bewildered. 'Edward Young asked me the same thing. Is this something to do with Mrs Thurgood?' he asked.

'Partly. She has a bee in her bonnet about it. That's why I wanted a fresh eye on the subject. What do you think?'

Charles looked so worried that Carl was tempted to laugh, but refrained.

'Well, you must remember that I come from a country with plenty of space, and we do tend to have large rooms, I suppose. But I like smaller places, like your English cottages, and I should say that the communal room, as you call it, was just about right for those few people.'

Charles Henstock looked relieved. 'That's a comfort to know. Now, I won't keep you, but we must make a date for your visit to St John's. It is well worth seeing.'

The early part of October was clear and fresh, with that

pellucid quality which is peculiar to fine days in early autumn.

Young pheasants were now strutting about the fields and woods, and occasionally stepping haughtily in front of motor cars in the country lanes, to the dismay of nervous drivers.

Harvest mice, refugees from the denuded fields, were looking for comfortable hibernation quarters in the sheds, barns and lofts of unwelcoming householders.

Gardeners were busy cutting down the dying foliage of perennials, and hustling the tender plants, such as geraniums, into the shelter of greenhouses.

The brave show of Busy Lizzies, fuchsias, petunias and lobelias which had adorned the troughs and tubs and hanging basket outside the Two Pheasants and elsewhere were now being dismantled, and tulip and hyacinth bulbs planted in their place, all with high hopes of glory in the spring, which were somewhat mitigated by the knowledge that mice, birds and other nuisances would no doubt make inroads on this bounty so generously offered.

It was on one of these gentle afternoons of mild sunshine that Connie took her refractory aunt to pick up crab-apple windfalls along the road to Nidden.

The old lady was well wrapped up, and had even submitted to wearing gloves. She was in high spirits as she sat beside Connie, who drove to the appointed place.

'I suppose I must have been coming here for crab-apples for seventy-odd years,' prattled Dotty. 'My nurse used to bring me. In those days you called her 'Nurse'. None of this 'Nanny' nonsense. She was just fourteen when she came to work for us, and her first errand was to go to buy a feeding bottle for the new baby. That was me!'

'And how long did she stay?'

'Day and night. She lived in, up at the top of our house with me and my older brothers.'

'I really meant how many years,' explained Connie, halting to let a covey of young partridges bustle across the lane.

'Oh, heavens! She stayed in our family till she died. She went with my brother Oliver when his children came, and then she was with me and father. They died about the same time. That was some years before you married Kit.'

'She sounds a faithful soul.'

'I loved her dearly,' said Dotty. 'She taught me to knit, and to pop lime leaves with my mouth to make a really loud bang, and she could make lovely shadows on the wall by the light of the candle – rabbits and swans and Ikey–Mo, who was the local cats' meat man. She was simply wonderful, and I still miss her.'

She was beginning to sound a little tearful, something which had been occurring too frequently since her mishap, and which perturbed Connie quite a lot.

'Well, here we are,' she said cheerfully, drawing in to a farm gateway. 'Let's get the baskets.'

Dotty's spirits soon revived as she bent to collect the hard little apples on the grass verge.

Straightening up happily, she made for the gate.

'Give me a hand with this, dear,' she said, struggling with a strong snap spring.

'But we can't *trespass*!' protested Connie.

'Rubbish!' snorted Dotty. 'It's only old Bob Bennett's field, I went to kindergarten with him, and used to have to help him lace his boots. He was always an awkward lump. Still is, they tell me.'

Together they opened the gate, and went to collect the bulk of the windfalls that lay in 'the awkward lump's' property.

Dotty was enchanted at the sight. Connie, rather more conscious of trespass, only hoped that they would be unobserved.

Straightening her back, Dotty gazed across the field to the distant farmhouse.

'I remember,' she said speculatively, 'that the Bennetts always had lots of mushrooms in that field by their garden. I wonder if — ?'

'No,' said Connie firmly. 'We've quite enough to cope with when we get these apples home, without stealing mushrooms as well.'

'Just as you say, Connie dear,' replied Dotty meekly. 'But these are not really Bob Bennett's. They are simply the fruits of the earth, and we are *keeping them from waste*!'

Connie stowed the heavy baskets in the car, ushered her companion into the passenger seat, and drove home with what she could only think of as 'their loot'.

Winnie and Ella, setting off for an afternoon's walk, saw Connie and Dotty driving by on the other side of Thrush Green.

'Blackberrying?' queried Winnie.

'Crab-apples, more likely,' said Ella shrewdly. 'Dotty

never lets an autumn go by without raiding Bob Bennett's crab-apple tree.'

They crossed the grass to the lane leading to Nidden. Lately, the two women had seen much more of each other, for Ella now asked Winnie to check colours for her when she was engaged on much of her handwork, and Winnie had threaded many needles for her now that the other's sight was deteriorating.

Ella, in her gruff way, expressed her thanks, but Winnie brushed aside the gratitude.

'I used to read the clues for Donald's daily crossword, during the last few years of his life,' she said. 'He found newsprint trying.'

'You must miss him very much.'

'I do, of course. In fact, I wondered if I could go on without him, but one has to, and after a time one even begins to find a few small benefits.'

'Really?' Ella sounded startled at this admission, and Winnie laughed.

'Only little things! Not enough really to fill the gap completely, but I remember the relief I felt on taking down a photograph of Donald's mother, and putting it up in the attic. I felt guilty too, of course.'

'Did you dislike her? Or was Donald over-fond of her?'

'Neither really. She didn't particularly like me, but then she would never have considered anyone good enough for her Donald. I think there are quite a few mothers like that. No, it wasn't that. It was just that she was a plain woman, with a long horsy face and she looked so dreadfully disapproving in the photograph. As Donald fixed it at the head of the stairs you had to face it every time you went up.'

'You should have told him.'

'I didn't want to hurt him. Far simpler to say nothing,

my dear. You learn to hold your tongue when you are married.'

'And what other small comforts did you discover?' asked Ella, who found herself fascinated by these disclosures.

'Well, now what else? Donald was a stickler for having every meal at the table, properly set, tablecloth, napkins, the lot. Even for afternoon tea. Once the poor darling had gone, I took to taking my tea into the sitting-room on a tray, and then, quite often, my supper. I can't tell you how lovely it seemed, but I still felt guilty. Childish, isn't it? But then I suppose one finds comfort in little things whatever one's circumstances.'

They had now reached the farm gate where they usually paused to have a break.

'I think I've been lucky to be single,' mused Ella. 'I don't think I should have been unselfish enough to lead a married life. Always having to consider what the other person needed, or would think, would drive me mad.'

'But you lived quite happily with Dimity,' pointed out Winnie.

'Looking back,' said Ella, 'I reckon poor old Dim did the adjusting, and I took it all for granted. She's one of those people better off in the married state.'

'She picked the right man in Charles,' replied Winnie. 'As I did with Donald,' she added loyally.

'I don't know about you,' said Ella, 'but I reckon it's getting chilly. Come back and have a cup of tea with me. What's more, we'll have it by the fire, on a tray.'

The weather changed overnight. The mild wind which had blown from the south-west backed to the north-east and gained in strength as dawn approached. When the good folk of Thrush Green and Lulling awoke, it was to find the dead leaves bowling across the ground in a stiff breeze, and the branches above tossing vigorously.

The temperature had dropped. Harold Shoosmith decided that the time had come for the full-scale central heating to be turned on. Alan Lester, next door, was making the same decision for both his house and school, while Mr Jones, shaving in the pub bathroom, was startled to find that he 'could see his breath', and called across the landing to tell his wife so.

Nelly Piggott, hard by, was already buttoning up her winter coat preparatory to making her way down the hill to the Fuchsia Bush.

Now that she had come to terms with the fact that she was in charge of the business, in all its aspects, a wonderful strength had taken the place of her fears, and she was beginning to enjoy the feeling of power which her new status gave her.

She was the first to recognize the loyalty of the staff. Gloria and Rosa seemed to have shed some of their native lethargy, and were becoming much more enterprising. Even Irena seemed to take her more humble duties with the vegetable preparation with greater enthusiasm, and Nelly was quick to praise whenever possible.

It did not occur to her that her own energy had a lot to do with this change in the outlook of the staff. In fact, Mrs Peters, though an excellent businesswoman, had always been a little remote in her relationship with the girls, and understandably had been even more so during the long months of her last illness at the Fuchsia Bush.

Nelly, on the other hand, the girls recognized as 'one of them'. She had the same background, the same necessity to work for a living, the same tough philosophy of 'doing as you would be done by', 'taking the rough with the smooth' and all the other homely tags which governed their way of life. They might grumble behind her back at her sharpness and bustle, but they respected her high standards and the fact that she could – and did – turn her hand to any task which cropped up.

The difficulties which had so daunted Nelly when she first heard of her inheritance had largely been solved when a competent young woman from the accountants' office was put in charge of the business side of the Fuchsia Bush. Justin Venables' wise suggestion that Miss Spooner should be consulted about the transaction had given that lady enormous gratification, and she and Nelly had parted with great goodwill.

As Nelly made her way along Lulling High Street that blustery October morning, she felt well content with the general affairs at her place of business. But one difficulty confronted her, and that she was determined to tackle that very morning.

When some years earlier Mrs Peters and other shopkeepers had approached Miss Violet with complaints about her older sister, it was all very embarrassing. The Lovelocks had been respected for all their long lives in Lulling, and no one wished them harm. Violet had tackled her duties with sense and courage, and Bertha's kleptomania had seemed to be controlled. But to Nelly's dismay she had noticed that the basket of tiny jamjars, bright as jewels, and the sort of thing which would catch the eye of any magpie or jackdaw, bird or human, was suddenly half empty after a visit from the three sisters.

Nelly had questioned Rosa.

'Oh, I expect it was that Miss Bertha,' replied Rosa nonchalantly, 'I think she nicks one now and again.'

'This isn't *one*!' retorted Nelly. 'It's a good half-dozen, and we can't let it go on.'

She decided to ring the house next door at about ten

o'clock. The old ladies were not early risers, and took considerable time dressing, as she well remembered from the days when she worked there.

Soon after that hour, she closeted herself in the privacy of the office and rang. Luckily, Miss Violet answered, much to Nelly's relief. Apart from the fact that she was the only one of the three who was not deaf, she was also the only sister who had some sense.

With what tact she could muster Nelly explained the problem.

'Oh dear, oh dear!' sighed Violet. 'Not again, Mrs Piggott!'

'I'm afraid so,' responded Nelly, noting that she was now 'Mrs Piggott' and not 'Nelly' to her former employers. 'Rosa had noticed it before this, I gather, but didn't like to say anything.'

'I shall look into it straightaway,' promised Violet, 'and come and see you later this morning.'

The telephone was put down. Nelly returned to her kitchen, and Violet went to her sister's bedroom.

Bertha was in her petticoat. She was sitting in front of the mirror rubbing face cream across her wrinkled cheeks.

'I want to look through your coat pockets,' said Violet, with commendable courage. 'Mrs Piggott next door has been missing things.'

'Really?' said Bertha, sounding bored. 'What sort of things?'

'Little things that could be picked up easily and put in pockets,' retorted Violet, swinging open the heavy wardrobe door.

There were several coats hanging there, all with capacious pockets. Violet plunged her hand into the deep patch pockets of the tweed coat which Bertha frequently wore. There was a chinking of glass against glass, and Violet

pulled out four small jamjars from one pocket, and three
from the other.

She put them in front of her sister on the dressing-table.
'Well, Bertha?' she demanded.

'They're not mine,' said Bertha, still busy massaging her
face.

'I'm well aware of that! They come from the Fuchsia Bush.'

'Then you'd better take them back,' responded Bertha.

Her off-hand manner and the assumption that Violet
could clear up any difficulties, no matter whose fault they
were, infuriated Violet who normally faced life with great
equanimity.

'*You* are taking those back *yourself* this time,' she told her. 'You stole them, Bertha! You are no better than a common thief, and if Nelly Piggott wants the police brought into this affair I shall back her to the hilt.'

A red flush suffused her face, and Bertha too began to look agitated.

'Someone must have put them in my pocket,' she quavered. 'I don't remember anything about it.'

'Then you will have to try and remember,' said Violet. 'The police will ask lots of questions.'

Bertha put down the jar of face-cream among the tiny jamjars and bowed her head. A tear splashed among the pots.

'You wouldn't really call the police, would you, Violet? Not to your own family?'

Violet, almost in tears herself, did her best to sound firm. 'If you don't return Nelly's property, and apologize to her, I shall certainly think about the police,' she replied.

Leaving her sister to her sniffling, Violet returned to her bedroom to find a handkerchief for her own tears. How would this end, she wondered?

Just before twelve o'clock, Bertha descended the stairs, dressed in the incriminating tweed coat, and holding a small carrier bag, which chinked as she moved, and presented herself to Violet.

'Are you coming with me?' she asked in a low voice.

'Do you want me to, Bertha?'

'I think I should like a little support,' said Bertha.

Without a word, Violet fetched her own coat from the hall stand, and the two sisters made their way next door.

Nelly welcomed them as politely as ever, and ushered them into the privacy of her office, and firmly closed the door against any prying eyes.

'She's got the stuff in that bag,' observed Rosa to Gloria. 'I heard the jars rattling.'

'Would have done the old girl good to have it all thrashed out in public,' said Gloria, rather miffed at being denied a first-class row.

'Nelly's too soft by half,' agreed Rosa, and then noticed Irena peeping through the kitchen door to see what was going on.

The pair advanced upon her menacingly.

'And what do you think you're doing?' demanded Gloria.

'I saw them Lovelocks coming in,' faltered Irena who, like the rest of Lulling, knew of Bertha's little weakness.

'And what, pray, is that to do with you?' asked Rosa loftily. 'You get back to your sink, my girl, and don't poke your nose into other people's business.'

Irena retreated, and the door was closed.

'I just can't abide people *prying*,' said Gloria to Rosa, as they returned to their own territory.

'Quite right, dear,' agreed Rosa.

The sudden cold spell brought more customers than usual into the Fuchsia Bush, seeking the comfort of coffee or something more substantial. Nelly had said nothing about what had gone on behind that firmly closed door on the day of the Lovelocks' visit, much to the chagrin of her staff. However, they realized that the matter was closed, even if only temporarily.

The cold weather was to Connie's liking, for she could make sure that Dotty stayed in the warm as Dr Lovell had directed, and as there were masses of crab-apples awaiting attention, the two ladies set about the task away from the bitter wind that raked Thrush Green.

Flossie slept tranquilly in her basket by the stove, and even Bruce seemed content to stay inside out of the unkind breezes that disturbed his usual haunts.

Connie was rinsing the fruit at the sink, and Dotty busied herself cutting the small apples in half and hurling them into a gigantic preserving saucepan ready to be simmered into a fragrant pulp. Overnight, the jelly bags would drip, and the serious business of apple jelly would be on its way.

'That letter you brought me this morning,' Dotty said, 'was from poor Audrey.'

'Why "poor Audrey"? Is she ill?'

'No, no. She's worried about Lucy, her daughter. She's just got engaged.'

'And she doesn't approve?'

'Audrey seems doubtful. He's Irish, you see.'

'You and I know plenty of nice Irishmen,' Connie pointed out, lifting the last of the washed fruit from the sink. 'Look at the O'Briens! They're dears.'

'I know all that,' said Dotty testily. 'But the O'Briens have lived here for years! This man is only just over here, and has had no time to lose that Celtic roguish charm which Audrey finds so suspicious.'

'Does she think that Lucy has fallen for the roguish charm?'

'Definitely! She is most upset.'

'Well, there's not much she can do about it,' said Connie philosophically. 'Daughters usually do what they like, in the end, and I expect Audrey will come round, and fall for that roguish charm just as Lucy has.'

Carl Andersen was due to fly to Scotland at the end of the week, and invited Ben and Molly, Joan and Edward to dinner at the Bear before he departed.

He had collected quite a number of photographs and other memorabilia about Mrs Curdle, and showed some of it to his guests as they enjoyed their coffee.

'The Millers gave me these,' he said, handing over some ancient group photographs. 'I'm getting them copied. By the way, I had a look at that common room again. What worries you?'

'It isn't exactly a *worry*,' replied Edward untruthfully. 'It's just that having extended that annexe I resent the recent criticism about the need for more space.'

Joan broke in. 'Edward can't help it,' she said with a laugh. 'He's a born worrier, especially if his work is criticized.'

'I know how he feels,' said Carl. 'I'm the same.'

'It could easily be made bigger,' went on Edward thoughtfully. 'I roughed out a plan some time ago when this business cropped up.'

'You must show me sometime,' said Carl. 'I must say, I thought it looked perfectly adequate for the needs of the old folk at the moment, but I suppose a larger space would give them more seating accommodation, and there could be more room for plants and so on.'

'I can't see it coming off,' said Molly. 'Mr Henstock was talking about it the other day. He seemed a bit worried. I believe Mrs Thurgood had been at him.'

'Mrs Thurgood,' snorted Edward, 'is a public menace! She caught me outside the Fuchsia Bush not long ago, and harangued me about the matter. It was a good thing I could tell her categorically that we had no money for the project.'

Conversation turned to Carl's work in Scotland, and he and Edward became deeply engaged in technical details about stresses and strains, and the problems of frost, wind, rain and all the other weather hazards which would have to be considered when dealing with the costing of this enormous undertaking.

Ben and the women were more parochially inclined, and

the affairs of Thrush Green and Lulling engaged their attention until the time came for them to part.

As they walked to the car Edward and Carl fell behind a little.

'Are you on the board of Rectory Cottages?' asked Carl.

'I'm a trustee, yes.'

They walked through the chilly darkness, and Carl spoke as they drew near to the car.

'If the money were available, would a bigger room be a good idea, do you think?'

The two men stopped, while Edward considered the question.

'Yes, I really believe it would. Looking to the future, I think it would be desirable. There's already talk of adding more residential accommodation some time, but that's way in the future.'

'I'll see you when I get back,' said Carl. 'I've enjoyed this evening so much.'

'A splendid dinner,' cried Joan, 'and a thousand thanks.'

'See you on your return,' called Ben.

The men shook hands. Carl kissed the women, and they drove off.

Later, as they prepared for bed, Molly said dreamily, 'Carl does kiss lovely!'

Ben looked startled, as he peeled off his socks. 'Better than me?'

Molly, hanging her petticoat neatly over a chair back, paused for a minute to look abstractedly across Thrush Green in darkness.

'Different, Ben. Just sort of *different*.'

November

No shade, no shine, no butterflies, no bees,
No fruit, no flowers, no leaves, no birds –
November!

Thomas Hood

It was the custom of Thrush Green to celebrate Guy
Fawkes night with a roaring bonfire and a plentiful
supply of fireworks.

Carl Andersen, who knew little of such things, privately
thought it amazing that such a law-abiding community –
or nation, for that matter – should see fit to remember one
who had been about to blow up the Houses of Parliament.
However, he was wise enough to hold his tongue, and
simply hand over his pence to the few children who
petitioned him in Lulling High Street as they pushed their
guy around in an ancient pram.

Preparations had been going ahead for two or three
weeks, and a splendid pile of flammable material, such as
pieces of wood, small branches, cardboard boxes and the
like, stood towards one end of the green, well away from
Rectory Cottages and other habitations.

To be sure, it was rather unsightly, and at one time the
local council had threatened to ban the bonfire altogether.
At this there was such an outcry from the residents of
Thrush Green, even those who had condemned the pile as

an eyesore earlier, that the council withdrew its objections, and celebrations were allowed to take place.

The arrangements, by ancient custom, were in the hands of the scoutmaster and his zealous troop. Also, by ancient custom, potatoes for baking in the hot ashes were provided by the Hodge family, and the morning before Guy Fawkes Day found Percy Hodge sorting out some great beauties ready for the festivities.

His sister, Mrs Jenner from next door, had called in on her way down to the town and came upon her brother in his shed, counting potatoes as they lay in long rows on the bench.

'They look good, Perce,' she commented approvingly. 'What might they be?'

'Willjar,' said Percy.

'How do you spell it?'

'W-I-L-J-A,' said Percy, after some thought.

'I think,' said his sister, 'that you pronounce it "Veelya".'

Mrs Jenner had come across a number of foreigners during her wartime nursing, and had a smattering of various European tongues.

Percy poured brotherly scorn on such fiddle-faddle. 'If W-I-L-J-A don't spell Willjar,' he maintained, 'I'm a Dutchman.'

'Well, whatever you call 'em,' said Mrs Jenner in a conciliatory tone, 'they look as though they'll eat a treat, Perce.'

And with that she went on her way.

November had come in with grey skies and a depressing stillness. Trees dripped, and a light mist gathered overnight in the little valley by Lulling Woods and was slow to clear.

The clocks had been put back at the end of October, and

now the darkness descended at about five o'clock, adding
to the general murkiness of people's spirits.

The old folk at Rectory Cottages became querulous as
they were obliged to spend more time indoors than they
wanted. The roads were slippery with dead leaves and
general dampness. Despite good lighting in the rooms,
everywhere seemed gloomy, and reading was difficult.

Jane Cartwright did her best to cheer her charges,
arranging a birthday party for one old lady in the communal
room, and persuading a local pianist to entertain the residents one evening. But attendance was poor on both
occasions, and Jane just hoped that the dreary weather
would lift, and the spirits of the little community would
follow suit.

The prospect of Bonfire Night gave some cheer. There
was usually a party of the old folk from the Cottages
standing by the blaze, and enjoying the excitement of the
fireworks.

'I hope to goodness it doesn't rain,' said Jane to her
mother. 'That would be the last straw. The poor dears are
so low that I'm praying for a dry starry night to cheer
them up. Has Uncle Percy looked out the potatoes?'

Mrs Jenner assured her that all was well in hand, and
said that, in her opinion, they would have a fine night for
the celebrations.

It was usual for the more active of Jane's charges to help
in providing some of the sausage rolls or sandwiches
which supplemented the potatoes to enjoy round the bonfire. This had been a considerable help in raising the spirits
of her little flock during the doldrums at Rectory Cottages,
and Jane encouraged all their efforts.

The schoolchildren were in charge of the guy for the
great night, and the question of its identity was hotly
discussed. Alan Lester could remember a guy of his child-

hood representing Adolf Hitler which had swung from a nearby tree before hurtling to his funeral pyre amidst patriotic cheers from the war-weary onlookers.

Various names had been put forward. They included an unpopular local councillor, a school inspector who had been on a recent visit and Alan Lester himself. It seemed best, he decided as he listened to their suggestions, that a strictly impersonal guy would be a more diplomatic choice, and his decision was respected.

Two afternoons were spent happily stuffing a sack with some of Percy Hodge's straw for the torso and head, and four long stockings for arms and legs. It was the clothing of their puppet which caused the greatest anxiety.

All agreed that the pointed hat so recently worn by one of the girls, who had been to a Hallowe'en party as a witch, was perfectly in order for Guy Fawkes' headgear. Alan Lester had looked out an illustration showing costume of the time, and considerable ingenuity was used to make Thrush Green's guy look as much like the original as possible.

The snag was the extraordinary difficulty in thrusting the straw-filled arms and legs through sleeves and trouser legs, and buttoning garments round the bulging torso. After a great deal of frustration, it was decided that he should wear a cloak which would disguise any blemishes.

The dressing-up box was ransacked and a grubby and moth-eaten cape found which had clothed Red Riding Hood in a school play some twenty years earlier.

It was agreed that it was time that this unhygienic garment was consigned to the flames, and the school guy was finally dressed to everyone's satisfaction.

It slumped on a chair at the front of the class, and far more attention was given to it, during its two-day wait for incineration, than any lesson that Alan Lester could produce.

The gloomy weather continued unabated, but to everyone's

relief November the fifth was no worse than the preceding
days. In fact, for a brief period in the afternoon a watery sun
was visible, and raised the spirits of young and old.

The festivities began at six-thirty, which meant that
most of the people would have had a meal after work, and
could enjoy the celebrations and the extra pleasures of the
snacks and Percy Hodge's potatoes should they still have
any pangs of hunger.

The children, of course, were always ready to eat. The
Rectory Cottages contingent reckoned that the refreshments provided would be quite adequate for their elderly
digestions, and thankfully reckoned to do without their
usual supper on Bonfire Night.

The bonfire roared away. Bright sparks flew up towards
the damp trees. Children capered round the crackling blaze,
waving sparklers, and the guy was lowered, amidst cheers,
to his fiery end.

The firework organizers included such stalwarts as

Harold Shoosmith, Edward Young, Percy Hodge and Alan Lester, all capable of handling the pyrotechnics with safety, and rockets, Catherine wheels and squibs blazed into the darkness until the fire began to die down, St Andrew's clock struck nine and it was deemed fit to close the proceedings.

The old people straggled away first, becoming tired of standing on the damp grass. Parents rounded up their offspring. The scoutmaster rallied his troop for the final effort of damping down the remains of the bonfire and clearing up the litter around it.

There were many black hands and scorched faces that night, and clothes worn then would reek of wood smoke for days to come, but everyone went home that night with raised spirits.

'Better than ever,' said Alan to Harold as they helped to clear up.

'Thank God it didn't rain,' commented Edward, rubbing his hot face with a black hand. 'And your potatoes were better than ever, Percy.'

'Ah! Willjars, they were,' said Percy much gratified. 'We'll have them next year. I'll see to that!'

It was striking midnight when Harold drew back his bedroom curtains and looked out into the darkness. The night was still and damp. He remembered the rosy glow of the bonfire and smelt a whiff of wood smoke in the air.

There was something very exhilarating, thought Harold, about this mixture of the elements, fire, air and water. It had done them all good.

Greatly content, he climbed into bed.

Carl Andersen had not been present at the Guy Fawkes jollifications for he was immersed in the main purpose of his business in Scotland.

But before his departure, he had had an interesting conversation with Edward Young. He had asked Edward if he could have a private talk, and Edward had invited him to his home one evening when Joan was engaged at a reunion at her old school.

It was the cold dark night of the first of November, and the two men enjoyed the log fire at their feet, and the drinks in their hands.

Edward had wondered about this request for privacy which Carl had mentioned. Before, he had always blown in, cheerful and informal, glad to see both Joan and Edward, and any other Thrush Green people who were present.

Perhaps, thought Edward, he wanted to discuss some point connected with the Scottish project, and felt that people generally would be bored by technical details? Perhaps there was a personal problem of health, finances, accommodation or of dealing with local or national officialdom?

The truth of the matter, when it was revealed, was a complete surprise.

Carl began by talking about his mother and Mrs Curdle.

'As you know,' he began, 'my ma felt she owed a lot to the old lady. She talked about her often, and particularly during the last months of her life. It was the reason for my coming here in the first place, and the fact that I managed to take back so many mementoes of Mrs Curdle gave my ma enormous pleasure.'

'She always had a great name here,' agreed Edward, 'and it's good to know her influence spread so far afield.'

'The thing is this,' went on Carl. 'My ma wanted me to do something practical to honour her godmother. I know you did something for Nathaniel Patten, your local missionary, some years ago, but I don't think a statue of Mrs Curdle would be quite the thing.'

'Perhaps something for the church?' suggested Edward. 'A plaque or an urn, or something of the kind, for her grave?'

Carl looked doubtful. 'I gather from Charles Henstock that the old lady was not much of a church supporter. I talked it over with Ma not long before she died, and she wanted something practical done for people living in Thrush Green.'

'A trust fund? Something like that, for people in need?'

Carl shook his head. 'As a matter of fact, you gave me the idea yourself.'

'I did?' Edward was startled.

'Yes, when you told me your worries about the annexe at Rectory Cottages. Why not make a really handsome addition to that and call it after Mrs Curdle?'

Edward was still flummoxed. 'It's a fine idea,' he said at last, 'but it would cost several thousand pounds. It's a pretty big project.'

Carl sighed. 'Look, I don't want to seem boastful, but the money doesn't matter. My old dad left a heap of dollars, and my ma had more than she ever needed when he went. Mind you, he deserved every cent he made. He worked like a Trojan for the firm and it rewarded him handsomely. My job, as I see it, is to do what my ma asked me to do, and to do it properly.'

'It does you credit,' said Edward, still bemused.

'I thought I'd broach it with you first,' continued Carl, accepting a refill to his glass, 'because we talked about the possible enlargement of that place, and because I could sound you out about how my idea might be received. What d'you think?'

'I can't think of anything more suitable as a tribute to both your generous mother and dear old Mrs Curdle,' said Edward warmly. 'What do you want me to do?'

Carl rubbed his chin thoughtfully.

'I know you are one of the trustees, but I wondered if it might be best to sound out one or two privately before a meeting. I'd like to have a word with Charles Henstock, for instance, but I'm off to Scotland tomorrow night.'

'I'd do that willingly,' offered Edward, 'if you are sure. It's a big undertaking.'

'If you do that,' said Carl rising, 'we'll take it from there when I get back.'

'We have a trustees' meeting some time at the end of the month,' said Edward. 'When do you expect to be back?'

'It all depends on the state of progress,' replied Carl. 'I must have a day or two in London as well. There's someone there I must see urgently, but I'll ring you while I'm away.'

Edward watched him stride away to his car, and then returned to his fireside. He turned over a log very carefully with the poker.

'What a shock!' he said to the dancing flames. 'But what a wonderful one!'

Ever since Dotty's escapade in Lulling Woods she had been a little more amenable about taking an afternoon rest.

This was a source of great relief to Connie and Kit, and also much appreciated by Flossie, who soon realized how comfortable it was lying on Dotty's eiderdown with her old stiff back propped against the warmth of her mistress's legs.

The two dozed for an hour or so each afternoon, much to the relief of Dr Lovell, as well as Dotty's friends and relatives, who knew what a refractory patient she had always been.

Dotty herself came to enjoy this tranquil hour of the day. Her active mind, a rag-bag of assorted thoughts from 'ships and shoes and sealing-wax' to 'cabbages and Kings', seemed to move more slowly these days, and sleep often overcame her when she sat down to rest. It was not long before she realized that her ancient bones appreciated the benison of her afternoon rest.

One grey afternoon the two old ladies composed themselves on the bed, one under the eiderdown, and the other stretched out on top. Peace reigned and neither snored, nor stirred. Only a bird chirped now and again in the still garden. At the other end of the house, Connie sat alone doing the crossword puzzle, while Kit had gone to the dentist.

It was half past two when Dotty came to her senses. Still drowsy, she lay relishing the warmth of her bed and the familiar weight of Flossie's body against her legs.

After a time, she put out a hand to feel the familiar silky head. Flossie enjoyed having her ears caressed.

But something was wrong. Something was different. In alarm, Dotty struggled up to investigate.

Flossie's weight was heavier than usual. She seemed just as peaceful, eyes closed, limbs comfortably stretched along the eiderdown, but Dotty knew at once that she had died. Gently, quietly, without stirring, Flossie's heart had stopped, and she had gone for ever.

Silently Dotty stroked Flossie's head and fondled those long silky ears which could feel nothing now. A tear or two rolled down Dotty's wrinkled cheeks and splashed upon the much-loved head.

Friends must part, thought Dotty, searching for her handkerchief.

A day or two after Carl's departure to Scotland, Edward called at St John's vicarage to see his old friend.

Charles Henstock was in his greenhouse, busy picking a few dead leaves from his geranium cuttings.

Edward joined him in the peaceful dampness and told him that he had a message from Carl.

'Dear fellow,' commented Charles, putting a few dead leaves to join others in a flower pot. 'I had an idea he was off about this Scottish building job.'

'He went a couple of days ago,' said Edward, 'but asked me to sound you out.'

'Sound me out?' echoed Charles. 'What about?'

Edward told him about Carl's idea of a tribute to Mrs Curdle, and his mother's wishes. Charles drew out an ancient stool from under the bench, and sat down upon it suddenly.

'But we can't possibly accept it!' he said at last. 'It would cost a fortune!'

Edward tried to explain. 'He's a very wealthy man, Charles, although he is so modest and unassuming. I feel just as you do, but he says he's determined to do what his mother would have wanted, and money is no object.'

'I really don't know what to think,' said Charles, wiping a muddy hand across his brow, and leaving a dirty mark upon its pinkness. 'Would it be feasible to enlarge that room further? As an architect, what's your opinion?'

'Nothing simpler.'

'We should have to confer with the other trustees, of course, about this marvellous offer.'

'Naturally, but I don't think anything should be done until Carl returns. And then he should put this idea into writing, if he still feels the same way.'

'No one else knows?'

'No one. I just said that I would speak privately to you on his behalf.'

'Then we must keep silent until he is in touch again. I really am quite flabbergasted, Edward. If it goes ahead I hope you will feel able to take on the job.'

'That's for the trustees to decide,' said Edward. 'I hope they won't think I'm pushing myself forward. Not everyone seems delighted with my last effort.'

He sounded bitter, and Charles put a grubby hand on his friend's sleeve.

'You did a splendid job, and we all appreciate it. Any man in the public eye has to face the fact that he is sometimes an Aunt Sally, and I regret to say that there are unkind critics even in Thrush Green.'

'Don't I know it!'

Charles put down the flower pot, and pushed the stool back under the shelving.

'Time for coffee, Edward, and I believe Dimity has been making Welsh cakes to go with it.'

'Lead me to the kitchen,' commanded Edward, greatly cheered.

The dismal weather continued, and the people of Thrush Green and Lulling, in company with most residents in the British Isles, were heartily sick of having the lights on all day to counteract the gloom, and of having to curtail their outdoor activities because of heavy showers.

At the village school the children were as frustrated as the old people at Rectory Cottages.

The fact that preparations for Christmas were already in progress at the school did a little to mitigate the general depression, and calendars, bookmarks and Christmas cards were being manufactured with some zest.

Of course, there were drawbacks to these preparations, and for Alan Lester the most grievous was the revival of those noisy dances which Miss Robinson so enjoyed. The weather was too unreliable to banish the infants to the playground for their rehearsals, and Alan Lester was obliged to conduct his lessons with a background of clapping and stamping from next door which made the partition between the two rooms shudder.

The Remembrance Sunday service, with its sad splendour, took place in pouring rain, and like many thousands of villages in the land, the poppy wreath seemed to be the only glowing spot of colour against the grey wet stone of the memorial cross. It was a sorrowful time, with the glory of autumn wasted away and Christmas too far ahead to give any real cheer.

The first of the winter colds were beginning to afflict young and old alike. The talk was all about cough cures, injections against influenza, and seasonal ills.

News of Flossie's death, of course, had flown round Thrush Green very quickly, and had added to the general gloom.

As soon as Albert Piggott heard it the next morning, he was rapidly on his way, spade on shoulder, to dig the grave he had been waiting to prepare for some months. He had already chosen the site. It was towards the end of a long bed beside an old hedge where several other of Dotty's former pets had their last resting places.

He found Dotty in her kitchen stirring a large saucepan containing food for the hens. It smelt rather good, thought Albert, although he knew that the contents were only scraps from earlier meals. By the time Dotty had added bran and some poultry spice it would be fit for anyone, flesh or fowl, to eat.

He had the delicacy of feeling to prop his spade outside the back door before he entered, and Dotty welcomed him warmly, waving to a kitchen chair with an enormous wet wooden spoon.

'I've sad news for you, Albert,' said Dotty.

'Ah! I heard. Poor old Flossie! Still, she had a good life and went very peaceful, I understand.'

'That's quite right,' said Dotty with a slight sniff. She rubbed an eye with the back of her hand, and a dollop of chicken food fell to the floor, which Dotty ignored, but which was hastily consumed by Bruce who emerged from under the kitchen table.

'I brought me spade along,' said Albert, 'just in case you was needing it. I know just the place to put her if you'd like me to make a start.'

Dotty left the saucepan and came to sit down at the table. She looked earnestly at her visitor.

'Albert! You are so kind, but dear Kit insisted on burying her at once. He didn't want me to be upset. Not that I should have been. Death comes to us all.'

Albert was seriously affronted to hear of Kit's officiousness in taking over a rightful gravedigger's job, but did his best to hide his feelings.

'I daresay you was upset at the time,' said Albert, determined not to be completely thwarted of funereal misery.

'Well,' conceded Dotty honestly, 'of course I had a little weep when I realized she'd gone, but dear Bruce is being such a comfort.'

Hearing his name the little terrier wagged his stumpy white tail. His mistress bent to pat him.

'I'm sure he misses Flossie, but it seems to have made him more *responsible*. He seems to be looking after me as Flossie used to do in her heyday, the dear boy.'

'Well, he knows he's top dog now,' said Albert nastily, still smarting from Kit's impertinent hastening of Flossie's interment. 'If you don't need me to do anything I'll be getting back.'

Dotty, quite unconscious of his hurt feelings, wished him goodbye, and he retrieved his spade from outside the back door, and set off homeward.

He was not only offended, he was real hungry, he told himself. That chicken food smelt a treat.

He heard the church clock strike, and quickened his pace.

The Two Pheasants would be open now.

Betty Bell brought the news of Flossie's demise to the Shoosmiths.

Isobel was much distressed on Dotty's behalf. 'Poor darling! Dotty will miss her so much. Such a faithful little dog, and so gentle.'

'She's taken it on the chin,' Betty informed her, rummaging in a kitchen drawer for a duster. 'She's a tough old party, you know, and she's got young Bruce.'

'But he's so *boisterous*,' protested Isobel. 'I wonder if Dotty can manage him.'

'He'll calm down as he gets older,' Harold assured her. 'A lot of his exuberance was simply looking for attention. I think he was always a bit jealous of Flossie.'

'You're right there,' said Betty, flapping a duster round the toast rack. 'You finished your breakfasts? Want me to wash up before I do your study? Willie Marchant's on his way, so you might get a load of letters any minute.'

'I'll do the breakfast things,' said Isobel, pushing back her chair.

'D'you know,' said Harold, 'Willie told me the most remarkable thing about his cousin Sidney. He picked up a fountain pen on Narrow Hill and it turned out to be his brother's.'

'I know,' said Betty, 'Uncle Stan told me.'

'Uncle?' queried Harold.

'Well, Willie's my cousin and Sid's another, so his dad is my Uncle Stan.'

'I might have known,' said Harold, who had never really understood the vast network of relationships in Thrush Green.

'And another thing,' said Betty, 'this makes the third.'

'Third what?'

'Deaths.'

'I'm not with you Betty,' confessed Harold, passing a hand across his brow.

'You know what I told you months back? That nice Mr

Andersen's mum passed on in America, and Mrs Peters at the Fuchsia Bush was taken, and I said at the time, "Who's going to be third?" and it's our poor old Flossie. See, it always goes in threes, death does. D'you remember me telling you?'

'Yes,' said Harold meekly. 'I remember it well now. You are always right, Betty.'

Much gratified, she whisked off to wreak havoc in Harold's study.

Carl Andersen kept his promise and rang Edward one evening from Scotland.

'Charles was as overwhelmed as I was at your offer,' he told Carl. 'But once he got over the shock he was all in favour of your marvellous idea.'

'Good! Well, I suppose the next move is to put it to the trustees.'

Edward told him about the advisability of putting his suggestion in writing so that the committee could study it, and Carl agreed.

'I shall have to get in touch with my lawyers in the States, but they know a little about these plans, as I got their advice before I came over this time.'

'Any chance of seeing you soon?'

'In about a week's time, I hope,' said Carl. 'I've a few things to sort out here, and I shall make a stop overnight in London, but I'll give you a ring before I set off.'

'So far,' said Edward rather diffidently, 'I have only told Charles about this business, but would you want me to sound out anyone else?'

There was a brief silence, and then Carl said, 'I should rather like Harold Shoosmith's reaction. He's a wise guy, and will keep his own counsel until I get back.'

Perceptive as ever, he had guessed that Edward, always

a worrier, could do with a little support under the weight of the secret with which he had been entrusted.

'I'll do that,' said Edward. 'I quite realize that the fewer people who know about it, at this early stage, the better.'

'Well,' laughed Carl, 'I've soon got to realize that any news in Thrush Green gets around pretty smartly.'

'And of its own volition,' agreed Edward. 'It's an absolute mystery, but one has to face facts. Secrets don't stay secrets for long in a village.'

'I know you'll do your best,' Carl assured him. 'I'm sorry to put a burden on you.'

'No *burden*, but an *honour*,' Edward said with emphasis. 'Come back soon, Carl. We're all missing you.'

The gloom of November's early days had lifted a little, and a watery sun began to struggle through the clouds in late morning and survived for an hour or two in the early afternoon.

This raised everyone's spirits. Alan Lester was able to recommend that rehearsals of the ear-shattering country dances could be held in the fresh air, preferably at the farthest end of the playground, and so obtained a little relief from this trouble.

Preparations were already in hand for Christmas at the school. Alan's own class was busy rehearsing the Mad Hatter's tea party and trying to find a youthful actor who could remember his words and yet might be small enough to stuff into a cardboard teapot.

Handiwork lessons were devoted to the making of Christmas gifts. Older boys were trying their hand at simple woodwork, and teapot stands, pipe racks and dolls' house tables stood at crazy angles on the shelf behind Alan's chair, and were the object of many admiring glances from the manufacturers.

Christmas catalogues were being pushed through letter-
boxes, and the shops in Lulling High Street were already
displaying 'Acceptable Gifts For Christmas' signs, which
most people decided were much too early to heed.

Nelly Piggott at the Fuchsia Bush already had a great
many delicacies made for Christmas, but they were stored
out of sight, for she was one of those who deplored the
too-early fever of Christmas.

'Time enough when December comes,' she told Rosa,
who had suggested that it might be a good idea to start
sticking blobs of cotton wool on the windows to simulate
snow.

'We always done it for Mrs Peters,' she said resentfully.

'Not in November you didn't,' retorted Nelly. 'You go
and give the tables a good rub up if you're short of a job,
and let Christmas look after itself.'

Nelly now was in complete and happy command. Her
early fears had vanished as she found that all ran smoothly
under the new arrangements.

Business was brisk. There were more orders for Christmas provender than in previous years, and jars of her
homemade mincemeat and Christmas puddings were carefully stored at the back. Orders for Nelly's superb mince-
pies were already being noted in the order book, and if the
premises had been larger she could have provided for the
Christmas office parties of several local firms.

But the time for such expansion was not yet ripe. One
day, Nelly mused, if things went on as prosperously as
they were doing, she might think of it.

Meanwhile, she knew that she was running the business
competently and with ease. It was the personal touch
which her customers valued, and she was wise enough to
see that this was where her strength lay.

The gold chain which hung about her neck, always

concealed by her clothes, was a constant reminder of her lost lover. Sometimes her thoughts were sad when she fingered it, but on the whole it was a source of strength.

Hadn't she overcome that grief? Hadn't she come to terms with betrayal, humiliation and loss? Wasn't she now a busy happy woman, doing the work she loved, and respected and appreciated by all Lulling?

Such thoughts often came to her as she bustled from kitchen to shop, from morning to night. Life for Nelly Piggott had never been so sweet.

Harold Shoosmith was as staggered by Edward's disclosure of Carl's plans as Charles Henstock had been. But, once over the shock, he was filled with appreciation for Carl's generosity and enthusiasm for the idea in general.

Edward explained about the letter which Carl was proposing to send to the chairman of the trustees, Charles Henstock, with a copy for each member of the committee at the meeting which was to take place very soon.

'Has Ben been told about this?' asked Harold. 'He is the closest relative.'

'Not yet,' said Edward. 'Carl particularly wants to tell him himself, once the meeting has taken place. After all, the offer may not be welcomed.'

'I can't see that happening,' commented Harold. 'Do you think it would work? Architecturally, I mean?'

'I can't see any real problem.'

'Could you do it?'

Edward looked unhappy. 'I don't want people to think I'm pushing for a job. I don't want the trustees to feel that just because I am one of them I should be handed the thing. The idea makes me cringe.'

'Naturally,' said Harold. 'Sorry I mentioned it.'

They sat in silence for a moment or two, then Harold spoke again: 'It does seem an outstandingly generous offer, and I wonder if Carl quite realizes how much this may cost.'

'He's in a far better position than we are to judge that,' Edward pointed out. 'He's doing this sort of thing all the time. His aim is to do what his mother asked him to do. It's really as simple as that.'

'Well,' said Harold standing up, 'it's a wonderful thought, and we'll have to see how the trustees react when they read Carl's letter next week.'

The night of the meeting was cold and bright. As the eight trustees assembled, blowing on their freezing fingers, they were glad to see the blazing fire in the Cartwrights' sitting-room, which the couple had handed over for this evening's business.

They themselves did not take part in these meetings, but were kept well-informed of any decisions taken, and their own views were much welcomed by the committee.

Charles, as chairman, had wondered if the letter from Carl should be sent to each member of the committee in advance of the meeting, but had decided against it. Far better to get the initial response round the table, he felt, and so it was arranged.

Having gone smoothly through the agenda, the all-important Any Other Business brought Charles to his feet as he bustled round the table putting a copy of Carl's letter before his friends.

'We'll have a few minutes to read this to ourselves,' he said, 'and then have comments.'

The trustees applied themselves to their task diligently, and silence fell upon the little company as they read the letter before them. It said:

To Those Whom It May Concern

My mother, who died recently in Michigan, was the god-child of Mrs Curdle, well-known in Thrush Green. Ben Curdle, who still lives there, as you know, is her grandson.

My mother loved and respected Mrs Curdle and always wanted to pay tribute to her by way of a memorial. She asked me to find out the most suitable remembrance, and this was the main reason for my visits to Thrush Green.

I have looked and listened, and it seems to me that the most suitable tribute would be the enlargement of the present sun room at Rectory Cottages, and perhaps, if agreed, to name it 'Mrs Curdle's Room'.

All expenses would be my concern, and I should be happy to provide this tribute to Mrs Curdle, as my mother wished.

'Well,' gasped Mrs Thurgood, 'what an amazing letter!'

'A most generous offer!' commented Justin Venables. 'We should have to look into the legal side, of course.'

There were other comments of amazement as the letters were lowered again to the table, and the trustees looked bemusedly about them.

'I should like your comments,' said Charles.

As expected, Mrs Thurgood was the first to burst into speech.

'Well, as you know, I have always maintained that the present annexe, or "sun room" as Mr Andersen calls it, was far too small.' She turned to Edward. 'If you remember, I said as much when we had our little discussion in the High Street.'

Edward felt that 'little discussion' hardly described his capture and incarceration by a strategically placed shopping trolley, but he remained silent. It would have been a waste of breath to try to quell Mrs Thurgood.

'So,' continued that lady, 'I heartily welcome this offer.'

'Hear, hear!' came from her fellows round the table.

'It seems to me,' said Charles, 'the most wonderful gesture. I only question the expense of the project. One wonders if perhaps Carl would allow us to contribute part of the funding.'

'My daughter,' began Mrs Thurgood eagerly, 'would be very pleased to have an exhibition—'

She was cut short by Charles who interrupted her with uncharacteristic firmness.

'Not now, Mrs Thurgood! What do you all feel about this?'

Edward spoke. 'Carl mentioned this matter to me in confidence, and I did question the very considerable sum that such an undertaking would need. He was quite adamant that he wanted to meet all expenses himself, and I think he would be hurt if we suggested that we muscled in – shall we say? – on his very personal offer. He is anxious to carry out his mother's wishes, and I think we should respect that.'

There was agreement over this, and after a little more discussion and general appreciation of Carl's offer, the motion of acceptance was put and carried.

It was then that Harold made the suggestion that the Cartwrights' opinion might be sought.

'After all, they will have to cope with the building and general upheaval, and the comfort of their charges.'

'You think I should write?' queried Charles, 'and perhaps send a copy of Carl's letter?'

'What 's wrong with calling 'em in now,' said Edward. 'They're only in the kitchen washing up, and we've never stood on ceremony with Jane and Bill.'

And so the Cartwrights were summoned to their own sitting-room, provided with their own chairs, and offered one of their own biscuits which were ready on a side table to eat with the coffee which came when the meeting was over.

Charles explained about the incredibly generous offer, and how pleased the trustees were. Had they any comments? Were they happy with the idea? Nothing yet had been done about replying to Mr Andersen, but he would be writing immediately on behalf of the trustees.

Bill took his wife's hand and looked at her delightedly.

Jane was starry-eyed.

'It's the best news in the world,' she said.

'She's right,' agreed Bill. 'Tell Carl when you write, that we send all our thanks and love.'

'And now,' said Jane, jumping to her feet, 'if you've nearly finished, I'll get the coffee.'

When the company emerged from Rectory Cottages, the stars were bright above, and frost was beginning to form. The grass was already crisp, and their breath billowed before them as they made their way to their cars, or on foot to nearby homes.

'Come in for a drink?' invited Harold to Edward, but the latter shook his head.

'I promised to ring Carl as soon as the meeting was over. He'll be waiting for a call.'

'He'll be delighted with the outcome, I've no doubt. What a success the meeting was! Even Mrs Thurgood was pleasant.'

'Naturally! She's got her own way again,' said Edward laughing.

'And we shan't have to have an exhibition of her daughter's ghastly daubs,' agreed Harold. 'When's Carl back, by the way?'

'Ben's fetching him the day after tomorrow.'

'Good! I've no doubt Ben will be told all about it then.'

Edward stopped suddenly beside one of the great chestnut trees near his house.

'D'you know, it was under this tree that Mrs Curdle always put her caravan. It's nice to think that her memorial will be standing so near.'

'Halfway,' mused Harold looking across the green, 'between her caravan site and her grave. I like the idea.'

'So will everyone,' said Edward heartily.

Walking alone to his own house, Harold thought that he had never seen Edward quite so happy before.

He, and all at Thrush Green, had Carl Andersen to thank for that.

December

Let joy be unconfined;

Lord Byron

A welcome change in the weather heralded the arrival of December. The weather-vanes of Lulling and Thrush Green veered to the north-east, the skies cleared and a wintry sun emerged for part of each day.

Spirits rose. Christmas shopping began in earnest, and all those loved ones in far-flung quarters of the globe were remembered with lightweight parcels sent by air mail, if they had been forgotten earlier in October, when presents should have been despatched by surface mail by prudent donors.

In Lulling High Street the Christmas decorations were being draped across the road by men balanced on long ladders.

Nelly Piggott allowed Rosa and Gloria to stick morsels of cotton-wool on the windows of the Fuchsia Bush, much to their satisfaction, and a small Christmas tree stood in a prominent position just behind the snowfall.

At Thrush Green there were more modest decorations. The Two Pheasants had a string of varied coloured lights round the door, and Mr Jones's two bay trees, one each side of the entrance, were also decked with fairy lights.

In St Andrew's church the crib stood in the chancel.

Winnie had washed the figures of the nativity, as she did yearly, and she and Ella had put it all in order and set it up in its appointed place.

At the school the making of paper-chains went on apace. Jars of almond-smelling Gloy gave forth their fragrance, and paste brushes were plied with feverish zeal. Already the infants' room was criss-crossed with many-splendoured pieces of handiwork, and the fact that every now and again one link would give way and a shower of paper rings would descend upon the makers only added to the general enjoyment.

Rehearsals for the Mad Hatter's tea party and the thunderous country dances went on apace, and although Alan Lester and Miss Robinson adhered valiantly to the timetable, there was no doubt that rather less knowledge was imbibed than usual.

'Never mind,' said Alan philosophically, 'Christmas comes but once a year.'

It was at this time that more news came of Bruce's owners. They were indeed in South America and in one of those countries which did not recognize the usual international necessity for returning malefactors to the country of their origin in order to expedite justice.

Stern letters had crossed the Atlantic. Diplomats had argued. Letters from outraged readers had enlivened the columns of the local newspapers, but all was in vain.

The couple were allowed to remain in the country of their choice, living, no doubt, on their ill-gotten gains and spreading happiness among the local traders.

'It is deplorable, of course,' Dotty said to Betty Bell, 'but at least we know they won't come back.'

'Good riddance to bad rubbish!' agreed Betty.

'And in any case,' added Dotty ferociously, 'I should

never have given Bruce back to such dreadful people. My
father would have put them to rights, I can tell you!'

Carl Andersen returned, much to the pleasure of his friends,
and one of his first visits was to see Ben and Molly.

Now that his plan had been accepted by the trustees, he
had the freedom to discuss it openly.

Ben was much touched by this honour to his grandmother, and said so with unusual eloquence.

'It's exactly the sort of thing she would like,' he said.
'You see, she always had a soft spot for children and old
people, and I think children get much more attention these
days than the old folk.'

'That's right,' agreed Molly.

'What's more,' went on Ben, 'she would have known
some of those folk at Rectory Cottages, and certainly some
of their forebears. It's a lovely idea. We shall be very proud
to have a Curdle room.'

Edward Young had told him about the general delight
expressed at the trustees' meeting.

'It is a magnificent idea of yours,' he said. 'You have no
second thoughts about it? No doubts? We feel it is going
to be such an expensive undertaking.'

Carl laughed. 'I've been into it all most carefully, both
here and back home. It's what I dearly want to do, and to
be given the go-ahead was all I wanted.'

'I'm sure you will be asked to a trustees' meeting very
soon, so that they can tell you how they feel and to discuss
the best way of putting the work in hand.'

'Good,' said Carl. 'And I want to involve as many
Thrush Green people as possible in this affair. Ben and
Molly, for instance, will be the chief guests at the opening,
and I hope you will take on the job of architect.'

'*Please*,' begged Edward. 'I know it's an honour, but it

must come from the trustees. I should be embarrassed to have this automatically given to me.'

'I understand,' Carl assured him. 'I'll be discreet.'

'Are you able to stay for Christmas?' asked Edward. 'Joan and I hope you'll stay here.'

'Nothing I'd like more,' said Carl, clapping him on the shoulder, 'and now I'm off to see Charles.'

The news of Carl's offer had been relayed to Barton-on-Sea by telephone from Isobel Shoosmith to her old friends.

Dorothy and Agnes discussed it with much enthusiasm.

'She was a great influence, was old Mrs Curdle,' said Dorothy. 'Everyone respected her, and this project of Carl Andersen's will get everyone's support.'

'George was a dear little boy,' responded Agnes wistfully. She often looked back to her teaching days at Thrush Green with considerable nostalgia. Dorothy, made of sterner stuff, seldom looked back. The future was what interested her, and she broached it now.

'Do you know that Eileen is contemplating moving? I don't know what Teddy feels about it, but I told her straight that I thought it *quite wrong*!'

'But surely,' quavered Agnes, 'it is their affair? And why should you think it is wrong?'

'Poor Teddy is used to his surroundings. He knows where the steps are in the house, and which way the doors open, and all·those important things for a person without sight. I told Eileen so, and I didn't mince my words either.'

She thumped down a saucepan on the draining board to emphasize her resolve. The two ladies were washing up their lunch pots and pans.

Agnes was deeply disturbed. Dorothy could be so thoughtless. She might have offended Eileen. It was true that Teddy would have quite a problem in adapting to a new environment, but was it Dorothy's place to point this out?

Agnes's heart had leapt when Dorothy spoke of this proposed move. It would come as a relief to know that Teddy was safely removed from Dorothy's attentions.

She had certainly been much more restrained in her dealings with Eileen and Teddy since Agnes had pointed out the desirability of discretion on their visit to Thrush Green earlier in the year. But this news might well inflame those feelings which Dorothy had made some effort to calm, and who knows what might happen?

'It's surely their business,' said Agnes diffidently. 'I'm sure they would have talked it over thoroughly before making such an important decision.'

'Teddy is so *unselfish*,' declared Dorothy, dropping a handful of kitchen cutlery on to the draining board with a resounding clatter. 'If Eileen wants something, then Teddy will give way to her.'

'Well, of course, they consider each other,' pointed out Agnes reasonably. 'Married couples have to make their plans jointly.'

Dorothy wrung out the dish cloth with excessive vigour. Agnes saw, with dismay, that her neck and face were getting flushed, always a bad sign.

'There's really nothing we can do,' she continued soothingly. 'In any case, I'm sure they will tell us if they do decide to move.'

Dorothy gave a gusty sigh, and folded the dish cloth with care.

'I suppose we must just be patient,' she said. 'Very irksome, I find it, but you are quite right, Agnes dear. It's just that I am so fond of Teddy – in just a *friendly* way, you understand – that I don't care to see him *exploited*.'

'I quite understand,' replied Agnes.

One frosty December morning Carl called at St John's vicarage to see his friends the Henstocks.

Dimity was busy rolling out pastry, but paused to put floury hands round his neck and give him a hearty kiss.

Charles, less demonstrative but equally delighted to see him, led him into his study.

'I'm juggling with the Christmas services for all four parishes,' he explained, pushing a sheaf of papers to one end of his desk. 'Such a joyous festival of the church, but *very* difficult to arrange.'

'I can imagine,' said Carl. 'I won't hold up the good work, but I just wanted a word about the trustees' meeting.'

'Of course, of course! I can't tell you how excited and grateful everyone is. We are having an emergency meeting here next week. I hope you'll be here too.'

He began to shuffle his papers.

'Somewhere I've got a letter here from the trustees thanking you,' he said with some agitation. 'Now where— ?'

Carl broke in. 'I'll be there without fail. Which day is it?'

'Half past seven next Tuesday,' replied Charles. 'And we're having it here this time. You can tell us all your plans, and we can tell you how we feel about this marvellous offer.'

Carl began to tell him how anxious he was for as many Thrush Green people to be involved as possible.

'Perhaps the trustees will bear that in mind,' he said. 'There must be good builders, electricians, plumbers and the like who could tackle the job.'

'Indeed there are,' agreed Charles.

'And I should very much like Edward to be the architect,' added Carl, 'but he's very diffident about taking it on. He says it must be the trustees' decision.'

'I quite understand his natural feelings over this,' said Charles. 'I'm sure it would be the general wish that he took on the enlargement. He made an excellent job of the first stage.'

'Well, make sure you tell him that,' said Carl. 'I think he feels that he let you down by not making it bigger in the first place.'

'Oh poor Edward!' cried Charles, his face puckering with dismay. 'I'd no idea he felt like that. He has no need to reproach himself.'

'So I tell him,' replied Carl, getting up. 'Just see the message gets across. I'll see you next Tuesday then.'

The next Tuesday was as bright and clear as the days which preceded it, and, very cheerful, the good people of Lulling and Thrush Green were to be able to do their Christmas shopping without the hazards of deep puddles, dripping awnings and umbrellas.

Carl drove from Woodstock, where he had taken up his old room, and crunched across the gravel of the vicarage drive to attend this important confrontation.

As he waited for the door to be opened he gazed at the great spire of St John's church silhouetted against a luminous sky scattered with stars.

Near by a small animal, vole, mouse or shrew, rustled among the dead leaves under the shrubs. It was very quiet, and the serenity of his surroundings calmed the slight agitation which had been with him on the short journey to this destination.

This would all be here when he had gone. When the projected new annexe had gone, for that matter. Other men, a hundred years hence, would look up at that noble spire and those eternal stars.

The door opened, and Charles welcomed him in.

The meeting began on time. Charles took the chair, and invited Carl to sit beside him. Edward sat alone at the foot of the table and the rest of the trustees were ranged along the sides.

'I have apologies from Justin Venables,' said Charles. 'He has one of his chesty colds.'

There were murmurs of sympathy for young Mr Venables, but, as Mrs Thurgood pointed out, one must face these things in one's seventies.

'Good old camphorated oil takes a lot of beating,' said Harold.

'A bit whiffy,' commented another, and the rival merits of such remedies as friar's balsam, blackcurrant lozenges, gargling with salt water, as well as such modern medicaments as Vick, Night Nurse and Benylin were being briskly discussed when Charles, who was quite used to these digressions at meetings, called them to order, and explained, although they already knew, just why they were there.

His little speech of thanks to Carl was a model of its kind, and warmly supported by all present. He responded by explaining that it was going to give him enormous pleasure to fulfil his mother's wishes, and continued by saying how much he wanted as many Thrush Green people as possible to be involved in the work.

He then paused, and Charles took up the theme.

'That is what we should all like,' he said, 'and it will involve everyone more closely with such an intimately local project. As you know, Edward here made a wonderful job of the original building, and I think it would please everyone if he were invited to take on this work.'

'I propose that,' said Mrs Thurgood promptly. 'Nobody better!'

'And I second it,' said Harold Shoosmith.

'Would you like to make a comment?' asked Charles of the silent figure at the end of the table.

Edward was looking unhappy. He raised his eyes and saw Carl's intent gaze upon him. There was silence round the table.

'Please,' said Carl gently.

Edward looked at the waiting faces, and smiled. 'If that is what you want,' he said, 'I should count it an honour to take on the job. And I promise to do my best.'

There was an audible sigh of relief. The motion was carried unanimously, and twenty minutes later Dimity appeared with glasses and the vicar's best port to celebrate.

Carl was obliged to return to his Scottish affairs the next day but had a chance to tell Edward how relieved and delighted he was at his acceptance of the work.

'I've been thinking about the design,' said Edward, 'and it seems to me that a large shallow bay with a really comfortable window seat round it would be useful as well as attractive to look at. And we must have plenty of light. It makes such a difference to old people's reading.'

Carl was relieved to see him so happily engaged, and Joan, out of her husband's earshot, told Carl how Edward's spirits had revived.

'You are a greater benefactor than you know,' she told him, 'and the news is already cheering people with the prospect of more work to do.'

She was right. Carl's present to the community was warmly welcomed, and the thought of such a practical tribute to dear old Mrs Curdle of hallowed memory pleased everyone.

Nelly Piggott, as a Thrush Green resident, had many comments made to her on the subject by customers of the Fuchsia Bush.

Christmas shopping was now in full swing, and Nelly and the staff were uncommonly busy when one morning the three Lovelock sisters made their appearance.

Instead of seating themselves at one of the tables as Nelly expected, they approached her with smiles on their wrinkled faces and hands outstretched. Bertha Lovelock, the collector of unconsidered trifles such as small pots of jam, was holding a little parcel wrapped in Christmas paper.

'Do come into the office for a minute if you can spare the time,' said Nelly, conscious of inquisitive glances from the customers and guessing, rightly, that this was an offering for herself.

They followed her obediently into the inner sanctum where so recently Bertha had made her apologies in the stern presence of her sister Violet.

'No, no. We won't sit down, Mrs Piggott. But we wanted you to have this little Christmas present with our very best wishes.'

Nelly unwrapped it with care. It was a charming little silver dish, oval in shape, called, she believed, a bonbon dish, and she remembered polishing it in days gone by when she worked for the old ladies.

'This is much too good for me,' she exclaimed, holding the pretty thing.

'Nothing is too good for you,' pronounced Bertha. 'It is a little memento of three old friends.'

Nelly was much touched. It was old, it was lovely and had been much cherished. It had cost these three old ladies a great deal to part with it.

'I can't begin to tell you how much I appreciate it. I'll always treasure it, believe me.'

'We know it is in safe hands,' said Violet.

'Do go and sit down, and let me bring you some coffee,' urged Nelly.

'No, really,' protested Ada.

'Please. It's the least I can do, to give you a cup of coffee in return for this wonderful present.'

The sisters exchanged glances.

'In that case,' said Violet inclining her head graciously, 'we should be delighted to accept such a kind offer.'

Nelly followed behind them, and summoned Rosa to fetch coffee 'and in the best cups, please'.

The Youngs were expecting Carl to come to them on Christmas Eve, and Molly and Joan were busy the day before making up a bed for him in the spare room when the telephone rang.

It was Carl. He sounded agitated, quite unlike his usual self.

'Something's cropped up,' he announced. 'Pretty serious too, I guess.'

'Are you ill? What's happened?'

'We reckon there may be a fault on site. We've got the surveyor and a whole heap of geology guys testing like crazy everywhere. The thing is, Joan, I'll just have to stay here, and I'm real sorry to miss Christmas with you.'

'I can see it can't be helped,' said Joan. 'Edward's out, but he'll be as disappointed as I am.'

'I'm sick about the whole thing, but we must get this sorted out. Luckily they don't seem to worry too much about the Christmas break up here. Something called Hogmanay next weekend or so seems to be their knocking-off time.'

'Any idea when we might see you?'

'None at the moment, but I'll keep in touch. I'll probably go straight to Woodstock if I can get away, but I can see it won't be until after Christmas now.'

They wished each other well and Carl rang off.

Sadly, Joan returned to the bedroom to tell Molly the news.

Christmas Day was bright and clear. The bells of St John's

were the first to be heard, and later the answering peals from Thrush Green and the villages around were plain to hear through the frosty air.

Above St Andrew's church the rooks wheeled and cawed, as the parishioners made their way to morning service.

Winnie and Ella met at the church gate and Ella asked her if she would like a trip to Woodstock when the shops opened again after Christmas.

'I'd love to come,' said Winnie. 'Is there any particular reason?'

'That nice woman in the wool shop rang yesterday to say she had a late delivery of the wool I'm using for my rug. You know, that thick stuff I'm using for that tied-brick stitch.'

'How's it getting on?'

'Slowly. I don't really care for this coarse handiwork, but it's no good pretending I can see to do anything finer.'

Winnie was sympathetic. They entered the church, and as they knelt together to say their first private prayers Winnie thought how bravely Ella was tackling her problem of diminishing sight.

The ancient Mini which had served Ella for so many years had already been sold, and Winnie knew how much Ella missed her independence and the joy she had always felt in forays into Lulling and the surrounding countryside. Winnie herself had never driven, for Donald had enjoyed taking the wheel and she had been more than content to be a passenger. Since his death she had become familiar with the local bus timetable, and now, it seemed, Ella had to do the same.

Charles Henstock took the service. He had already celebrated early communion at St John's at eight o'clock and matins at ten o'clock. From there he had driven to Thrush Green's service at eleven fifteen, and rejoiced in his work.

St John's had looked splendid. The great nave had echoed to the grandeur of a full choir and an organ loud in triumphant rendering of 'Adeste fideles'. The flower ladies had excelled themselves, and swathes of greenery, branches of berried holly, great mop-headed chrysanthemums and Christmas roses added to the splendour. It was a noble church, thought Charles, nobly tended as it had been for generations, and he was proud to be the incumbent of such a fine and famous parish.

And yet, thought Charles, looking fondly about the modest interior of St Andrew's as the country voices sang 'Hark, the herald angels sing' beneath the pitch-pine rafters, there was something very endearing and very personal about this building.

It was not beautiful as St John's was beautiful. It had been built in Victoria's reign by less skilled men with less time and money. But it was the church in which Nathaniel Patten had worshipped and where that fine missionary's benefactor, the Reverend Octavius Fennel, had conducted his services just as he was doing this Christmas morning.

It was here too, at Thrush Green, thought Charles, that he had lived for a number of years, at first alone, until he had met and married his dear Dimity who had changed his life so wonderfully.

'Amen!' resounded round the church, and Charles returned to his duties, with a thankful heart.

Winnie Bailey and Ella Bembridge had decided to catch the bus from Thrush Green to Woodstock.

'If we catch the two o'clock,' said Winnie, 'we shall be there in good time, and after we have picked up the wool I suggest that we have a walk in Blenheim park.'

'Good idea,' said Ella. 'I think Blenheim Palace looks at its best in winter, and it should still be light. After that we will have tea in Woodstock and catch the five o'clock back.'

The two looked forward to their outing. They had always been good friends, but since Donald's death and Dimity's departure to the vicarage at Lulling, they had seen more of each other and enjoyed their meetings.

It was dry and still, but there was no sunshine as they waited for the bus to mount the hill from Lulling. Outside the Youngs' house a bed of nerines glowed pinkly against the Cotswold stone house. In local gardens the bulbs were already pushing their noses through the soil, and winter jasmine starred the cottage walls with yellow blossom.

'Soon be spring,' said Ella cheerfully.

The bus arrived. One of the Cooke boys, who had started life in a council house along the Nidden road less than half a mile away, welcomed them aboard and took their fares. He was driver and conductor combined.

They visited the wool shop, inspected the goods, paid for them and arranged to pick up the parcel after their walk.

By now a weak shaft of sunlight was showing through the clouds, and brightening the ancient street.

Two people were crossing the road from the Bear.

'Look!' cried Winnie. 'There's Carl!'

The two came towards them. Carl was accompanied by a tall elegant woman in a long black coat with a fur collar, and a dashing little black fur hat to match.

'How lovely to see you,' said Winnie. 'We thought you were still in Scotland.'

'We arrived here late last night,' said Carl smiling. 'But let me introduce you. This is Elizabeth Winsford and we are getting married very soon.'

'What news! Congratulations Carl!' cried Winnie.

She held out her hand to the elegant stranger who was laughing at the excitement she was causing.

'And mine too,' said Ella warmly. 'This is tremendous news. All Thrush Green will rejoice with you.'

Winnie interposed anxiously, 'Unless it is a secret, of course?' She looked questioningly at Elizabeth.

'No indeed,' said the girl. 'Carl has just been telling Joan and Edward Young and we are going over there now to see them.'

'In fact,' said Carl, 'we're just slipping across to the florist to buy a belated Christmas present to take with us. Can we give you a lift back?'

But the two ladies explained about their proposed walk and the parcel waiting to be collected, and the couples parted with renewed congratulations and in high spirits.

By the next day it was common knowledge in Thrush Green, and even in Lulling, that Carl was engaged to be married. His fiancée had only been glimpsed the day before, so that descriptions of the lady varied from 'proper skinny, and all in black' (Albert Piggott), 'a real lady with furs on' (Mrs Cooke) and 'elegant, I'd say, and what a pair they'll make' (Nelly Piggott).

The use of the word 'black' in Albert Piggott's comment, was soon translated by those who had not seen the lady into conjectures about whether Carl's bride-to-be was black or white, but everyone agreed that whoever Carl had chosen would be wholeheartedly welcome in the neighbourhood.

Joan and Edward, as the first people to welcome the couple, were overjoyed and set about arranging a celebratory party as soon as possible. It had to be planned very quickly, as Carl was taking Elizabeth to America to meet his relatives. They were to be married there, which was a disappointment to Charles Henstock as well as the rest of

Thrush Green. After a brief honeymoon they would return to Scotland for a short time while Carl continued with his work there.

The Saturday after the news had broken was chosen for the party, and the telephone wires buzzed from the Youngs' house to all parts of Thrush Green and Lulling. On this day Nelly Piggott was busy in the kitchen of the Fuchsia Bush filling trays with delectable tit-bits to accompany the drinks.

It was a clear dry evening when the first guests arrived at six o'clock. The stars twinkled above St Andrew's church and the bare branches of the horse-chestnut trees. Underfoot the ground was crisp. There was going to be a hard frost.

But inside all was warmth and happiness. Carl and Elizabeth stood by the Youngs to welcome, and be welcomed by, their friends.

Nelly Piggott was in Joan's kitchen supervising sizzling pans of miniature sausages, while Gloria and Rosa had volunteered, with rare enthusiasm, to act as waitresses, a tribute to Carl's charm.

About twenty or so guests made the room hum with excitement. Ben and Molly Curdle were there. Charles and Dimity Henstock, the Shoosmiths, Ella, Winnie and Jenny, the Cartwrights and a number of Carl's friends from Rectory Cottages swelled the throng.

At last the time for informal speeches and toasts arrived, and Edward gave a short, elegant and warm-hearted tribute to Carl and Elizabeth, amidst general applause.

Carl, flushed, happy and handsomer than ever, responded, his arm around Elizabeth's shoulders. He spoke movingly of his mother who had waited at Woodstock for her American to return after the war to claim her as his wife.

'That wouldn't have happened,' he said, 'but for Mrs Curdle. In fact, I shouldn't be here at all, if it were not for her advice to my mother, as some of you know. So would you raise your glasses once more, my friends, to the immortal memory of the great Mrs Curdle.'

'Mrs Curdle,' came the hearty response.

'Thank you,' said Carl when the toast had been drunk.

He smiled at Elizabeth, and added: 'As you see, we Andersens always come to Woodstock for our wives.'